ONE LAST SHOT

ALSO BY TODD E. CREASON

Non-fiction

Famous American Freemasons: Volume I

Famous American Freemasons: Volume II

A Freemason Said That?
Great Quotes of Famous Freemasons

ONE LAST
SHOT

A NOVEL

TODD E. CREASON

Moon & Son
Publishing

ONE LAST SHOT
A Moon & Son Book

Published by Moon & Son Publishing
Fithian, Illinois

ISBN 978-0-9831156-0-1

PRINTED IN THE UNITED STATES OF AMERICA

To those members of the
O.T.H.S. Class of '85
known simply as the B-Crew

This one's for you.

1

"Hey, Levi!" Brittany squealed through the window screen. "You're going to be on TV!"

Levi Garvey was finishing his breakfast on the front porch of his Savannah townhouse. Sighing, he ignored her as he leaned back in his chair, sipped his coffee, and watched the early morning joggers and dog walkers on Pulaski Square. Dressed, as usual, in a cotton button-up shirt with the sleeves rolled up to the elbows, blue jeans, and tennis shoes, he took it all in from under the brim of his ever-present Panama.

The morning light in Savannah, Georgia, was especially breathtaking in Pulaski Square, one of the beautiful town squares in the historic district. The sun's golden rays beamed down wherever it could find an opening through the live oaks draped in Spanish moss. The gauzy light illuminated the purple wisteria blossoms, the cobblestone sidewalks, and the palm trees. Early morning was Levi's favorite time of day.

"Levi, come quick! You'll miss it! They're going to talk about your book," Brittany called again from inside the house.

Glancing at his German shepherd, who was sleeping at the top of the porch steps, he said, "Come on, Rosco. Let's go see what Brittany is so excited about."

The dog never flinched.

"Rosco!" he said louder.

Nothing.

Grinning broadly, Levi got up from his chair, walked over to Rosco, and nudged him with his foot. Rosco's brown eyes blinked open. He raised his head and looked around slowly, not sure what had disturbed his nap. When he finally realized his master was standing behind him, his ears went up and his tail wagged, but he never got up.

"I just wanted to make sure you weren't dead," Levi said as he leaned down to scratch Rosco's head. "You have to be the laziest dog I've ever seen. You're good for nothin'."

Levi walked across the porch to the screen door and disappeared into the house. Rosco looked after him for a moment, then put his head back down on his paws, and fell asleep again.

Brittany was sitting on the arm of the couch, eating Lucky Charms right out of the box. She was the kind of girl most men dream of—young, blonde, and blue-eyed with a perfect tan on a perfect body. The slogan on the skin-tight t-shirt she was wearing described both her strengths and her weaknesses in one short statement—I wish these were brains.

"See, I told you," she said, pointing at a morning news program.

Levi was a bit surprised to see Brittany watching the news. She probably ran across it by accident while looking for SpongeBob SquarePants, he thought.

The cover of his most recent book was on the screen behind the critic. Brittany smiled, her eyes blinking brightly as she munched on the cereal and watched the commentary.

". . . and after reading his first book, *But for the Grace of God,* back in 1999, I truly believed Levi Garvey was well on his way to being one of America's great writers. I found that same powerful storytelling ability and tense prose in his second book, *Fear No Evil*, in 2005. These were books readers not only enjoyed reading but also continued to think about long after they turned the last page. The popularity of his first two books skyrocketed again when they were adapted into blockbuster Hollywood movies. But after reading Garvey's latest book, *Thou Art with Me,* I think it's obvious that he's lost his touch. This book has very little to offer fans of his previous books besides disappointment. Levi Garvey has gone from genius to hack in just three books."

"Is hack better than genius?" Brittany asked.

"No, Brit. Being called a hack is not a good thing," he said.

"Oh," she said, cocking her head and looking a bit perplexed. The wheels turned ever so slowly. "So he didn't like your book?"

"No, he agrees with everyone else that it sucks."

Thinking that during the past few weeks had caused butterflies in his stomach to flutter. Saying it aloud caused him real pain.

Brittany's short attention span was quickly whisked away by a buzzing sound. "Hey, your cell phone has been ringing every five minutes," she said, pointing to it as it vibrated on the coffee table.

Levi picked it up, glanced at the number, and shoved it into his pocket without answering it.

"I think I'll take a walk, Brit. Maybe down to the Gryphon."

As he walked towards the door, Brittany said, "Hey, Levi, what channel are the cartoons on again?"

I know that girl way too well, he thought as he shook his head and grinned. "Channel 162," he called back over his shoulder.

Rosco was still sleeping at the top of the porch steps—no big surprise.

"Rosco, you want to go for a walk?"

Rosco's eyes opened sleepily, but he never raised his head. The answer was pretty clear.

"Suit yourself," Levi said as he quickly descended the steps and walked out into Pulaski Square.

Levi loved walking in Savannah. He'd learned a lot about the history of the city in the past ten years. The city's twenty-two squares in the historic district were just beautiful. In the center of each city square was a block-sized park with perfectly tended gardens, park benches, and, of course, the live oaks and Spanish moss for which the city was known—picturesque and historic places that were favorite sites for family picnics and weddings.

Many of the squares were named for famous Americans—Franklin, Washington, Greene, Warren, and Madison. However, one of the original squares, Liberty Square, was named after a founding principle of America. It was a parking lot now. Levi considered it ironic that Liberty Square was one of two original squares lost since liberty was so often sacrificed in the name of progress.

Many of the squares featured fountains, statues, and memorials, each as visually stunning as it was rich in history. Most of the houses, churches, and buildings surrounding the squares were original. The squares were often used in Hollywood films, especially those that were set during the Civil War era. One of Levi's favorite movies, one set in modern times, had also been filmed there. He wasn't too far away from the square where Forrest Gump had sat on a park bench, waiting for a bus while telling the story of his remarkable life to those waiting with him.

Savannah's historic district was an American success story. After decades of neglect, many of the oldest blocks had fallen into disrepair—the district becoming a ghost town with block after block of abandoned mansions and townhouses from America's past boarded up and forgotten. It was only through the dedication of the Savannah Historic Society that many of the houses were saved through renovation and restoration. In order to own the historic homes, owners had to agree to maintain them exactly as they were when they were built. The district had gone from an abandoned relic to a thriving community again. The great success story of the renovation had encouraged many more historic cities to do the same thing.

Levi's townhouse on Pulaski Square was part of that success story. His home looked exactly as it had when it was built in 1844. Inside, however, it had all the modern conveniences along with five bedrooms, three baths, original fixtures, and hardwood floors—all that for a hefty price tag he could afford, thanks to his first two books and the movies that followed.

As he cut across the square, Levi's phone chirped in his pocket—a text message. Reluctantly, he pulled out the phone. He froze as he read the message: U better answer!

"Oh, shit," Levi said.

It was Wanda Sterling, his agent. And she was angry. He'd been dodging her calls for a couple of weeks. If he kept dodging her, he knew she'd show up in Savannah.

Seconds later, the phone vibrated in his hand, startling him. That was quick, he thought. He sat down on a park bench, stared at the phone reluctantly for a moment, then flipped it open, and said, "Hello, Wanda."

She never said hello, and she never said goodbye. She said what she had to say, and when she was done with the conversation, she hung up. That was her style.

"What the hell is wrong with you?" she snapped.

Levi knew her well enough to say nothing. He heard her inhale deeply. He could almost see her in New York, sitting at her desk behind mountains of paper, chain-smoking and slugging coffee. She was one of the most successful agents in the business, and she was not a woman easily ignored, especially since she'd been in publishing longer than he'd been alive—a fact she reminded him of often.

"I don't know what the hell you've been doing," she said, "but you picked a hell of a time to go off the radar. You don't show up for two signings, you miss an important interview, and your publisher is not very happy about it."

"I'm sorry," Levi said. "I figure I've written my last book. Right?"

She sighed. "Although the critics hate *Thou Art with Me*, your adoring readers are buying it by the tens of thousands. This book could actually wind up being another bestseller for you. Don't get me wrong. We both know it was terrible, but as long as it sells, Moon & Son is willing to move on. You'll lose a few readers, but you can easily come back after one bad book—you just can't come back after two. You have one last shot, Levi, so don't waste it. Write another clunker, and you're done. You'll never see your name on the new release shelf in a bookstore again."

"I don't know if I can write another book, Wanda," Levi said flatly. "I've been thinking about it. I don't think there is another book in me. I should never have written the last one."

Silence. He heard her take a drag off her cigarette. He heard her sip coffee.

"You don't really have a choice in this, Levi. You're going to write another book," she said gruffly. "You and I have a contract, not to mention the publishing contract with Moon & Son. You'll have to write one more. Now it's up to you whether you write a good book or another bad one. Look at this as an opportunity to redeem your tarnished reputation as a writer."

Leaning back on the park bench, Levi pushed his hat back on his head. "I don't know, Wanda," he said, shaking his head.

"You can do this. I've seen it a thousand times. You've just let yourself get swept up by the fame and fortune, and the most important thing, the writing, has suffered. I've seen lots of writers pull out of a slump and go on to write great books again."

Ah, the inspirational speech, Levi thought.

"I don't know what you need to do to get back to that place where you can write a great book. If you're drinking, then stop drinking. If you don't drink, then maybe you should start up. Maybe you need a new age-inappropriate girlfriend—or do that Hugh Hefner thing and get two more girlfriends. Maybe you need to go back to the place where you got that first idea. Whatever it is, you need to start thinking about the next book right now. Are you listening to me, Garvey?"

"I hear you," Levi said.

He took off his Panama hat and wiped the sweat off his forehead. His hand was shaking slightly. It was suddenly very warm in Pulaski Square.

"Then stop all this self-pity garbage and get back to work," she snapped. "You're a gifted writer. That should be obvious considering the quality of your agent. Believe in yourself."

"You're right, Wanda." He said the words, but he wasn't sure he really believed them.

"And, Levi."

"Yeah?"

"If you think you have problems now, you try ignoring my calls again. Don't think for a minute I won't come down there."

Levi couldn't think of anything more unpleasant than a personal visit from Wanda.

"I'm sorry, Wanda. I've been—"

But the phone was dead. Wanda was done speaking, and the conversation was over. He stared at the phone for a moment before putting it back into his pocket. He could feel his heart pounding in his chest and the pain in his stomach. It was all coming undone.

Levi glanced around the square, trying to decide if he was going to walk back to the house or finish his walk to the Gryphon Tea Room as he'd originally planned. The Gryph, as he called it, was one of his favorite places to think.

He got up and began walking towards Bull Street where the Gryphon Tea Room was on the first floor of the Savannah Scottish Rite Temple.

2

"Something seems to be on your mind today," Ray Billings said casually, looking at Levi over the top of his teacup with his dark gray eyes. The cup looked tiny in his massive hands.

Levi said nothing at first. The remark surprised him since it was unlike Ray to pry. Ray set his teacup down and leaned back in one of the trademark orange wooden chairs of the Gryphon Tea Room. The chair creaked under his massive athletic build. In the morning light streaming through the front windows, his badge gleamed brightly from the pocket of his perfectly pressed khaki shirt.

Ray, who was in his mid-fifties, kept his head shaved clean, but his most defining feature was a handlebar mustache, which he kept waxed and curled up at the ends—the kind of mustache not seen much anymore. Ray crossed his arms over his chest, looking confident that his assessment was correct.

"Why do you say that?" Levi replied.

"Levi, don't bullshit a bullshitter," Ray said with a chuckle. "I'm a trained observer with more than twenty-five years of experience. Little gets past me, as you should well know. When I pull over a teenager, I can tell by his mannerisms if he has beer in his trunk. I'm so good, in fact, I can usually guess how many."

Levi grinned. Ray was good. Levi was often mystified by his friend's powers of observation. He'd often thought of himself as Watson to Ray Billings' Sherlock Holmes.

"You're a wise man, Officer Billings. What gave me away? What little hint did I give you that something is wrong? "

The giant man smiled broadly. His size and demeanor were intimidating, but when he smiled, all that melted away in an instant. He had a face people instantly trusted, a trait that served him well in his job.

"It was pretty easy, actually. You probably could've figured this one out yourself," he said, chiding Levi.

"Really? So easy even *I* could've figured it out? Oh, please, share."

The great observer thought for a moment about how he would reveal the answer.

"How long have we known each other, Levi?"

"I met you shortly after I moved to Savannah ten years ago."

"Has it been ten years since that night I caught you and that young lady in your car in the parking lot of the Crystal Beer Room? Come to think of it, you never did tell me what you and that girl were doing in that car."

Levi grinned. "Nothing, thanks to you."

"I believed your story."

"That's what you say now, but it sure didn't stop you from running me in back then. And, by the way, I maintain the same story I told you that night—I had no idea the young lady was a hooker."

Ray shook his head, smiling at the memory, and continued, "And on the following Monday, I ran into you here."

"And I was *thrilled* to see my arresting officer again so soon. Of course, you invited yourself to join me at my table," Levi said, sarcastically. "And you ate all my damned scones."

Ray ignored him. "We got talking, and we became friends. And since then, we've met here just about every Monday"

"True," Levi said. He had no idea where Ray was going with this.

"I'd say we've missed maybe one or two Mondays a year when you were off on speaking engagements or frying chicken with Paula Deen on her show or signing books somewhere." Ray often teased him about his celebrity. "So we're talking about what? Five hundred Mondays all told that we've met here at the Gryphon?"

Levi nodded. "You're pretty close."

"And yet, when I came up behind you today and said 'good morning' as I always do, you jumped a damned foot. You didn't expect to see me here on our regular meeting day. Now I know you come up here a few times a week, but your reaction means either you didn't know it was Monday, or you are so preoccupied with something else you forgot it was Monday."

As with Holmes and Dr. Watson, when the answer was revealed, it was always more obvious than expected.

"True," Levi said, smiling and shaking his head.

"So what's bothering you?"

Levi's smile faded. There were few men on earth he trusted more—maybe none. Ray had started out a jackass cop, but he'd wound up a friend and later a brother. Levi glanced down at his gold ring which featured a red stone with the gold square and compass emblem embedded in the stone. Ray wore a Freemason ring just like it. In fact, two stories up from where they were sitting at the Gryph, in a lodge room in the Savannah Scottish Rite Temple, Ray had raised his new friend a Master Mason. Levi had since become a 32° Scottish Rite Mason as well.

"I think life is about to change for me," Levi said. "I'm forty-two years old, and I've been successful, but I'm hemorrhaging cash, and I think the cash cow is about to dry up."

"Ah," Ray said, "what a strange day. We're on a topic we never discuss. We're talking about your books—right?"

The strength of their friendship was based on the fact there were some things they seldom discussed. One topic that seldom came up was Levi's books. Ray always got the feeling Levi wasn't completely comfortable with his celebrity. Even upstairs, amongst his Freemason friends, Levi didn't want to be known as "the famous writer." He bristled every time someone introduced him that way or brought up the fact he was a published writer. Ray didn't understand Levi's reaction, but he respected his privacy.

Levi's past was another topic they seldom discussed. Levi was very adept at steering conversations away from his history. Ray had picked up a few things over the years since Levi had occasionally let comments slip. For instance, Ray knew there were problems with his parents and that Levi hadn't been home in nearly two decades. And, of course, there was a ten-year gap between the time Levi had graduated from the University of Illinois and when Ray had met him—a blank slate about which Levi had never dropped even one hint. Ray knew he could find out more if he wanted to, but again he respected Levi's privacy.

Ray leaned back in his chair, sipping tea as he listened to Levi's story about the declining quality of his three books. He knew Levi was getting to the crux of the problem.

"The book I just published, *Thou Art with Me*, isn't very good. My agent tells me it will sell, but another crappy book will put me out of business for good."

Ray finally leaned forward and looked Levi square in the eye.

"So you wrote two good books and one bad one. Write another good one," he said simply. "Try harder. Spend a little less time chasing tail and a little more time writing books. I mean, that was the problem last time, right?"

Levi looked at him blankly. He'd just heard this same lecture from Wanda. When Levi didn't say anything, Ray suddenly understood the real problem.

"Ah, I get it. It's deeper than that, isn't it. You, Mr. Garvey, are going through a mid-life crisis. You've reached that age when you begin to think your best years are behind you. You think you've already reached the peak of your craft, and everything to come will pale by comparison. You don't think you can write another good book."

"Another good book?" Levi snorted. "That's the problem, Ray. In all honesty, I've written only one good book. I spent years thinking about *But for the Grace of God* before I wrote it. I don't mind saying it was a great book. The second book was a variation on the same theme—a cheap knock-off. The third book was another carbon copy. Each incarnation of that same theme has been a little weaker than the one previous. In truth, I've had only one brilliant idea and one good book. I've been plagiarizing myself ever since."

Ray nodded. "You've been half-assing it because you never really believed that first book was anything but a fluke. You've been riding that success for all it's worth. That's why we don't discuss your success—you don't think you deserve it. And now that you've ridden it as far as you can, you realize it's time to either put up or shut up, and you're scared shitless. You don't have another idea, and you aren't convinced you'll ever have one."

Levi was stunned. Ray had nailed it.

Ray leaned forward and took a scone off the table. He took a large bite, then leaned back and chewed it as he eyed Levi. There was a long pause as Levi waited for more, but Ray had said what he wanted to say.

"So what do you think I should do? You can't buy book ideas at Wal-Mart."

"Well, think about it," Ray said. "How did you get that first book idea? You said you thought about it for years. Where were you? What were you doing? What was the one experience you had that got you thinking about writing a book? You weren't a writer when you got that idea, but once you got it, you couldn't stop yourself from thinking about it. You were just going through life, and that one thing stuck. Right?"

Levi thought for a moment, then slowly nodded his head.

Suddenly, Wanda was there, her words echoing from their conversation an hour before—"Maybe you need to go back to the place where you got that first idea."

"You're a good friend, Brother Billings," Levi said.

"Did I help?" Ray asked.

"Oh yeah," Levi admitted. He reached for his Panama, which was sitting on the edge of the small table between them, and picked up the newspaper he'd bought from the machine outside. "If you're not doing anything, why don't you come by tonight and bring a few beers. We'll sit on the porch."

"Sounds good. I'll be there."

3

There was actually one phrase that would wake Rosco out of one of his deepest naps, and that was, "Hey, Rosco, wanna go for a ride?"

Rosco loved rides, especially to Bonaventure Cemetery, a beautiful place unlike any Levi had seen before. It was another place he went when he wanted to think. Levi loved the peace and quiet of the cemetery.

The cemetery, which sprawled for acres, was full of ornate and unique stones, statuary, and mausoleums. It was rich in history as well. Levi sat down on a bench that marked the grave of the famous musician Johnny Mercer. From under the shade of the moss-draped live oaks, he watched Rosco sniff around.

When Rosco finally tired of sniffing around, he came over to Levi and put his head in Levi's lap. Levi fished a treat out of his pocket. Rosco wolfed it down and settled at Levi's feet for a nap.

"You're something else, Rosco," Levi said with a chuckle.

Rosco had a nickname, Rosco the Lethargic. He wasn't the first Rosco. In fact, he was the fourth German shepherd Levi had owned named Rosco. And they'd all had nicknames.

He'd gotten the first Rosco when he was a scrawny ten-year-old in a small Midwestern town. His Uncle Ed brought him home, a gift from a friend of his at the Beer Chaser—the local watering hole in Twin Rivers, Illinois. The pup was about six weeks old when Ed presented him to Levi as a birthday present. Levi named him after the fumbling sheriff on his favorite TV show, *The Dukes of Hazzard*. Within months, Rosco was constantly on the hunt, kicking up pheasants or chasing ground squirrels. More times than he could count, Rosco had tried to catch a skunk. Those episodes always ended badly for Rosco. Levi loved that dog.

One day, while Levi was attending class at Twin Rivers High School, Rosco chased a rabbit across the yard and into the road. He was killed by a passing school bus. Uncle Ed buried him in Grandmother Lucille Garvey's yard under the elm tree where he'd so often napped during the heat of the day. Uncle Ed marked the grave with a blue-gray granite boulder on which he'd engraved "Rosco the Hunter."

Every dog Levi had owned since had been a German shepherd named Rosco, but none had quite measured up to Rosco the Hunter.

Levi leaned over and scratched Rosco the Lethargic on the head. "Poor dog, you can't help it you were born with tired blood. There must be a little hound in you from somewhere in the family tree."

Levi rose to walk around Bonaventure. It was time to think, and it wasn't long before he'd made a few decisions. It was time for a change of scenery, and he knew exactly where he was going on his vacation. He had business to take care of in Illinois. He was going back to Twin Rivers—the hometown he'd left more than twenty years ago. Grandmother Garvey had died in November and left her estate to him, including the house where he'd grown up. It was a beautiful old Victorian house that sat on the edge of Twin Rivers on six rolling acres. The locals referred to it with great reverence as the Garvey House.

Levi knew why she'd made that decision. It certainly wasn't because he was such a good grandson. Even though he'd called her every Saturday night and talked for at least an hour, he'd never gone back to see her. He just couldn't bring himself to go home again, and he always felt bad about that. That choice, however, didn't have anything to do with her.

His grandmother had been the most important person in his life—his anchor. She'd raised him. She'd instilled in him some of his best attributes. She'd paid for his college. She'd been a fan of his books—had even told him, years before he realized it himself, that he could do much more as a writer. She'd tried in her own way to tell him that copying a working formula would take him only so far.

Smart lady, he thought. She knew years ago that this was going to happen.

When Lucille Garvey had come to see him in Savannah several years earlier, it was the first time he'd seen her in years. One evening while she was there, they'd sat on the porch and had a few beers.

"Your father was my first born," she said, stroking Rosco's head as she gazed out on Pulaski Square with her deep blue eyes, her snow-white hair pulled back in a bun. Rosco, who'd fallen in love with her, was at her side constantly, his head in her lap.

"I indulged your father more than I should've. I was young, and I didn't know anything about raising children. Whatever he wanted, I gave to him. He grew up with a sense of entitlement. He knew we had farmland, but he never understood we didn't have lots of money. What little money we had, we earned by working hard. We didn't inherit anything from your great-grandpa but a massive debt. It took years to pay that off, and we struggled to keep the house and farm intact. We farmed, we raised livestock, we picked apples from our orchard. I baked pies and made jam that I sold to local restaurants. We didn't start getting ahead until the mid-sixties. Your dad never understood that there is no such thing as a free lunch, and once that attitude is engrained in people, they never get over it. He's never done a damned thing with his life but try to figure out how to get something for nothing. He's selfish and self-absorbed, and he's never given a moment's consideration to anyone but himself. Your mother is the perfect mate for him. It breaks my heart."

She glanced over at Levi as tears welled up in her eyes. "It's my fault your father is a jackass."

"Here I always thought it was my fault," Levi said with a smile.

When his grandmother left him the estate, Levi wasn't surprised. He knew exactly why she'd done it. She didn't want his parents to have a nickel of what she'd worked so hard to get.

Her decision, however, had widened the rift between Levi and his parents into a chasm. When they learned the details of the will, they were furious that they hadn't inherited the property—especially since their son had accumulated so much wealth and they had so little themselves.

"It's not as if you need it," his father had said several months ago when he'd phoned Levi.

Levi could still hear the anger in his voice. It was the last time he'd been in contact with his parents, but that was nothing new. He hadn't actually seen his parents in years.

Levi still hadn't done anything with the Garvey House, which had been sitting empty. He was having a difficult time deciding what to do with the estate. He was the last in a long line of Garveys who'd lived on that property since the 1860s. He knew how hard his grandparents had worked to keep the farm and estate intact. Now it fell to him. He would be the one to dispose of what had taken four generations to build. But he didn't have a choice. It was time to go back home. It was time to settle the estate and put the house on the market.

After talking to Ray at the Gryphon Tea Room, he'd remembered something else as he walked back home. He'd gotten an invitation to his 25th high school class reunion a few weeks earlier. He'd found it after rummaging through his desk and brought it with him to Bonaventure. He pulled it out of his pocket and sat back down on the bench. It was a nice invitation, done in the school colors, purple and white, with a highly stylized metallic foil comet streaking through the year 1985—the Twin Rivers Comets. The reunion was taking place at Twin Rivers High School on Saturday night.

My God, has it been 25 years? he thought.

Suddenly, it seemed to Levi that the stars and planets had aligned. Now was the perfect opportunity to go back to Twin Rivers. He could kill two birds with one stone. He'd settle the estate and finally face the one person who'd kept him away from Twin Rivers—Tori Buchanan.

Tori was the missed opportunity in his life he'd never gotten past. He'd fallen in love with her the first moment he saw her in the sixth grade. But she hadn't felt the same way about him—at least he hadn't thought so. But there had been one minute, just one minute, when it seemed that maybe Tori did love him. But the moment had passed. He'd let it pass, and the memory had haunted him ever since. It was the last time he'd seen her—the day of their high school graduation. He wanted to go back to that one minute and do it over again. Each time he replayed the memory, the pain of that mistake, of that missed opportunity, was as fresh as it had been the moment it'd happened.

By the time he'd graduated from college, he knew he'd made the biggest mistake of his young life, and he intended to correct it. He went home to see his grandmother and to find Tori. He had to convince her that they were made for each other.

Shortly after he arrived, he went to Harv's Diner for a cup of coffee and a piece of chocolate meringue pie made by Harv's wife, April, who was, in the opinion of most of the local residents, the best pie baker on the planet. At the diner, he ran into an old friend, Jay Snider.

"It's been a long time, but I kind of figured I'd see you this week," Jay said as he shook Levi's hand and took the stool next to him at the counter.

"Why's that?" Levi asked.

"Aren't you back for Tori's wedding this Saturday?" Jay replied.

The news was devastating. He'd left town that evening.

A few months later, he received the invitation for the five-year class reunion, but he knew he couldn't go. He didn't want to see Tori with another man, he didn't want to be friends with her husband, and he didn't want to find out she was pregnant with their first child. He didn't want to hear about them building the new house or remodeling the summer home. He just wanted Tori. But it was too late.

Then came the invitation for the ten-year reunion, and he could see her raising children and living this perfect life with another man. When the fifteen-year reunion arrived, he entertained the idea of taking his twenty-something girlfriend along, but even after fifteen years, he couldn't do it. He didn't want to hurt Tori. He just wanted that one minute back—that one minute on the tailgate of his old truck at Kingery Pond after their graduation in 1985.

Then came the twentieth . . . and now the twenty-fifth. As always, Tori was the first thing he'd thought about when the invitation arrived in the mail.

My God, I'll bet she has children graduating from college by now. She might even have grandkids, he thought.

The sun was dropping low in the west when Levi finally stood to leave. The decision was made. It was time to go home again. As difficult as it might be, he had to see Tori. It was time to stop running and face the fact he couldn't change the past. It was time to accept reality.

And just maybe Wanda and Ray were right. Maybe the change of scenery might get his creative juices flowing again. Maybe during what was likely to be an emotionally draining week, some little idea might begin to perk—something brand new and unique.

But that's probably a little too much to expect, Levi thought.

4

"I'm flying out in the morning, and I'll be gone a week to ten days," Levi said from behind his massive antique oak desk in the library.

There was a pile of paid bills propped up against the Tiffany lamp, ready to go out in the mail. Brittany, wearing nothing but a long t-shirt, was sitting on the front edge of his desk. She wasn't paying much attention since she was focusing on her fingernails, which she'd just painted. But she'd at least heard the word *gone*.

"I don't have to feed that dog, do I?" she said, wrinkling up her nose.

She didn't care much for Rosco, who was napping in Levi's leather wingback chair. His head popped up when she said *dog*—he knew she was talking about him.

"Rosco will be coming with me," Levi said.

Seeming relieved, Rosco put his head back down. Brit went back to examining her fingernails.

"Anna will keep the fridge stocked, and she'll cook for you if you want her to, but you'll need to tell her what meals you're going to be eating in. I also left her some cash, which she'll dole out to you if you need it."

Brit became suddenly interested in what he was saying. Her head popped up much like Rosco's just had.

"How much?" she asked.

"I think $5,000 will get you through the week," Levi replied shortly.

The topic of money irritated him, especially her interest in it.

"Anna is to give you only $500 at a time. Don't give her any grief about it. And Brit, when that's gone, it's gone. Don't be calling and giving me some sob story about a big sale somewhere."

Brit rolled her eyes as if that had never happened before, but Levi knew it had. He just couldn't remember if it was with this girlfriend or another one.

Brit slid off the desk and sat on Levi's lap. She'd seen the sour look on his face as they discussed money.

"I'll miss you. It'll be awfully lonely around here."

She wrapped her arms around his neck and gave him a kiss that made his pulse race.

"Don't stay up too late with Ray. I'd like to give you a little something to think about while you're gone."

She got up and walked across the library towards the foyer.

"Brit," Levi said, stopping her in the doorway, "are you wearing anything under that t-shirt?"

She had to think for a moment before she shook her head.

"We've had this conversation before, haven't we?" Levi said sternly.

"Yes," she admitted.

"This is my house and my rules. What have I repeatedly said about you running around the house half naked?"

She smiled broadly. Seconds later, the t-shirt hit him in the face.

"Don't do anything half-way," she said with a giggle.

She posed nude in the doorway, a breathtaking picture of youthful perfection. After a moment, she turned and began walking across the foyer towards the stairs. Levi watched her with rapt attention, wishing he hadn't made plans for the evening.

Suddenly, Levi heard a tremendous crash. Brit jumped and turned toward the front entrance. Levi was on his feet, racing to the foyer, in an instant.

Ray Billings was standing frozen on the other side of the screen door. His hand was raised in a fist as he prepared to knock. His mouth was hanging open, and his eyes were wide. At his feet was a smashed grocery bag with beer fizzing out in a growing ring of liquid around his shoes.

"Oh, hello, Ray!" Brit bubbled cheerfully as she stood before him, completely naked. "You startled me."

She turned quickly, revealing a perfect ass, and disappeared up the staircase. With great amusement, Levi leaned on the foyer wall, watching Ray watch Brit climb the stairs.

"How could you, Ray?" Levi said.

Ray was dazed. He looked at Levi with a mixture of confusion and guilt on his face.

Pointing down at the ever-widening circle of beer at Ray's feet, Levi said, "That's alcohol abuse."

"You ready for another *can*," Levi said with a chuckle as he reached into the cooler.

"I'd rather have a bottle."

"Oh no, I've seen what you do to bottles," he said, cocking a thumb toward the wet spot on the porch in front of the door.

They were sitting in Adirondack chairs with a stack of empty cans on the low table between them. The only light was from the front windows of the house behind them. Ray had often wondered why Levi owned such a large house since it seemed that he spent most of his time in the front three rooms—the library, the den, and the front porch.

Ray popped the top of his beer with a hiss.

"So you're going," he said

"Yep," Levi said, popping his beer.

Ray looked over at him. All he could see was Levi's darkened profile in the light from the windows, his hat pulled down low over his eyes.

"You've never talked much about your family—except your grandma and Uncle Ed."

As soon as he said the words, he regretted them. Levi tensed up and set his beer down on the table. Ray didn't think he was going to say anything, but finally, he spoke.

"When I was a kid, we lived with Grandma Garvey in her huge house. My dad worked this job and that, and my mother . . . well, my mother did as little as possible. Dad would work at a job for a while and then claim he got hurt. He was the kind of guy who had a disability attorney on speed dial. He never worked anywhere for too long, and Grandma paid all the bills.

"When Dad was between jobs, my parents would take off on a trip—always without me. They'd run off to Las Vegas or Atlantic City or Cancun. Grandma paid for these trips. I figured out later that she wanted to get them away from me—that and to get my mother away from her. I think it was as much a vacation for her as it was for them. Besides, Grandma wanted me to be raised right—the way a Garvey should be raised.

"But there was a huge blow-out the summer before my freshman year of high school. My dad lost his job in a local plant, a job Grandma had gotten him because she was friends with the man who owned it. Dad started another bogus disability claim against Grandma's friend with the same shyster lawyer he'd used at least a half-dozen times before. That was the proverbial straw that broke the camel's back. Grandma finally decided it was time for a change.

"There was a huge fight. Dad thought maybe it would be good for him and Mom to leave until things cooled off. They'd always dreamed of visiting Paris. He suggested that if Grandma would pay for the trip, they'd go only for a month. I'll never forget it. Grandma collected little ceramic pigs. She picked one up that was about the size of a coffee cup and bounced it off the side of Dad's head. It shattered into a million pieces.

"Dad and Mom started packing ten minutes later. Suddenly, Dad knew a guy who could get him a job down in Tennessee, so off they went. Of course, in *my* best interest, they thought I should stay with my grandma in Twin Rivers so I could graduate with my friends."

"Probably better off," Ray replied.

"Well, I didn't have a choice in the matter," Levi snapped.

Suddenly, a side of Levi came out that Ray had never realized existed. There was bitterness in his voice. Levi took a sip of his beer, leaned back in his chair, and took a deep breath.

"When they left, they left. They didn't come back—not for high school graduation, not for college. I've seen them three times since they moved out of Grandma's house nearly thirty years ago."

"And what would you have done if you'd been given the choice? Would you have gone to Tennessee with your folks?" Ray asked.

"That's not the point," Levi snapped again.

Levi was quiet for a moment. Ray knew there was more, so he waited.

"The last time I saw them was shortly after my first book hit the best-seller list. I'd stayed on in Urbana after I graduated. I liked it there, and I got a job. I'd written my first book during evenings and on weekends. Anyway, Dad and Mom showed up out of the blue. They were so proud of me! They'd read that my book was a huge success. I was really happy they'd come so far to see me, but that feeling quickly changed. Within ten minutes, I got the story about Dad's bad back and how he couldn't get on permanent disability and how they were about to lose their house in Tennessee."

"And it was a bullshit story. Right?"

"Yes. I knew why they were there. Success equals cash, and

they'd smelled it all the way down in Tennessee. I'd just gotten my first royalty check that week—I hadn't even cashed it yet. I wrote them a check for $30,000."

Ray whistled.

"That was about the amount of the first royalty check. Even though I knew more money was coming, I kept working as a—"

Levi suddenly stopped himself.

Ray knew Levi was hiding something. This was one of the few times Levi had ever talked openly about his family, and it was also the first time he'd even mentioned his life in the ten years between college and moving to Savannah. And yet, even as frank as he was being, there was still something he was intentionally hiding. Ray knew better than to press it.

Levi realized he'd nearly said too much, so he backed up his story and started again. "I'd gotten a state job after graduation, so I kept working my job a little longer, and the book money soon followed. Of course, I didn't hear a word from my parents for a year."

"But they called again," Ray said knowingly.

"Of course, they did. I'd just moved to Savannah. It was right before I met you. They had another sob story, another crisis, and that one was bullshit, too. I wrote them another huge check for some reason."

"They're family," Ray said.

"After I wrote that check, I never got so much as a thank you note from them. It wasn't six months later, they had the nerve to call me up to ask for more."

"So you cut them off," Ray said.

"You bet I did," Levi said sharply.

"That sure explains why they were so pissed off when you got your grandma's house," Ray remarked.

"Sure, they expected a huge inheritance. They'd been waiting for Grandma to die for thirty years so they could get their paws on it. But she left it all to me—the house, the farmland, the money. I don't need it, but I promise you one thing. My parents will never see one nickel of it because that's exactly what Grandma wanted."

But something wasn't adding up for Ray.

"So why haven't you been back in so long? Obviously, it wasn't your grandmother. And your parents were in Tennessee."

Levi looked troubled for a moment and then looked at Ray. "No, it wasn't my grandma. It wasn't my Uncle Ed either—he was more of a father to me than my father was. Let's just say it's very complicated."

Ray nodded. "It's gotta be a woman then."

Levi's head snapped towards Ray. It was spooky how Ray did that. It was impossible to hide anything from him.

"Let's just say Twin Rivers is haunted."

Ray smiled. He understood. It was obviously a subject Levi didn't want to talk about. Since he'd pushed Levi hard on several topics that day, it was time to leave it alone.

Ray glanced at his watch, tipping it to catch the light from the window.

"Maybe that's a story for another time. It's getting late, and you've got a big travel day tomorrow," he said, standing up. "If you don't mind, I think I'll leave my car where it is and walk home."

"Probably wise," Levi said, motioning toward the pile of cans on the table.

"Goodnight, Levi. Enjoy your trip," Ray said. "And beware of those ghosts in Twin Rivers. Remember what happened to Ebenezer when he finally had to face the ghosts from his past. He went from being a miserable, lonely man to the happiest man in all of London in one night."

Levi smiled at him. Ray walked to the top of the steps and paused to scratch Rosco's head. Then he descended the porch steps and walked across the street into the square.

Still sitting, Levi called after him, "We'll do this again when I get back!"

Without turning, Ray waved and called back, "*If* you come back!" Then he disappeared into the shadows of Pulaski Square.

Levi shook his head. "If I come back?" What a strange thing to say, he thought as he stood up.

"Come on, Rosco. Ray's right. It's time for bed."

Rosco got up from his spot next to the porch steps, stretched, and walked slowly into the house as Levi held the door. Rosco was barely through the threshold when he plopped down on an area rug just inside the entryway and went back to sleep.

"Rosco, you're never going to survive the rigors of travel," Levi said to the sleeping dog.

5

Levi couldn't believe he was back in Champaign-Urbana, Illinois, after so many years. He finished his breakfast in the morning sun outside the Courier Café under the umbrella of a sidewalk table, feeding the last of his ham to Rosco, who wolfed it down eagerly and looked up for more.

"Sorry, Rosco, that's all the ham," Levi said.

Rosco continued to look at him with sad brown eyes, cocking his head to one side, his ears standing up. Levi set his plate on the ground, and Rosco began aggressively licking what remained of the fried eggs and maple syrup from his "cake and egger" breakfast—a staple of the cafe's breakfast menu. Except for the umbrella tables outside on the sidewalk, the Courier Café was unchanged. When Levi had lived right up the street, he'd been a regular there.

The cafe was a simple two-story brick building that at one time had housed the offices and printing press for the long defunct *Courier Newspaper*. After the paper went out of business, the building sat empty for decades. In the early 80s, it was bought and extensively restored to become a trendy eating spot on Race Street. The seating inside was intimate low booths for couples and small families and antique round tables and stick chairs around the edges for larger groups.

The Courier's decor included a huge antique regulator clock, a gumball machine, and a ceiling fan shaped like a bi-wing airplane. Of all the antiques, Levi particularly loved the stained glass panels that hung in the windows, panels which had been saved from an old church in nearby Danville. It was especially nice in the morning when the sun, streaming into the Courier, painted the interior with the multi-colored light.

But what made the Courier so memorable was the terrific food. The café had nailed the flavor of the Midwest. It'd been one of Levi's favorite restaurants during the thirteen years he lived in Urbana. Even years later, when he was eating some of the best cuisine in Savannah, he still craved a Race Street Burger with a side of sweet potato chips from the Courier Café.

Levi had flown into Champaign-Urbana the evening before. He'd rented a car at the airport and parked it at the hotel. Even before checking in, he'd taken Rosco for a walking tour of the campus quad. They must've walked three or four miles. They'd sat until twilight on the steps of Foellinger Auditorium, the domed theater that graced the southern-most end of the quad. He knew all the buildings surrounding the campus quad and had taken classes in many of them—Lincoln Hall, the English Building, Henry Administration, Altgeld Hall, Noyes Lab, the Foreign Language Building. Little had changed on the quad in twenty years. It was like going back in time.

Levi had sat for a long time, looking out over the wide grass center of campus, which was intersected at strange angles with sidewalks. Wide pedestrian avenues canopied with shade trees ran down both sides. He knew those random sidewalks that crossed the center had been laid out like that intentionally—he remembered that little detail from the tour of the campus he'd taken with Grandma Lucille just after he was accepted. Those sidewalks were originally laid out over the muddy paths made by students in the lawn as they traveled between buildings for classes in the early days of the University. At the far north end of the quad, the massive brick edifice of the Illini Union loomed, the heart of student life at the University of Illinois. He'd spent many happy hours in the basement of that building, bowling and playing pool with his friends.

The sound of breaking glass snapped Levi out of his thoughts. Rosco had licked the plate he'd given him across the sidewalk and over the curb into Race Street.

"Rosco, damnit."

Suddenly, the shadow of a waitress descended on him. He blinked up at her with his deep blue eyes.

"You know, we reuse those plates, believe it or not," she said.

The face was familiar. He smiled broadly as he realized who she was.

"Audrey?"

"Hi, Levi," she said with a smile. "Welcome back. You've sure got everyone talking inside."

"Really? I didn't think anyone would know me anymore."

"Oh, you're a big celebrity now."

"I can't believe you're still here," he said.

She sighed and shook her head. "Twenty-two years I've been waiting these tables."

Her brown hair was tinged with gray, but she wore it the same way—pulled back tight into a pony-tail.

Levi grinned. "I'd like to introduce you to my dog. Meet Rosco."

She looked at him, eyebrows raised. "You're pulling my leg, Levi. That's not Rosco. I *knew* Rosco."

"You knew *a* Rosco. This is another Rosco—Rosco the Lethargic."

She laughed out loud. "Oh boy, you sure haven't changed much."

"So what does breakfast and a broken plate run at the Courier these days?"

"Less than twenty bucks," she said.

He pulled a hundred dollar bill out of his pocket and held it up between two fingers. "Keep it," he said.

Snapping the bill out of his hand, she said with a grin, "I think I like rich Levi way better than poor Levi. It's good seeing you again. Come back real soon, and don't forget your wallet."

She waved the bill at him, then ascended the steps into the Courier and was gone.

"Okay, Rosco, this is where the fun begins," Levi said, pulling the invitation out of his pocket and laying it on the restaurant table.

He unclipped the cell phone from his belt and dialed the number on the RSVP card. Almost immediately, a hesitant female voice answered, "Hello?" Obviously, she'd seen the unfamiliar number before she'd answered.

"Is this Christine White?" he asked.

"Yes?" She didn't recognize the voice.

"I don't know if you remember me, but this is Levi Garvey. We graduated from high school together back in—"

"Of course I remember!" she exclaimed. "It's so good to hear from you! You know you're quite the local celebrity!"

"Oh, well, thanks," Levi said. He was already beginning to regret this decision. "I was hoping it wasn't too late to RSVP for the 25th reunion on Saturday. I know the date to contact you has passed, but I may be able to come, and I wanted to make sure I still could."

He heard her gasp. "Of course you're not too late! I'd love to have you come! In fact, I'd love to get you to say a few words to the class at the dinner if you wouldn't mind!"

Ah, Jesus, he thought, she's still a cheerleader with every sentence ending with an exclamation mark. He could see her in her purple and white cheerleader uniform with the short skirt. He wondered momentarily if she still had the big hair and lip gloss, then decided that of course she did, and she probably still tried on that cheerleader uniform at least once a year to make sure it still fit.

"Well, I'd rather not do that," Levi said. He couldn't think of anything more pretentious than speaking at the dinner at his own high school in front of his own class. "If I can make it, I'd rather keep it as low key as possible. I'd just like to meet up with some old friends and have a nice evening without any hoopla."

"Oh, I see," Christine said without an exclamation mark and with obvious disappointment. "I apologize. I get carried away. It's just that you are such a distinguished member of the Twin Rivers Class of 1985." She said that as if graduating with that prestigious class was an even greater honor than being a two-time bestselling author.

"Great, I hope I can make it," Levi said with false cheerfulness, hiding his thought that he couldn't believe he was actually doing this.

"And Christine?"

"Yes?"

"As you know, it's difficult for me to travel without drawing attention from the media, especially considering I just released my latest book. I'd appreciate it if you could keep this to yourself. I'd like to stay off the media radar. I'm sure I can trust your discretion. And I'm not positive I can come."

"Of course, I will keep it on a *need to know* basis," she said, sounding as if she'd just been entrusted with a national secret.

"I do appreciate it," Levi said.

He knew, of course, that the phones would be ringing off the hook in Twin Rivers two seconds after he hung up. That's why he'd called her. He needed to see Tori, and that phone call pretty much guaranteed that if Tori still lived within a hundred miles of Twin Rivers, she would know in a matter of a few hours he was coming.

"I hope to see you at six on Saturday!" Her bubbly enthusiasm had returned.

"Hope I can be there, Christine. Goodbye."

Levi tucked his phone into his pocket and looked at Rosco.

"Well, Rosco, you ready?"

Rosco looked up at him with big brown eyes, ears straight up.

"Come on. Let's go home."

As soon as he said it, Levi paused. Though the words sounded strange coming out of his mouth, he couldn't believe how easily they'd popped out. He hadn't thought of Twin Rivers as home in a long time, but obviously, some part of him still saw it that way. He wondered, am I going home? Is that what Ray had meant? "If you come back . . ."

They crossed Race Street to the parking lot where his rental car was parked. It was a two-hour drive to Twin Rivers, and Levi realized, to his own amazement, that he could hardly wait to get there.

6

Even before Levi had turned onto the interstate, Rosco was snoring loudly in the seat next to him. Levi hadn't realized how tired he was until he'd gotten into the car. He'd stopped at a Starbuck's in Urbana for a venti coffee. To say it was a strong was an understatement.

It was never easy, flying out of Savannah. Since there were no direct flights from Savannah to any major metropolitan city, connecting flights were always involved. It was no easier driving in and out of Savannah since there was only one major route. The locals were pleased with this fact and often bragged that there was no possibility anybody could ever accidentally find Savannah—people had to *want* to go to Savannah.

Yesterday's travel had been especially grueling because he'd booked it online at the last minute, and he'd had to take what he could get—Savannah to Raleigh to Cincinnati to Chicago to Champaign-Urbana. Four stops and four planes and a couple of long layovers had taken a toll on him—twelve hours all together, and only about five had been spent in the air.

Levi glanced at his sleeping dog. If the trip had been hard on him in first-class, he could only imagine how it'd been for his traveling companion—Rosco was cargo.

To help stay awake, Levi was scanning for a good channel on the radio when he heard a snippet of a familiar guitar riff from one of his favorite songs from twenty-five years ago. He quickly went back to it.

Smiling broadly, he shouted, "Van Fuckin' Halen!" which is what all his friends had shouted years ago whenever a Van Halen song had come on the radio.

The song, "Panama," transported him back to a life he didn't think about much anymore—back to high school and Twin Rivers. The familiar sounds of Eddie Van Halen's blistering guitar solo filled the car. Levi knew every note by heart. He remembered the first time he'd heard the song. In Old Blue . . . with Tori.

The music brought back a flood of memories—skipping school with Tori on the day *The Empire Strikes Back* opened at the Comet Theatre, shooting bottle rockets out the window of Tori's Vega, eating cheeseburgers at Harv's Diner, sitting on the tailgate of his truck and splitting a six-pack with her at Kingery Pond . . .

Saturday June 1, 1985

"I still can't believe you guys did that," Tori said.

Levi had backed Old Blue up to the edge of the cliff on the south end of Kingery Pond—the spot they called the overlook. The cliff towered seven stories over the black surface of the little round pond below. The moon was full, and the silver light reflected off the water. With the moon and stars, the light was nearly bright enough to read by. They were sitting on the tailgate of Levi's 1960 Ford F-100 pick-up truck, sharing a six-pack of Budweiser from a cooler in the bed. Music was playing on the radio in the cab. This was something they'd done often.

But tonight was different. A few hours earlier, they'd graduated from high school.

"You bunch of dorks. I can't believe you mooned the entire school board at graduation," she said, grinning and shaking her head.

"It begged to be done, Tori. I mean they always sit up there in the front row at graduation."

"So you had to moon them?"

Levi looked at her as if she'd said something stupid. "Well, yeah!"

They sat silently for a few minutes. Finally, Tori turned to him. "Now what, Levi?" she said.

"Well, Jim and I were talking about that earlier. We have a dream. We'd like to moon a Presidential motorcade. We're thinking the best location would be on top of an interstate overpass as the motorcade is driving under. I think Ronnie would see the humor in it, but I'm pretty sure Nancy would disapprove. She'd probably start another campaign—this one would be 'Just Say No—to Crack!'"

Tori laughed out loud, her voice echoing out over the pond below. Levi could always catch her off guard.

"No, you moron, I meant now that we've graduated."

"Yeah, that," Levi said with a sigh as he looked out over the water.

After a few moments, he looked over at Tori. In the light of the moon, her skin looked as if it were glowing. She was beautiful. Her blonde hair was long and naturally curly. As long as he'd known her, she'd had one wild ringlet of hair that always got loose and fell down over her face. It was hanging there now, a perfect spiral. He reached over and tucked it behind her ear. In that moment, he tried to take a mental picture of her. He wanted to remember everything—her deep green eyes, her hair, and the way she always wore rock band t-shirts they'd bought together at the concerts they'd gone to. He memorized her mannerisms, like kicking her legs as she sat on the tailgate, her voice, her laugh.

"It changes everything," Tori remarked.

He knew what she meant. Graduation had changed everything.

She was going to school at Purdue, and he was going to the University of Illinois. He could hardly think about being apart from her. Within days of meeting her in sixth grade, they'd become inseparable friends. They *knew* each other. They were the same person in many ways, with the same likes and dislikes. They both covered pain with humor, and they'd both had their share of pain. Tori lived with an alcoholic father, and Levi had a lot of anger towards his parents for abandoning him. They shared that pain with each other and only with each other.

Levi was in love with her. He had been since the first time he'd seen her. But as their friendship became so important to both of them, it became difficult—impossible actually—for him to tell her how he felt. The more they shared, the more he realized he'd rather have her as a friend than risk losing her if he told her how he felt and if she didn't feel the same way. He had tried very hard not to let his true feelings show, but he never stopped looking for signs that she loved him, too. But there was never an indication from Tori that she was anything more than just his best friend.

"Are you going to miss me, Levi?" she said, looking at him. Her eyes were shiny with tears.

"Of course I will," Levi admitted. He wanted nothing more at that moment than to lean over and kiss her, but she sat, as always, with space between them.

"Can I ask you something?" Tori said. "After this summer, we probably won't see each other for awhile, and there is something I'd like to know."

"What?" Levi said, taking a sip of his beer.

"Why didn't you ever try anything with me?"

Levi's head snapped towards her. "What do you mean?"

"You know what I mean, Levi. I know you aren't queer since you've dated other girls—just not me." Levi noted her choice of words.

"I've thought about it, but it might be weird since we're friends.

If it makes you feel better, I never tried to kiss Jim either," Levi said, using humor to cover up his feelings as he so often did.

She smiled. "Afraid you might like it?"

Levi laughed. "No, I was afraid he would."

Tori laughed. "I'm sure you're right about Jim. You're probably a pretty good kisser," she said, crushing her beer can and tossing it into the bed of the truck. She got another one out of the cooler.

Levi looked at her. He could feel his face getting hot and his heart beating more rapidly. What is she doing? Does she want to know? he wondered.

There was an uncomfortable silence between them. They both looked out over the pond, wondering what to say next.

I've got to know, Levi thought. I'm going to take this as a sign. If I don't, I'm going to regret it.

Levi slid over closer to Tori and took her hand in his.

"Listen, Tori. I'm not good sometimes at saying what I'm really thinking, and there are a few things I've never told even you."

Tori looked at him intently. She blew the stray strand of hair that had worked itself free again out of her face. "So tell me. What *are* you thinking, Levi?"

Levi sighed. How do I say it? he thought. Do I just come out with it? Do I tell her I've been in love with her for as long as I've known her, that I can't imagine living a life she's not a part of? Good God, how many hours have I spent thinking about this?

"I've always thought we make a pretty good team," Levi said.

Tori smiled and leaned into him. "We do."

"And . . . well . . .

Just say it! he thought. This could be your last chance. Tell her you're desperately in love with her and don't want to lose her. Ah, screw it, I'll just kiss her. We'll just see how that goes.

He leaned in towards her, and to his surprise, she leaned closer to him.

They were inches apart when headlights cut across them as a

truck slid to a stop on the gravel road in a cloud of white dust. The boom-boom-boom and screaming guitars of Def Leppard filled the air. The bed of Jerry Davis's white truck was full of their recently graduated classmates, all of whom were flashing their bare asses at them and laughing hysterically.

"Hey Levi! Hey Tori!" It was Jim Anderson shouting from the bed of the truck, cackling like a wild man. Obviously, he'd been enjoying a few beverages. "I knew you'd be up here. Thought you'd enjoy *another* full moon."

Everyone in the truck laughed as if that were the funniest thing they'd ever heard.

"Come on. We're going over to Shelia's bonfire! The band starts playing in the shed at ten! They got the Metal Cowboys to play!"

"I think we'll just stay here," Levi said.

"Suit yourself," Jim laughed.

Jerry gunned the accelerator, and the truck threw gravel in all directions as he cut a donut and fish-tailed back down the lane. Levi heard a few rocks hit Old Blue. Instantly furious, he jumped off the tailgate and ran to the edge of the road, yelling after them.

"You ding my truck, you stupid son-of-a-bitch, and I'll beat your sorry ass!"

As the truck roared down the lane, all he could hear was music and laughter fading off as the taillights disappeared into the woods.

Tori handed Levi the last beer, but the moment was gone. They talked until the beer ran out about going off to different schools. Levi noted Tori never mentioned that the two of them could stay in contact with each other. She never suggested that they could visit each other weekends although the distance between Lafayette, Indiana, and Champaign, Illinois, wasn't great. Levi took that to mean that they were friends, high school friends, and now that that phase of their life was over and a new one was about to begin, it was time to move on.

Levi took her home.

She walked slowly up her driveway as Levi watched her, Old Blue idling on the street. He never left until she was in the house. Then she turned, walked back to the truck, and leaned in the passenger window.

"What am I going to do without you?" she asked.

Levi fought the lump in his throat. "You'll be fine. It's going to be tough for both of us."

Tori nodded. Levi saw tears in her eyes.

"Goodbye, Levi," she said, turning suddenly and walking quickly up the driveway.

Levi sat in front of Tori's house long after she'd disappeared inside.

"Goodbye, Tori," he finally said to himself as he put Old Blue in gear and drove home.

He never saw Tori again after that. A few days later, she left for a summer job in Lafayette. Even though there hadn't been a day in the last seven years the two of them hadn't seen or called each other, after that last night at Kingery Pond, Tori never called him, and he never called her.

But in the twenty-five years since, there hadn't been a single day when Levi hadn't thought about her.

7

Christine White swung her black Ford Expedition into a parking space in front of the First National Bank of Calloway. She was sideways across the dividing line, taking up two spaces instead of one, and she'd managed to roll one tire up on the curb. One of the spaces was a handicapped spot. She knew that, but she was busy and couldn't be bothered with such a little detail. She hung up her cell phone, took a sip of her Starbuck's Frappuccino, checked her makeup and hair in the rearview mirror, and climbed out.

An old man sitting on the bench in front of the bank glared at her and shook his head. Christine smiled at him broadly—a smile she'd perfected over decades—and strutted into the bank. But the smile didn't work on the old man. He'd been on Iwo Jima. He'd seen many of his friends go home without arms or legs. There were few things that pissed him off more than idiots who parked in handicapped spaces—even attractive idiots wearing high heels and tight jeans.

As soon as Christine walked into the lobby, the bank president spied her from the window of her office. Oh, crap, she thought, what did I do to deserve this today!

Tori Buchanan very slowly got up from behind her desk and crept across her office toward the window that looked out into the bank. She intended to pull the wooden venetian blinds and hide out in her office until Christine left. She knew it was cowardly, but she didn't care. Tori had made it only half way across her office when Christine spied her and motioned for her to come out.

Damn. It's my own fault, Tori thought. I should have heard the circus music playing right before she came in.

Putting on her best smile, Tori waved back at Christine. She straightened her blazer and tucked a loose spiral of hair behind her ear. Taking a deep breath, she opened her office door and walked out confidently to meet Christine in front of the teller windows. Every man in the bank turned to watch as Tori crossed the lobby.

"Hi, Tori!" Christine bubbled. "I just stopped by to see if you were coming to the reunion this Saturday. I don't remember seeing your RSVP."

Tori smiled warmly as she thought, you dumb bitch, I never go to those.

"I hadn't planned on coming," Tori said, thinking as quickly as she could for an excuse should she need one.

"You really should. This one is going to be very special," Christine said, lowering her voice into a conspiratorial tone.

Tori didn't care about the gossip, but Christine was unlikely to leave until she'd shared it.

"Really? Why is that?"

"We'll be having a very special guest Saturday. . ."

She paused, hoping Tori would drag it out of her. But Tori didn't care.

"Christine, I've got a conference call in a few minutes."

Frustrated by Tori's lack of interest, Christine blurted out, "It's a best-selling author we both know very well."

That news caught Tori off-guard. She hoped her face hadn't betrayed her feelings since she knew Christine would be looking for any reaction.

"Levi is coming?"

Christine was studying Tori's face. It'd long been rumored that there had been something between her and Levi.

"He called me himself this morning," Christine said as if celebrities called her every day.

Tori held her emotions firmly in check, but she could feel a bead of sweat running down the back of her neck. She knew why Christine was there—she was looking for fuel for her gossip machine.

"Well, thanks for sharing. I'm sure Levi will have a great time. He hasn't been home in a long time," she said evenly, smiling as naturally as she could. "I'm sorry, Christine, but I've got to take that call."

Tori walked back to her office and quickly shut the door. As soon as she was alone, she leaned heavily against the door and let out a long breath. She reached over and snapped the blinds shut.

So Levi's finally coming home, she thought.

She walked over to the desk and sank into her leather chair. Opening the bottom drawer, she took out Levi's first book, *But for the Grace of God*, and turned it over to look at the picture on the back. Levi was standing in the doorway of an old building with his arms crossed in front of him, flashing the smile she remembered so well from under the brim of a Panama hat. His soft blue eyes were crinkled at the edges with a few crow's feet, and his hair was beginning to show some gray at the sides. But even after all those years, the impression of that smile hadn't changed. When he smiled like that, he looked as if he'd just pulled off the best prank ever, and nobody knew about it yet. Whenever she'd seen that smile, she'd come up behind him and whispered, "What did you just do?"

As she looked down at the picture on the book jacket, a spiral of hair worked itself loose from where she'd tucked it behind her ear and fell in front of her face.

I'm not going, she thought. It's just a rumor—probably started by Christine to get people to go to the reunion. Levi has got better things to do than chitchat with old forgotten friends.

Tori put the book back in her drawer and slammed it shut decisively.

Little did Tori know that three blocks away at Hillbilly Bob's Convenience Store, Levi Garvey was sitting on the hood of his rental car, sipping stale gas station coffee out of a foam cup and wearing the same Panama hat he was wearing on the book cover. He was waiting with increasing impatience as Rosco sniffed and circled the only tree in the lot beside the convenience store.

"Rosco! There's only one damned tree out there! You're going to pee on it. I know it, and you know it. Lift your leg and let's go!"

8

Harv Jenkins was wiping down the coffee counter as he had twenty or thirty times a day, just about every day, for the past forty years. His wife, April, was in the kitchen doing dishes. It had been a slow morning. There had been a lot of slow days at Harv's Diner in the past few months, so they'd let their waitress go and the dishwasher, too. Like in the old days, it was just the two of them from sunup to sundown every day.

Glancing out the front windows, he saw the white tow truck pull into a space in front of the diner. He yelled, "Hey, April, you want to toss a piece of ham on the grill and three eggs."

Harv heard the sizzle when they hit the grill. Moments later, she came through the swinging door, adjusting her apron, as Ed Garvey walked in through the front door. The bell over the door jangled cheerfully.

"Mornin', Ed," Harv said.

"Good morning, Harv. And good morning to you, April."

Smiling broadly, she set a cup of coffee in front of his usual seat at the counter. Ed smiled back at her, remembering a time when she was the most beautiful girl in River County. In many ways, she still was.

"Your eggs will be up in a minute," she said, looking at Harv with a side-long glance, "if Harv gets back there before they burn up on the grill."

Harv was tying on his white apron. He was a big man, six-foot-four and pushing three hundred pounds. He was struggling to tie the strings on his apron which barely met in the back.

"Now, April, how many eggs have you known me to burn in the last forty years?"

Ed Garvey chuckled as he settled onto his stool. He had the stunning blue eyes that ran in the Garvey family. His hair, which April remembered back when it was blonde, had gone silver. He was still in good physical condition, considering he'd just turned seventy. First thing in the morning, he was so clean he almost squeaked, and he always smelled like aftershave when he came in. April sometimes thought he pressed his t-shirts and jeans. By lunchtime, it would be a different story. Ed would be streaked from head to toe with grime, grease, and oil from stripping parts off the old heaps at his junk yard.

The bell over the door jangled again. April looked up. "Morning, Jack. Morning, Bill."

"Morning, April," they replied as they settled at their usual table—the big round table in the center of the diner called the farmers' table. "We'll have the usual."

April glanced at Harv, who was still fiddling with his apron. "I know, I know, two half-orders of biscuits and gravy," he said as he bumped through the swinging door into the kitchen. Ed could hear him muttering in the kitchen as April took coffee out. "You'd think this was my first damned day workin' here."

Ed grinned as he sipped his coffee. It was the same thing every morning. Everybody in town knew the arguing was part of the entertainment—Harv and April Jenkins were probably the happiest married couple in Twin Rivers.

April refilled his coffee. "So are you looking forward to seeing your nephew? How long has it been since Levi's been home?"

Ed looked at her blankly over his coffee cup.

"I'm sorry, Ed. I assumed you knew."

"I haven't talked to Levi," he said, taking a sip of his coffee.

"Well, it's just a rumor," April said. "Not the first time that rumor has gone around."

"No, it's probably true. I've been expecting him for awhile. He's got a little business to take care of here in town. I think he's been putting it off. Mom's house has touched off a battle between Levi and my brother."

The bell in the order window dinged brightly, announcing Ed's order was up.

"I know Larry Garvey's your brother, Ed, but I never liked him. He was always a very selfish man. And it's probably not my place to say so, but he certainly wasn't much of a father to Levi. You were more of a father to that boy than Larry was."

"April!" Harv bellowed. He was leaning through the order window. "You want to get these eggs out before they get cold?"

April spun around, "Harv Jenkins! How many eggs have you ever known me to let get cold before I served them?"

"About the same number I've burned up on the grill," Harv snorted back.

Ed grinned. Nice one, Harv, he thought. The two men at the table behind him laughed.

But April was right. Ed had raised that boy in his brother's absence as best he could, and he missed Levi. He knew exactly why Levi hadn't been back in so many years, and it didn't have anything to do with him.

9

Levi was parked at the end of the winding driveway. Three hundred feet in front of him sat the house he'd grown up in. It was a beautiful, massive, white Victorian house with stained glass windows, a turret on one corner, and a porch which surrounded three sides. His great-grandfather had built it on a hill at the edge of Twin Rivers in 1913 on the same site where the original Garvey home, which had dated back to the 1860s, had stood. When he was a kid, he thought the house looked like a giant wedding cake.

The six-acre property resembled a huge park with large shade trees surrounding the house. There was an apple orchard towards the back of the property with a stream running through it. As a boy, Levi had followed it to where it eventually flowed into the Calloway River, one of the two rivers which joined on the east side of Twin Rivers, giving the town its name.

His grandmother had kept the house meticulously maintained. The porch had been hung with ferns in the summer, and the gardens that surrounded the house had bloomed year after year with irises, gladiolas, Black-eyed Susans, larkspur, poppies, bleeding hearts, and chrysanthemums. Summer and winter, Lucille Garvey had flown an

American flag from the post beside the front steps, making sure it came in every night at dusk.

One of Levi's best memories was the early-morning aroma of coffee, mingled with the smell of pancakes, sausage, and eggs, and his grandma's voice as she shouted up the steps, "Up and at 'em!"

But the way Levi remembered Grandma Lucille's house and what he saw before him were two very different things. What he saw now was a place that needed a lot of work—maybe more work than he'd be able to do himself. He'd forgotten how long it'd sat empty. It wasn't just the six months since his grandmother had passed away. It was also the three years before that when she'd been in a nearby nursing home. The house had been empty for a long time. And it showed.

It needed a lot more than just paint. The rusty cast iron weathervane on the turret was leaning over. The rust had left a long brown stain across the roof shingles and down the scalloped siding. The front steps were sagging. There were boards over the large picture window behind where the porch swing now hung by only one chain—the window no doubt broken by the swing. Levi remembered that when a storm was brewing, the first order his grandmother gave was to take down the porch swing so the wind wouldn't blow it into the picture window. She'd been right about that.

The corner of the porch that bowed out around the turret room was screened in, making the perfect place to sit during summer evenings when the mosquitoes were out. But from the end of the driveway, he could see long rips in those screens. Even the white gravel driveway was grown over from lack of use.

Levi shook his head. He'd guessed the house would need some fixing, but this was a lot worse than he'd imagined. The feeling that it was a mistake to have come back had begun to nag at him as soon as he'd seen the rusted mailbox at the end of the drive leaning over at a forty-five degree angle in the knee-high weeds.

Slowly, Levi got out of the car. Rosco followed him. As he

approached the house, the nagging feeling became stronger as he saw the damage more clearly. Levi wished he hadn't come back. He wished he could've kept the memory of the house as it had been since the reality before him was too painful to see. The house looked dead, not alive. Now that he'd seen it in this condition, he'd never be able to picture it again as he'd remembered it. He felt the knot forming in his throat.

Grandma really is dead, he thought, and this isn't home anymore.

But Rosco didn't know that. He'd sniffed around some before finding the perfect spot for a nap beneath an old elm tree.

Staring at the house, Levi made a decision—the same one he always made when things got complicated. I'm getting the hell out of here, he thought. There is nothing here for me anymore.

Levi walked back toward the car, then turned when he realized he'd forgotten something. As loud as he could, he shouted, "Rosco, let's go!"

Rosco didn't hear him, and Levi couldn't see him.

"Damnit," Levi said as he climbed into the car and drove further up the driveway toward the house. When he spotted Rosco sleeping beneath the tree, he rolled down the window. "Come on, Rosco! Let's go!"

No movement. Rosco snored on.

When Levi got out, rounded the hood, and leaned over to shake Rosco awake, he saw the blue-gray boulder. Tall weeds were growing around it, but he saw one piece of the engraving. "Rosco the . . ."

He knew what it said, but for some reason, he pushed the weeds back so he could read it all. "Rosco the Hunter. Faithful friend."

As tears blurred his vision, Levi sat on the boulder that marked the grave of his old friend and did something he hadn't done since the day his first faithful friend had died—something he hadn't done when he lost Tori or when his grandmother passed, something he hadn't done when his parents had shown their true colors or when he realized his career was on the ropes.

He cried.

The life he'd known long ago in this house was gone. His life of fame and fortune was collapsing around him. The house in Savannah would evaporate as soon as the cash did, right along with the little gold-diggers who kept him company. Levi suddenly felt very much alone in the world—with no idea about where to go and no idea about what the future held.

10

The bell over the door at Harv's Diner jangled. The muscular frame of Doug Malone, the chief of the Twin Rivers Police Department, filled the doorway.

April sighed.

From under the flat brim of his hat, Doug glanced around at the customers in the diner. They'd frozen for a moment when he appeared in the doorway. Doug Malone made everyone in town uneasy. He sauntered over to the counter with one hand gripping his pistol belt like some gunfighter in a bad Western. He slapped the other hand on the counter.

"Coffee to go," he ordered without looking at April.

She poured coffee into a foam cup and put a lid on it—loosely—hoping it would come off and spill all over his uniform. She set it on the counter along with a green order ticket.

Harv was driving a nail into the wall over one of the booths on the side wall of the diner. He caught Doug's attention.

"What are you doin', Harv?" Doug asked, taking a few steps toward him. "You get another wall-of-famer for your collection?"

On the back wall of the diner was a huge jukebox, a perfectly preserved example of 1950s memorabilia in neon, chrome, and colored glass. It hadn't worked for years, but for over forty years, Harv had covered the entire back wall from floor to ceiling with framed pictures of famous musicians—every one of them personally autographed. He'd gotten a couple of them himself, but most had come from his customers, who'd bring them to him from their vacations and from concerts they'd gone to. Harv would hang them on his wall of fame for the whole town to enjoy. He had pictures of everyone from Hank Williams—that photo had been his father's prized possession—to the most recent addition, Taylor Swift.

"No, I'm starting a new wall of fame—something a bit more local," Harv said.

Stepping back so Doug could see the wall, Harv wasn't disappointed with his reaction. Doug's face went instantly sour. Hanging over the booth was a large picture of Levi Garvey with framed copies of each of his three book covers above it.

"When he comes in here, I'm going to have him sign that picture," Harv said, nodding at the work he'd done.

"Yeah, like he's coming back here," Doug grunted as he turned back to the counter.

April walked past him. "Actually, Doug, the word is he's coming back for the class reunion and to settle his grandmother's estate."

Doug's jaw clenched tightly. Obviously, he hadn't heard that. "Well, he needs to do something with that god-damned eyesore."

"Oh, I forgot. You and Levi didn't get along so well, did you?" she said innocently.

Harv listened with great amusement as April yanked Doug's chain.

"What was it he did to you anyway?"

Doug waved it off. "It was a long time ago. I've let bygones be bygones. I don't even remember what it was, to tell you the truth."

"It must've been something, the way you used to beat him up all the time. I'm surprised Levi wasn't afraid of you, considering you were the big high school linebacker and he was lucky if he weighed a hundred pounds."

April rattled on aimlessly as she filled the napkin dispensers. "But I guess you beating him up didn't bother him very much, did it? It sure didn't stop him from antagonizing you." She smiled at the memory. "He was so smart, and that wit of his was so sharp— sometimes when he'd insult you in here, you didn't seem to understand how you'd been insulted. Sometimes I think you beat on him just because he made everyone laugh, and you were the only one that didn't get it."

Doug's ears grew redder and redder as she talked. She paused and looked at his face which was set as hard as a marble statue.

"Or was it because he dated so many of the prettiest girls? Lord, I remember thinking back then that Levi Garvey was in here every weekend with a different lovely girl. Of course, the prettiest of all of them was Tori Bucha—"

"You know, April, sometimes you talk too much," Doug said, his voice louder than he intended.

Everyone stopped eating and looked at him.

Before picking up his coffee off the counter, he snugged the lid down on top, giving April a suspicious glare. She looked back, wide-eyed and innocent. He walked out the door, leaving the green ticket on the counter. As Doug stormed across the street to the police department, April's innocent stare cracked as she suppressed a satisfied smile. Harv walked up behind her and kissed the back of her neck.

"You can be such a bitch," he whispered to her.

"I don't know what you could possibly mean," she answered as a brilliant smile lit up her face.

Harv picked up Doug's green ticket off the counter and waved it knowingly at April. She frowned as she shook her head. Those tickets were a sore subject between them. Harv dropped the ticket into a box in the cabinet beneath the cash register.

11

Levi stood up quickly when he heard the truck rolling up the driveway. He faced the house, trying to regain control of his emotions. He didn't want whoever was coming to know he'd been crying. He heard the truck door open. A man walked up beside him and put his hand on his shoulder. "Needs a little work, huh?" he said.

Levi recognized the voice instantly. A broad smile crossed his face even as a lump formed in his throat. From the time Levi was little, Uncle Ed had had an eerie sense of timing, always knowing exactly when to show up and exactly what to say—especially when Levi was dealing with something difficult. Whether it was a bad grade on a report card, a wrecked bicycle, or a broken window in the carriage house, Uncle Ed knew just how to help him put things into perspective. Levi could hardly believe how happy he was to see him. He'd never needed him more than he needed him right that minute.

Ed was looking up at the house with his pale blue eyes. Levi noticed how much he'd aged. The lines in his face were much deeper, and he was a bit heavier. He had dark circles under his eyes. But the most noticeable change was his hair, silver instead of blonde.

"A little work? Are you shitting me?" Levi said, shaking his head.

"It needs a wrecking ball."

Ed laughed, sounding a bit like a mule. Even though a lot about Ed had changed, the laugh hadn't. Hearing it snapped Levi back to the past. Levi had to fight another wave of tears.

"Don't be deceived, Levi," Ed said. "Your great-grandpa built that house like a fortress. It's as solid as a rock. He spared no expense, from the oak rafters to the poured reinforced foundation, which was a new technology in Twin Rivers back then.

"Do you have any idea how many tornados have ripped through here over the years? How many ice storms? Blizzards? Scorching summers? Sub-zero winters? This house will still be standing when the rest of the town is dust."

"Really?" Levi said skeptically as they started to walk around the old structure.

Ed nodded and looked at him. He was serious.

"It's just got a little surface damage from the wind and weather over the last few years. A couple days' work and a few minor repairs, and this place will look like home again. It's just been a little neglected."

Levi was doubtful. He knew his uncle possessed the family gift of bull-shit, but he wanted to believe him.

"Come on. When you see the inside, you'll feel better," Ed said, slapping him on the back.

They'd taken a few steps towards the house when Ed stopped and exclaimed, "Oh, no! Not again!"

His outburst surprised Levi. For a moment, he thought his uncle might be having a heart attack. But Ed was looking at something. Following Ed's line of sight, Levi spotted Rosco, who was still asleep next to the grave marker under the tree but now with his feet straight up in the air.

Levi grinned.

Changing his direction, Ed began walking towards the carriage house. "I'll get the shovel," he said.

"I'm glad to see you're still completely full of crap," Levi said, laughing. "That dog's not dead. He's just very sleepy."

Ed stopped to gaze at the dog. "Are you sure? I thought I was having a flashback."

"Rosco!" Levi shouted.

For the first time ever, yelling at Rosco worked. He sprang up suddenly, facing the opposite direction. He looked around for a moment, unsure about what had awakened him. When he didn't see anything, he plopped back down in the grass and closed his eyes.

"Nice dog," Ed said sarcastically as they began walking towards the porch. "You didn't pay money for that mutt, did you? Was there a sale at the animal shelter? Oh wait. You lost a bet, didn't you?"

Levi knew Uncle Ed hadn't changed at all. "Are you done yet, Mr. Funnyman?"

"No, not even close. I can't believe you named that worthless mutt Rosco. What the hell were you thinking? Rosco *was* an honorable name for a dog."

Halfway up the porch steps, Levi's foot fell through the riser. He pulled his foot back up through the rotten hole and looked at Ed. "Solid as a rock, huh?"

"Yeah," Ed said, scratching his head. "I didn't want to say anything, Tubby, but you've put on a little weight, haven't you?"

Uncle Ed had been right. The condition of the house wasn't nearly as bad as Levi had originally thought. His grandmother had done a lot of work on updating the house before she became ill. She'd had all the wiring re-done. She'd replaced the ancient fuel oil furnace with a new one and added central air conditioning. The kitchen had new counters and appliances—including a dishwasher. The bathrooms had received the same treatment. The old wood floors and the wood trim had been stripped and refinished. Even thought the house featured many modern conveniences now, she'd been careful to ensure it retained its original Victorian styling. Even though Levi had grown up in that house, it was difficult for him to tell what was new and what was old.

It was the outside of the house that needed work. It would be a challenge, but Levi thought he could do most of the work on the house himself.

"I may need a little help with the steps and the broken window," Levi said as they again stood on the front porch. "That's a little more carpentry than I'm capable of."

"I know guys that do that kind of work. I'll send them out," Ed said. "I'll get some fresh gravel hauled in, too. That driveway is an eyesore."

Levi was becoming excited about the challenge.

"The big thing will be scraping and painting," he said.

"You've painted this house before," Ed commented.

Levi smiled at him. "Yeah, but this will be the first time I've done it when I wasn't in trouble for something."

Ed laughed. Then he became serious. "Levi, the fact you're here is proof you're in some kind of trouble. The work will be good therapy for you. It'll give you a lot of time to think."

Levi nodded. His uncle was a smart man.

Suddenly, Uncle Ed snapped his fingers. "Ah, hell! I almost forgot something," he said, motioning for Levi to follow him as he stepped around the hole in the steps.

"What?" Levi said.

"Come on," he said, walking towards the carriage house.

The round building sat off the back of the house. There was a chain and a padlock strung between the door handles. Ed pulled a wad of keys out of his pocket, unlocked it, and slid one side open wide enough to walk through.

The interior was enormous—big enough to store a dozen cars. The floor was paved with flagstone. It smelled of grease and oil and old gasoline fumes. The carriage house appeared empty other than for an enormous riding lawn mower sitting in the center of the floor. It was exactly as Levi remembered it. The light from the cupola windows above cast soft rays of light in patterns on the floor.

Ed walked towards the back of the carriage house. Levi followed, his curiosity piqued. The natural light didn't reach that far into the shadows under the loft. It was dark back there. Ed stopped in front of what Levi thought at first was a stack of hay bales. As his eyes adjusted to the shadows, he realized it was something else covered in several old olive-drab tarps.

Ed leaned against whatever it was under the tarps and grinned as if he held the greatest secret in the world. Levi looked baffled as his eyes slowly ran over the object. There was something familiar about the shape. When Levi saw a glint of blue below the edge of the tarp, he gasped and took a step back.

"No way," Levi said, hardly able to believe what he was thinking. It couldn't be possible.

Ed had waited for just that moment of recognition. Like a magician, he pulled the tarps off one by one. Underneath was a blue 1960 Ford F100 pickup—up on blocks.

"Old Blue!" Levi exclaimed.

He was laughing as tears streamed down his cheeks.

"How is that possible? You sold it when I went to college. You sent me the money to pay for my books!"

Ed was grinning broadly. "Yeah, I know. I was the guy that bought it. I wasn't letting Old Blue get away. We'd put a lot of work into this old truck."

Ed had brought the old heap home from his junkyard in 1979—a few weeks after Levi's parents had departed so suddenly for Tennessee. It had looked like a disaster when he rolled in with it on the back of a flatbed truck. It was covered in rust and had weeds growing out of the cab. Ed and Levi had spent the two years before Levi got his driver's license restoring it. Old Blue was how the two had bonded. Working on the truck seemed to help take Levi's mind off his parents leaving him. They'd worked on it several hours every night for two years. When they finished, it was in the same condition it'd been when it'd rolled out of the showroom in 1960.

A week after they'd finished the truck, Levi walked into the house, proudly displaying his new driver's license. Ed threw him the keys. "It's all yours," he smiled.

Here it was decades later, and Ed tossed him the keys again.

"It's *still* yours, Levi. Fire it up," Ed said, grinning broadly.

"It runs?"

Ed looked at him as if he'd just asked the dumbest question he'd ever heard. He opened the driver's door and waved Levi into the truck. Levi jumped in, inserted the key, and turned it. Old Blue instantly roared to life. Levi laughed out loud when he heard the familiar sound of the motor. Ed leaned into the cab through the window.

"She runs better now than she used to. She'll go from zero to sixty in just under half a mile . . . unless you have a head wind."

Levi laughed. "I always knew you brought this truck home knowing I'd never kill myself in it."

Levi's face was glowing. He certainly looked a whole lot less gloomy than he had an hour or so earlier.

"Glad you came home?" Ed asked.

Levi nodded. "I can't believe you, Uncle Ed. I feel like a huge ass for having been gone so long," he said, forcing the words out around the lump that was in his throat again. "You know it didn't have anything to do with you. Don't you?"

Ed nodded.

They looked at each other for a moment. Ed suddenly realized he was about to leak a few tears himself. He turned away.

"Well, don't just sit there burning gas. Let's get the tires on. You're going to need Old Blue this week."

They had the tires on in ten minutes, and Ed slid the carriage house doors open. Levi drove Old Blue out into the sunshine that winked off the polished chrome. He parked Old Blue in front of the house.

As Ed walked down the drive, something caught his eye. The sun was glinting off something across the road, too. He put his hand over his eyes to see what it was. Ah, crap, he thought.

As soon as he noticed the car, cleverly concealed, it began to move. The cruiser pulled onto the road, slowly drove past the Garvey house, and turned at the corner back towards Twin Rivers. Levi noticed a strange look on his uncle's face as he joined him.

"Something wrong?"

Ed scratched his head as he looked towards the road. Levi turned to glance at the road, but there was nothing there. He looked back at his uncle, whose mood had changed.

"What is it?"

"There's something else I need to tell you, Levi," Ed said. The serious look on his face indicated that it was important. "It's about one of your old buddies."

12

Doug Malone had been sitting in his cruiser across from the Garvey house. He'd followed Ed's tow truck at a distance when Ed left town. Doug had pulled into a field access road where the car was practically invisible behind the tall weeds growing along the ditch. He'd been watching Levi and Ed for an hour. The coffee he'd picked up at the diner was cold. Reaching into the glove box, he pulled out a flask and topped off the cup with bourbon.

Levi and Ed had first walked around the house, Ed pointing at different things and sometimes both bursting into laughter. Doug was too far away to hear what they were saying.

Doug was sure Levi wouldn't be in Twin Rivers too long. He'd go to the reunion. He'd fix up the house and put it up for sale. That was what they were talking about—all the things they needed to do to get the house ready to sell. Levi had a life somewhere else. He was just home for a visit.

But Doug didn't like the idea that Levi was back at all. Years ago, Levi had delighted in making Doug look like a fool, and there had been little Doug could do to stop him. Heaven knows he'd tried. Doug had learned a long time ago that Levi couldn't be intimidated. He'd beaten Levi's ass so many times he'd lost count, and it'd had no effect on him at all.

At least Tori won't be in the picture, he thought. But he wasn't so sure about that. She was still around—working in Calloway, not Twin Rivers—but there was a good chance she'd run into Levi. Hell, she might even come to the reunion if she learned Levi was in town even though she'd never come to any of the other ones. With Christine blabbing the news all over the county, there was every likelihood Tori would hear that Levi was back.

Doug felt something wet on his shirt and looked down at the growing brown spot on his shirt. Without realizing it, he'd crushed the coffee cup.

Doug had watched Ed and Levi look at a dog beneath a tree before they walked into the house where they stayed a long time. When they reappeared on the front porch, Ed motioned for Levi to follow him to the carriage house. As they disappeared inside, Doug thought of an old saying, Keep your friends close and your enemies closer. He'd have to get on Levi's good side while he was in Twin Rivers.

Levi and Ed were in the carriage house a long time. Doug was about to leave when he saw Ed appear again and slide both carriage house doors open. Doug couldn't believe what he saw emerge from the doors of the carriage house.

Are you kidding? Doug thought. Old Blue?

He hated that truck almost as much as he hated its owner. He couldn't believe that old truck was still around. His blood pulsed at his temples. Instantly furious, he started the cruiser and pulled away from his hiding place.

He crept slowly past the Garvey house.

13

Ed and Levi were sitting on the porch swing they'd hung back up, drinking beers. Ed never went anywhere without a cooler. They were swinging back and forth with their feet up on the porch rail. Rosco was snoring at the top of the steps, the same spot he favored on the porch back in Savannah.

"I'm not too worried about Doug Malone," Levi said, sipping his beer and staring at his old truck.

The day was beginning to fade as the sun dipped towards the horizon. Levi hadn't been able to take his eyes off Old Blue.

"Well, I think you should watch him. He's not gotten any friendlier in the past couple decades—quite the contrary."

"I won't be here too long. I'll steer clear of him."

Ed nodded. "You two used to be friends. I mean a long time ago, back when you were in grade school."

"Yeah, we used to be very good friends. We used to explore the woods all the time or go fishing for catfish over at the river junction. I don't know what happened. It seemed like in about sixth grade we went from friends to enemies overnight."

"It happens like that sometimes," Ed said. He paused, then

continued. "Sixth grade—that was about the time Tori Buchanan and her dad moved to Twin Rivers from Calloway, wasn't it?"

Levi nodded, suddenly understanding what Ed was getting at. "You think that was it?"

Ed nodded. "She moved to town, and you two started hanging around together. You and Tori were inseparable from the day you met until you left for college. If you remember, Levi, she spent a lot of time out in the carriage house with us restoring Old Blue. But I think Doug liked her, and I think he was jealous. I think he lost a friend and a potential girlfriend all at the same time."

"There was nothing to be jealous about," Levi remarked. "Nothing ever happened between us."

"We could debate that," Ed said, looking at Levi knowingly.

Levi looked away. Ed knew that was a topic they wouldn't be discussing any time soon.

"That can't be it," Levi said.

"Well, it's my theory. Doug's a very angry person. He still hates you. To this day, I think people in town intentionally bring up your name sometimes when he's within earshot just to see his reaction."

"What are you saying? You think I did that? I made Doug who he is?" Levi said, looking at him questioningly.

Ed shook his head. "No, it was in his blood already. It would have come out eventually. Mean runs in that family like blue eyes run in this one. Doug's father was a vicious bastard, too. You see this scar on my head?"

Ed pointed to a small scar at the edge of his hairline. Levi had seen it many times, but he'd never asked about it.

"Doug's father, Randall, did that back in '65 at the Beer Chaser. We were playing pool, and I was winning the game. He was trying to bully me, trying to rattle me so I'd miss a shot and he'd win. We had $20 on the game—that was like a $100 today. I wasn't afraid of that jackass, but I should've been. The fact I wasn't afraid of him made him even angrier." He glanced at Levi. "You know what I'm talking about, right?"

Levi chuckled. Ed could have been talking about Doug Malone just as easily.

"Anyway," Ed continued, "when I sank the eight ball, Randall knocked my ass out cold with a pool cue."

Levi suppressed a grin.

"I never saw it coming," Ed remarked, rubbing the scar. "Hurt like hell."

Ed glanced at Levi, who was obviously trying not to laugh. They both burst into laughter.

Levi reached into the cooler, grabbed two beers, and handed one to Ed.

"I remember Doug's dad, Randall—I was smart enough to be afraid of him. He died when we were in seventh or eighth grade. Hunting accident if I remember right."

Levi looked out towards the horizon where the sun was beginning to set.

"He killed himself, Levi. He took his father's service revolver out in the woods, sat under a tree, and blew his brains out."

Levi looked at him in shock.

Ed nodded. "It's true. You kids didn't need to know the details. I don't think Doug knew the truth until he was in high school. The sad part of that story is that Doug's grandpa, Hank Malone, had shot himself in the family dining room after Thanksgiving dinner some years before with the same gun. The whole family was in the house when he did it. Nobody knows why. Doug was probably six or seven at the time. Hank was a mean one, too."

Levi sat quietly, suddenly understanding something about Doug he'd never known. "Damn, what a life," he said. "No wonder we always met in the woods. He never wanted me around his house."

Ed nodded. "Well, you need to remember that when you're dealing with Doug. There is a lot of pent-up anger in him. He's become his father and his grandfather rolled up in one. He grew up knowing nothing but violence and cruelty."

"You think he's dangerous, don't you?"

Ed nodded. "I think he could potentially be very dangerous. You know, I've seen some stuff in my life . . . before you were born."

It was a subject that came up very seldom. Vietnam, Levi thought, he's talking about Vietnam.

"When you go through experiences like that, you learn things about people. If you survive it, you get kind of a sixth sense. You get to the point you can look people in the eye and tell things about them. Sometimes being able to do that is a blessing and sometimes it's a curse."

Levi said nothing.

"I've looked Doug in the eye, and you know what I see?"

Levi shook his head.

"Fear," Ed said. "He has no confidence in himself. He makes up for that by pushing other people around. He wants everyone to see him as the big man in town, but he's terrified of being exposed for what he is."

"And what's that?" Levi asked.

"A coward," Ed said. "Fear is a very dangerous thing in a person like Doug. Fear makes people unpredictable, and Doug is a ticking time-bomb, Levi. Something is going to set him off one day. You coming back here after twenty-some years . . . well, you need to be thinking about how he might react to that. He hates you. You never backed down from him, and that scares him. He sees you as a threat because he knows you wouldn't be afraid to expose him for what he is."

Levi looked at Ed for a long moment. There was fear in Ed's eyes as well. It sent a chill through Levi. He'd never seen that in his uncle before. Ed wasn't afraid of Doug, but he was genuinely afraid of what Doug might do to Levi. What Ed had said made perfect sense to Levi.

Levi nodded. "I'll stay away from him."

Ed sighed. I hope you mean it, Levi, he thought.

14

It was just after the breakfast rush. April was wiping off the counter. There were a few coffee customers swapping stories at the farmers' table. Harv was standing behind the register, thumbing through the order tickets from that morning and shaking his head. It'd been slow again. Damned recession, he thought.

The chime over the door jangled when Levi Garvey walked in. Harv glanced over at April, who winked at him, a wink that said, I told you so.

Levi stood in the doorway for a moment, looking around. He smiled broadly. Little had changed. Even the farmers sitting at the farmers' table were the same guys that had sat there twenty-five years ago.

April set a cup of coffee in front of the first stool at the counter. Levi nodded at Harv, and Harv nodded back. He walked over to his favorite stool, sat down, and parked his Panama hat on the counter.

"Good morning, sir," April said.

Levi grinned. Oh, she's going to act like she doesn't know me, he thought. I guess two can play that game.

"Good morning, ma'am," he replied.

It seemed like everyone in Twin Rivers had gone gray since he'd left, including Harv. But April had barely changed at all.

"You look very familiar," April said, scratching her head. "Doesn't he look familiar, Harv?"

Harv grunted, "Kind of."

"Oh, I know," April said. "There was this young man who used to come in here all the time back . . . oh, twenty years ago probably."

"Really," Levi said, sipping coffee. It was fabulous.

"Yes, and he looked a lot like you," April said, looking at him closely. "Are you his father?"

The remark caught Levi off-guard. He laughed, shaking his head.

"Oh, is that how we're going to play this, April? Make fun of me because I'm middle-aged now?"

Harv roared along with the men at the farmers' table.

April leaned over the counter and kissed Levi on the head. "I knew you'd be in today," she said.

"You couldn't have possibly known that," Levi said bluntly.

"Would you like to make a bet?" April replied evenly.

She was challenging him. The diner went silent. Levi met her steady gaze.

"Now you might have known I was in town. I'm sure Christine White took care of that. But there's no way you knew I'd be in here this morning. I wasn't sure I was coming in here myself until fifteen minutes ago. I might've come in here last night or tomorrow or not at all."

April leaned on her elbows in front of him. "I not only knew you'd be in here, but I knew you'd sit right in that very spot," she said, grinning.

The truth was she hadn't let anyone else sit on that stool all morning—including Levi's Uncle Ed who favored that particular stool as well.

"I always sit here," Levi said, "and just wait a minute. You led me right to this stool by putting my coffee on the counter in front of it."

"It doesn't change the fact that I knew you'd be in, and I knew you'd sit right there."

"Prove it!" Levi said over the top of his coffee cup.

"If I didn't know it, then why was I up here until after midnight last night making this?" she replied.

She reached under the counter right in front of Levi's stool, pulled something out, and set it on the counter in front of him.

Smiling broadly, Levi put his coffee cup down as he stared at what was before him. "Oh, April," he said.

The men at the farmers' table jostled around, trying to see what it was. Sitting on the counter was a chocolate meringue pie with a note taped to the edge that said, "For Levi Garvey when he arrives at Harv's Grill on Thursday."

Harv chuckled as he scooted past April behind the counter. "Why do you do it to yourself, Levi? Don't you know there's no greater power in the universe than a woman's intuition?"

"I guess not," Levi admitted. "You win, April. You always win."

April cut a big wedge out of the pie, dished it onto a plate, and set it in front of him. Levi took a bite and smiled from ear to ear. It was amazing how a smell or a taste could bring the past back so quickly. Like the coffee, the pie was just as he remembered it—perfect.

"I think I died and went to heaven, April," Levi said.

He leaned over and began devouring the pie on his plate. Suddenly remembering his manners, he turned to the farmers' table behind him. "Anybody want a piece of pie?" he asked.

There was a stampede to the counter, and April quickly dished out pie to the eager customers.

Levi finished his pie, took a deep breath, and leaned back on his stool, coffee cup in hand. April had watched him intently as he ate it. She didn't make pies as often as she used to, but there was nothing that gave her greater pleasure than watching people enjoy them.

"Well?" April said.

Levi thought for a moment. "You know, I've traveled this country from sea to shining sea, and I've eaten pie in some of the finest restaurants in this nation made by some of the best chefs the country has ever produced. In fact, I count Paula Deen as a personal friend of mine—I've been on her television show, and I've eaten many fine meals at her restaurant, Lady & Sons, in Savannah. But I can tell you honestly, you'll never find a better piece of chocolate pie than this in America. When it comes to chocolate meringue pie, April, you *are* the master."

The applause from the farmers' table supported that opinion.

April's face flushed with pride, but she said, "You are so full of crap I can't believe you don't have brown eyes."

"I'm not kidding," Levi said. "That's the best piece of pie I've had since the last time I sat at this counter."

April shook her head. "I just wonder what you'd say, Levi, if your grandma was sitting on one side of you and Paula Deen was sitting on the other."

Leaning back, Levi thought about that one for a minute before he said, "I know exactly what I'd say."

"And what would that be?" April challenged.

"Thanks for the pie!"

The diner exploded in laughter, but when the bell chimed over the door, the laughter and conversation stopped in a split-second. Levi's back was to the door, but he saw April's face as she looked at the door. Her mood changed instantly. She looked at Levi with concern in her eyes. Levi didn't even have to turn around to know who'd just walked in.

"You want a piece a pie, Doug?" Levi said as he swiveled on his stool.

He was looking at Doug for the first time in twenty-five years. He was the same guy—at least 6'4" and pushing 250 pounds, but what had once been a muscular build was now beginning to lean toward the fat side. Square-jawed and flat-nosed, he had a single eyebrow which stretched from temple to temple over small brown eyes. The only thing that was different about him was the smile. Levi hadn't seen a smile on Doug's face in a long time.

"You bet! Is that chocolate?"

Doug quickly crossed the diner, slapped Levi on the back a couple times, and took the stool next to him. He took off his flat-brimmed hat and set it on the counter next to Levi's Panama. Doug's hair was also different. He'd sported a mullet back in the 80s, but what little hair he had left was cropped short and mostly gray.

April wasn't sure what to make of this friendly meeting and glanced at Harv, who shrugged. He had no clue either. She dished out a piece of pie on a plate and slid it in front of Doug, then turned to get him some coffee.

"April doesn't make pie very often anymore," Doug said with a barely concealed sneer.

April poured coffee into the cup in front of Doug.

"Well, Levi was always one of my favorite *paying* customers," she said.

The remark caused Harv to glance up suddenly, a surprised look on his face.

Doug's smile faltered as he stared at her coldly. She glared back.

Just as quickly, Doug switched on the smile again and said to Levi, "It's good to see you. Really good."

"It's been a long time, Doug. It's good to see you, too," Levi said.

April Jenkins never made just one pie. There were two more in the kitchen, just as perfect as the first. Levi was finishing his second piece and Doug his third when Doug finally gave up and pushed the plate away.

They'd been talking the whole time about old friends and times gone by. Doug didn't strike Levi as being nearly as disturbed as Uncle Ed had said. But he also noticed how stiffly April reacted to him, and he'd caught the brief animosity between them earlier. She doesn't trust him, and she doesn't like him, Levi thought.

"I saw that truck parked in front of the diner. I recognized it in a second. Still has the same tags on it—LEVIZ 60. So your Uncle Ed has had that old truck all these years?"

"Yeah," Levi said.

"I'll tell you the truth, Levi," Doug remarked. "I was parked across the road in the lane when you rolled it out of the carriage house yesterday. I wasn't that happy when I heard you were coming back to Twin Rivers for the reunion, and I was spying on you."

A sense of relief ran through Levi. "Well, I'll tell you the truth then. I'm relieved to hear you say that since I already knew. Uncle Ed saw you."

Doug laughed.

"We gotta get over that old high school crap, don't we?" he said. "Get back to being friends again."

"I won't be here too long, but let's do that," Levi said. "We were good friends at one time."

"Those were good times," Doug said, "exploring the woods and fishing the river with Rosco."

Levi nodded.

"I saw your dog sitting in your truck outside when I came in. I thought for a minute it was Rosco."

"What are you talking about? That *is* Rosco. The latest in a long line of German shepherds named Rosco."

Doug took a sip of his coffee.

"Well, he sure is a good guard dog. He probably thought I was trying to touch your truck. When I tried to pet him, he growled at me."

Levi looked at him. "Rosco growled at you?" he said as the hair on the back of his neck stood up.

"Yeah, German shepherds are pretty protective, aren't they?"

"They can be," Levi remarked, trying to sound nonchalant.

He was looking at Doug for any sign of deception, but there was nothing. His uncle's warning about Doug came surging back. And now Rosco . . . Rosco had never growled at anyone. He'd never done anything but wag his tail and lick the people he'd met.

"I sure wish I still had my old truck. I miss The Reaper," Doug said, changing the subject. "I'd do anything to get that old truck back."

Levi remembered the truck well. It was a black Chevy Silverado, back when they still had square hoods. Doug had souped his up with tinted windows and a dual exhaust. It could be heard coming from a block away. It had a chromed roll bar with lights mounted on top and a huge cable winch mounted on the front bumper. The most memorable thing about the truck was the chromed skull and crossbones mounted on the grill and the bug shield that ran across the front of the hood with the words *The Reaper* lettered across it backwards so it could be read in the rearview mirror.

The memory gave Levi a little shudder. He had seen it in his rearview mirror many times along with the skull, usually inches off his bumper.

"What ever happened to that truck?" Levi asked.

Levi looked at Doug when he didn't answer right away. His face had gone tight and unreadable. "I hate to admit this, but I wrecked it. Shortly after graduation, I took out a utility pole."

"We did some dumb shit, didn't we?"

"We did some dangerous shit."

"You mean like walking across the top rail of the railroad trellis bridge over the Calloway River or climbing the Channel 29 news tower?" Levi suggested.

Doug nodded. "We weren't good for each other, were we?"

"No," Levi admitted. "We weren't. It seemed like we were always challenging each other to do dumber and dumber stunts. You know the thing that scared me worse than any of that?"

Doug shook his head.

"You remember Kingery Pond? When we first discovered it?" Levi said.

Doug looked uncomfortable. Obviously, the memory still held power over him, too.

"I do," Doug said.

"I still think about it every so often," Levi admitted. "I've never been that scared in my entire life. I still have nightmares about that."

Doug's face had gone white. "I still can't swim in water if I can't see the bottom."

Levi nodded. He had the same fear. It hadn't been that long ago that he and Brit had spent a day on Tybee Island. He was wading up to his knees in the Atlantic when something brushed his foot. He'd bolted out of the water and up the beach in a full-blown panic attack. All he could think about as he tried to get himself under control was Kingery Pond.

Doug and Levi looked at each other for a long moment, each with the same haunted look in his eyes. For an instant, Levi saw Doug's brown eyes as they were when he was a ten-year-old boy, wearing a striped shirt that afternoon they'd stumbled onto Kingery Pond.

"I don't want to talk about this," Doug snapped suddenly.

"Maybe one day we should."

Doug rose from his stool abruptly. "Agreed, but let's not do it today."

Doug picked up his flat brimmed hat and walked out the door without another word. After he left, Levi noticed that his ticket was still sitting on the counter. He started to pick Doug's ticket up to pay for it when April snatched it off the counter.

"I'll catch up with him later," April said.

* * *

After Levi left, Harv walked over to April.

"April, you're poking the bear," Harv whispered—there were still customers in the diner. "I heard your little remark about 'paying customers.' Do you really want to piss Doug off?"

"Next time he comes in here, I'm going to charge him up front," April said in the same quiet tone.

Harv took a deep breath. He'd known this was coming.

"That would be a big mistake," he said calmly.

April snapped, "It's about time somebody stood up to him. He doesn't run this town. And Harv, this is a business, not a charity. Just because he's the local cop doesn't mean he has a right to free meals and coffee."

Harv glanced around the diner, but nobody was paying any attention.

"I'll take care of it," Harv said flatly. "You stay out of it."

"Like you've taken care of it up to this point?" April said accusingly. "It was a problem back when we were doing well. Now that things have gotten tight, it's inexcusable. He hasn't laid a nickel on that counter in fifteen years. You remember this conversation when we're trying to figure out how to pay our property taxes next month."

"I'll take care of it," Harv repeated.

April snorted. "Standing up to Doug Malone certainly didn't bother Levi Garvey. I think he was the last person in this town who ever did."

She stormed past him and slammed through the swinging door into the kitchen. The sound boomed through the diner, and a few of the customers looked up.

"Anybody need coffee?" Harv said, trying to sound cheerful as he reached for the pot.

Several mugs went up.

15

Doug and Levi were lost in the woods. Of course, as ten-year-olds, neither had brought anything to eat or drink. It wasn't the first time they'd gotten lost, but they'd never been this lost before. After not seeing anything that looked familiar for over an hour, they'd finally stumbled across an old road. They followed it with some trepidation since they figured it was an old Kingery Mining Company road. Following the road was better than being lost because they knew that eventually it would lead them out of the woods, but they'd been told many stories about the dangers of playing on the old mining property. The stories had worked—they'd never played there. As they worked their way down the overgrown road, they were stepping very carefully, remembering what they'd been told about unexploded TNT and bottomless holes. They hoped they were following the trail in the right direction, towards Twin Rivers. The last thing they wanted to do was to follow the road back deeper into the abandoned mining property, which covered thousands of acres.

Seeing something familiar, Doug had run ahead several yards.

His sweat-stained striped shirt was torn on one shoulder, and his Pittsburgh Pirates baseball hat sat askew on his head—his shoulder length hair hanging out underneath. They were both covered with bug bites, scratches, and cockleburs. Doug looked back at Levi with a broad grin on his dirt-smeared face.

"I know where we are now," Doug said, pointing excitedly. "That's Kingery Pond. My dad took me rabbit hunting out here when I was little. You should see this, Levi. It's pretty cool."

They walked to the edge of the water. The pond was circular, like a quarry pond. It was about two hundred feet across and surrounded on three sides by high bluffs that towered sixty or seventy feet above. The pond didn't look very deep. Levi could see the bottom clearly, except in the center, where there was a perfectly round black circle. The pond looked like a donut—a green donut with a deep, deep hole in the center.

"What is this place?" Levi asked.

"It used to be one of the coal mine shafts. The center is like a thousand feet deep. That shaft is how they brought the coal up out of the ground from all the tunnels they dug. They used to drive the trucks in and out of this side. My dad knew all about it—he wrote a paper about it in high school."

"It's creepy," Levi remarked.

Doug nodded. "Dad said there was a bad accident here, a huge cave-in, and a lot of miners got trapped down there, and they couldn't get them out."

"So they're still down there?" Levi asked.

Doug nodded. "There wasn't anything they could do with it after it caved in, so they just left it. Over the years, the whole thing filled up with water."

They looked at the water for several minutes.

"Let's go. I'm ready to get back and get some lunch," Levi said.

"I'm hot," Doug said, peeling off his shirt. "I'm going to cool off first."

"You're going to swim in there? Are you nuts? That water smells terrible," Levi argued.

"Ah, suck it up. I'm going to get wet," Doug said, stripping nude. "It's safe along the edges. The shaft is clear out in the center."

He waded into the water—the pond was only about two feet deep around the shaft. When he had gotten out about six feet from shore, he lowered himself into the water, resting his butt on the bottom.

"God, this feels good," he remarked.

Levi knew better, but the heat was sweltering and the water, as brackish as it was, was irresistible. He peeled off his clothes and was soon wading out towards Doug. The bottom was covered in green slime, and the mud squished like clay between his toes. The water felt as hot as the air.

"This water is warmer than a bath tub, and it stinks," Levi remarked, wrinkling up his nose.

"Come out a little further. It gets cooler the further out you get."

Soon they were both sitting on the bottom, up to their necks in the slimy water.

Levi looked at Doug. "You ready to get out of here?"

"Yeah, but not before I swim across that hole," Doug remarked, grinning.

Levi laughed. "You're nuts."

He knew Doug couldn't be serious, but suddenly, Doug stood up and began wading out towards the black hole in the center.

"Doug! Come on! This isn't funny!" Levi yelled.

"Oh, come on, you pussy! That hole is only about twenty or thirty feet across," he said as he continued plunging through the shallow water towards the center.

Levi stood up in the water and watched as Doug plowed forward.

"Don't get too close to the edge! It could cave in and pull you down!"

Doug waved him off, but Levi quickly splashed after him. Before he knew it, Levi was standing beside Doug several feet from the edge of the abyss in the waist-deep water.

"I'm getting out of here. I'm not doing this," Levi said.

"Look, we swim over the shaft on our backs. You won't even know you're doing it. Just keep swimming until either you feel the bottom or you hit the shore on the other side. No sweat! We swim further than that all the time."

"It's stupid," Levi said firmly.

"Ah, you're chicken."

"I'm not chicken," Levi said.

"Good," Doug said. He turned around so his back was to the shaft. "On the count of three, we push off, and swim on our backs until we hit the shore."

"I'm not going to—"

"One!"

"Doug! This is really dumb—"

"Two!"

"You've got to be kidding," Levi said turning around so his back was to the shaft, too. He knew Doug was trying to fake him out. Levi wasn't about to jump off on three. He knew Doug was trying to trick him into doing it while he stood there laughing at him. That was just like him.

"Three!"

To Levi's surprise, Doug pushed off and began swimming on his back towards the shaft. For reasons he never understood, Levi pushed off, too.

Levi swam as fast as he could. Within seconds, he felt the temperature of the water change. It was cold. He knew he was over the shaft. As he swam, he turned his head, and from the corners of his eyes, he could see the blackness below. He squeezed his eyes tightly shut. His heart was beating so hard he could feel his pulse in his temples. He couldn't believe how quickly he'd made such a stupid decision, but there was no stopping now. If he stopped, he was dead. He knew it.

He kept going with his eyes clenched shut for what seemed like a long time. He kept waiting to feel his head bump against the far shore. His arms were getting tired and heavy. He kept thinking, I've made it over the shaft. I've been swimming forever. I've got to be swimming in the shallows now.

He stopped and put his feet down, expecting to find mud below, but there was nothing there. He opened his eyes. There was nothing but blackness below him. He was in the dead center of the abyss. Have I been swimming in circles? he thought, his heart pounding wildly.

Now the panic really began to set in, but he was so tired he wasn't sure he could keep swimming. His head bobbed below the surface, and he got a mouthful of smelly water. That changed his mind. He'd either make it out, or he'd die trying. He began swimming furiously in the direction he'd come. He couldn't see Doug anywhere.

Suddenly, he felt something touch his foot. In fact, he thought something grabbed at his foot. He had a horrifying vision. Maybe what he felt was Doug drowning below him and trying to save himself by pulling him down, too. He'd learned about that in Scouts—that very often somebody drowning would drown the person trying to save him. The other thought was even more horrible. Maybe it was something else—something unimaginable and even more terrifying that lived in the depths below.

Levi was so scared he was thrashing more than he was swimming. He felt himself sinking in the water as he swam. Each time his face went below the water, he got another burst of energy and kept swimming. He could see ahead of him where the bottom turned from black to green—he knew that was the shallow water. It didn't look very far away, but it just didn't seem like he was getting any closer to it.

A sudden cramp in his side paralyzed him. As he began to sink, he could see the surface of the water getting further and further away, but the edge of the shaft looked so close, just a few feet away— a few feet, and he'd be standing on the shallow bottom around the edges instead of sinking into the black center. But he knew he couldn't reach it. So this is what it's like to drown, he thought.

A hand from above plunged into the water and grabbed his hair and pulled him up. Doug pulled and tugged until they were well away from the shaft. Then from a safe distance, they stood up in the shallow water and looked back at the ominous black hole.

"Something grabbed my foot out there," Levi said.

Fear flicked across Doug's face. "Let's get out of here," he said as calmly as he could.

Suddenly, a giant bubble erupted on the surface of the water in the center of the shaft, and toxic, choking fumes permeated the air.

In a split-second, the urge to flee seized them both. They turned and began running through the shallow water as fast as they could. They grabbed their clothes and continued to run. Neither looked back, but they both had the feeling that something was chasing them.

Levi sat bolt upright in bed, covered in sweat, his heart pounding in his ears. It took him a second to gain his bearings in the unfamiliar room. Then he remembered where he was—in his old room . . . at home.

He didn't know how many times he'd had that dream, but the most frightening part was that it had actually happened.

As his heart slowed, he took deep breaths, but even as the terror of the dream began to fade, he could still feel the grasp of something on his foot.

16

Feeling totally worn out, Levi was finished for the day. After he backed Old Blue into the carriage house, he stood at the double doors, admiring her. He still couldn't believe Uncle Ed had kept that truck all those years.

Smiling, he slid the doors closed, noticing that it took a lot more effort to close them than it had to open them that morning. He was so sore he could hardly move.

As he walked down the driveway with Rosco at his heels, he admired the work he'd accomplished on the house. He'd spent the entire day scraping paint and had gotten most of it done. If he spent a few more hours scraping in the morning—if he was able to move at all—he'd be ready to begin painting. Again, Uncle Ed had been right. The worst part was the front of the house, the weather side. The other three sides wouldn't require much prep work or scraping at all.

He stood near the corner of the porch, looking up at the house, which looked a lot better with all the peeling paint gone. Levi could envision how it would look with a fresh coat of paint. It was amazing what a difference one day had made in the appearance of the Garvey house. With the exception of replacing the front steps, Levi was certain he could do the rest of the work himself.

As promised, Uncle Ed had sent some friends to help out. They'd been showing up all day. There was a fresh layer of gravel on the driveway. The weeds were gone from the flowerbeds and from around the carriage house, and the brush piles had been hauled off. Ed had also sent out a friend from the glass company to replace the picture window the porch swing had knocked out. Levi was beginning to recognize the place again. And that felt great.

Despite having paint chips stuck all over him, blistered hands, a sunburned neck, and sore muscles from climbing up and down the ladder all day—despite all that, Levi had never felt better.

And as he worked, he'd been thinking about what he was going to do next. He was at a crossroads—he knew that. It was time to pick his path. He'd made at least one important decision—he was going to write another book. What kind? He didn't know yet. He needed to find a subject that was new and fresh. And because the memories in Illinois were so powerful, there was a good chance that what he needed for inspiration was right there.

Ever since he'd climbed off the plane in Champaign-Urbana, he'd been buffeted with strong memories and even stronger emotions. Some of these things he hadn't thought about in years, and others had come rushing back in perfect clarity. The University of Illinois Quad, tree-lined and peaceful at dusk. Audrey at the Courier Café. Uncle Ed and Old Blue, a gift from the past he thought had been gone for twenty-five years. The blue-gray boulder beneath the elm tree—Rosco the Hunter. The diner with Harv and April Jenkins, who never seemed to change. Chocolate meringue pie. The vivid nightmare of Kingery Pond. The Garvey house. His grandmother.

And Tori. Always memories of Tori—the sixth grade girl he'd fallen in love with. The friend he'd never forgotten and with whom he'd shared his deepest thoughts. The only girl he'd ever really loved and the one he'd never told. The love of his life who'd gotten away because of one lousy minute—one minute he'd let pass. That one minute he'd spent twenty-five years reliving and regretting again and again. Always memories of Tori . . ..

There is a story here, he thought, right here in Twin Rivers. I'll just need to recognize it when it comes along. But it's here.

So one decision had been made—write the book. But something else had been going on in his mind as he worked. Was he close to another decision? Decision two?

He'd caught himself several times imagining himself living in Twin Rivers—sitting on the front porch with his feet up on the porch rail and the fall leaves swirling around the front yard as he worked on his laptop, writing at the old roll-top desk in the library with a fire crackling in the fireplace as the winter wind howled outside.

He didn't seem to have any control over those thoughts, which would take him completely by surprise. Similar thoughts came in other forms. While eating his lunch on the roof of the porch, he'd thought, I really need to plant a couple of Colorado blue spruces beside the driveway. They'd look great with Christmas lights on them.

He'd wondered several times that day if his mind hadn't already made decision number two without informing him. This is home, he thought. I'm not going back to Savannah, am I? I've found a little retreat here. This is a place where I can think straight and work without distraction. It feels right, doesn't it? And I think Grandma knew that when she prepared this house for another generation. She did that for me. She knew I'd be back.

He smiled at that thought.

Maybe he'd stumbled on what every great writer needed—a quiet place. Hemingway had written from a hideaway in Key West. Stephen King plied his craft from a Victorian mansion in Maine, not that much different from the Garvey house. Ian Fleming had found his solace at Golden Eye, his private estate on St. Mary Parish in Jamaica.

I don't belong in Savannah, Levi thought. Ray Billings knew

that. He knew once I came home, I'd stay home.

The other thing that attracted him to Twin Rivers was that he could be anonymous there. In Twin Rivers, he wasn't Levi Garvey, the famous author and celebrity. He was just Levi Garvey, Lucille Garvey's grandson and a 1985 graduate of Twin Rivers High School. He could stay out of the spotlight and focus only on writing great books.

But then there was Doug Malone to consider.

Doug's putting on a pretty good act for me, Levi thought. But if I decide to stay, I think he'll quickly revert to the Doug I knew in high school. That could be a big problem. I've got to slow down and think this through. This decision is too important to make based on nostalgia.

He glanced down at Rosco. "You must be starving. I haven't fed you all day."

Rosco's tail began to wag enthusiastically.

"Come on," Levi said, carefully walking up the edges of the porch steps so that he wouldn't crash through the risers again.

17

Levi had changed clothes half a dozen times. He wasn't sure what to wear to the reunion. Finally, he pulled on a pair of jeans, a t-shirt, and a denim shirt. Looking in the mirror as he rolled up the sleeves, he thought, good enough. We're in Twin Rivers, so I won't be the only one in jeans.

"You going to be okay here by yourself?" Levi asked Rosco, who was snoring on the bed behind him.

The dog never flinched.

As he put on his Panama hat and started out of his bedroom, he paused for a moment to glance in the mirror one more time. The hat seemed a little pretentious for the reunion, so he took it off and tossed it onto the bed next to Rosco. He walked down the stairs into the foyer, grabbed the rental car keys off the table beside the door, then paused again. Smiling, he tucked those keys into his pocket and took the ones for Old Blue off the hook beside the door. After all, Old Blue hadn't been to the high school in a long time either.

It was a short drive to Twin Rivers High School. Levi wasn't surprised to note the high school hadn't changed very much, with the exception of the new electronic sign in front. In bright, flashing light patterns in the school colors, purple and white, the sign welcomed the Twin Rivers Class of 1985. He was, however, a little surprised when he pulled into the parking lot half an hour early that, other than a catering van, nobody else was there. He got out of Old Blue and walked toward the school.

When he arrived at the open gym, he was suddenly transported back decades. The reunion committee had recreated the decorations from the senior prom. The traditional crepe paper ribbons suspended from the ceiling formed twisted arches of purple and white which met in the center of the gym. Hanging as a centerpiece from the rafters was a huge papier-mâché comet. Hundreds of purple, white, and black balloons covered the entire ceiling of the gym with shiny foil streamers hanging below them to about ten feet above the floor. It was astonishing how closely the decorations matched what he remembered from the senior prom. This has got Christine White written all over it, he thought.

The only difference in the decorations was the posters that covered the walls all the way around the gym—there must have been a hundred of them. Christine had blown up the black and white pictures from the 1985 yearbook. There were group shots, individual senior pictures, and candid shots of various classmates horsing around in the hallways. Levi was impressed until he saw his poster. He shook his head and thought, Are you shitting me, Christine?

His was the only picture in the gym that wasn't taken from the yearbook, it was the only one in color, and it was nearly twice the size of any other poster. It was hanging right behind the head table. Christine had blown up the author photo from the back of his first book. Now he was really glad he hadn't worn the Panama hat.

There were about a dozen large round tables, crisscrossed with purple and white paper ribbons, with ten chairs at each as well as the long head table, up on risers of course, where all the class officers and the in-crowd would no doubt sit. Twenty-five years, Levi thought, and they still think being popular in high school was their most important achievement in life.

"Hello?" said a voice behind him.

Levi jumped. He turned to face an older woman who was wearing an apron and carrying a tray of coffee cups.

"Oh, hello," Levi said. "Doesn't the reunion start at six?"

"Yes, it does," she said. "There will be a social hour first with an open bar, and dinner will be served at seven."

"I'm surprised nobody is here yet," Levi remarked.

She looked at him questioningly, then glanced at her watch. "Well, it's only 4:30."

Levi stared at her for a minute, then looked at his watch. It was 5:30. Suddenly, it dawned on him. You idiot, he thought. You never changed your watch. You're still on Savannah time.

Smiling, he said, "Well, I seem to be in the wrong time zone."

She smiled politely and set her tray down on a table that had been set up as the bar. "You have a good time this evening," she said as she walked out the gym doors towards the cafeteria.

Levi strolled around for a few minutes. The tables all had place markers. Levi looked around for his name, but he couldn't find it. Suddenly, it occurred to him with sickening clarity where he'd find his marker. He climbed the risers to the head table. Sure enough, he found his name right next to Christine White's. Oh, this will never do, he thought.

There wasn't any question in his mind where he'd find his friends—the group known as the Zoo Crew. He walked straight to the table furthest in the back, finding, as he'd expected, all of his friends' names. Next to the Zoo Crew table was a collection of names he recognized as the dorks, nerds, and geeks from the class of 1985.

You know, this pisses me off, he thought.

Grinning wickedly, Levi walked back to the head table. It had never been a good thing when Levi Garvey got annoyed, and this annoyed him on many levels. He picked up the place marker with his name on it, and, as he tapped it on his chin, he began to plot a little social justice.

To kill an hour, Levi drove over to the Beer Chaser where he had a beer with Uncle Ed. When he returned to the high school, the parking lot was full. He parked Old Blue in the same spot he'd always parked in when he was in high school. He couldn't wait to see his old friends. He'd been looking forward to the reunion all day.

When he walked into the gym, what he saw made him grin broadly. It was like a three-ring circus. Finding a place next to the door, he leaned against the wall so he could take it all in.

He recognized Christine White instantly. She was right in the center ring, looking exactly as he'd expected with big hair hacked at odd angles to her face, long nails, sunken cheeks, big empty eyes, and store-bought boobs. She was wearing a skimpy black dress and wobbling on high heels. The dress was so tight Levi could tell from across the gym she was wearing thong panties.

And emotionally, she was somewhere between panic and tears.

She was standing at the round table right in the center of the gym, the table directly in front of the head table—what might be called the best table in the house. She was trying to pick up the place markers while waving her hands frantically. She wanted everyone at that table to get up and move to the back table. Of course, the Zoo Crew was completely ignoring her. Every time Christine leaned over their table to snatch a place marker, one of the Zoo Crew would stuff a dollar bill down her top.

"I didn't know there would be entertainment!" Jerry Davis cackled as he pulled dollar bills out of his wallet. "I'd have brought more singles! Don't get me wrong, Christine. You're still kinda hot for an old cougar, but before you get a fiver from me that top is gonna have to come off!"

The Zoo Crew roared with laughter.

Her face bright red, Christine stormed off towards Chuck

Franklin, the long-ago quarterback of the football team. She had a brief but animated conversation with him, her arms flailing as she pointed from the tables at the front to the table in the back. Obviously, she wanted him to go over and make the Zoo Crew move. He looked at her as if she were nuts, slowly shaking his head. He wasn't having any part of that.

Jim Anderson had just swiped an entire beer cooler from the bar and was rolling it over to the Zoo Crew table. Although the event had just started, his old friends had already started building a pyramid of empty beer cans on the center of the table—what they'd used to call a "beer-a-mid." Levi knew that by the end of the evening that tower would be at least three feet tall. He'd seen that particular brand of stupidity before, repeatedly. And tonight, they weren't at a back table—they were right in the center ring.

As Christine stormed away from Chuck, she noticed two members of the class from the dorks-nerds-and-geeks' table finding their place cards on either side of her place at the head table. Her face went absolutely pale. The idea they would be joining her at the head table was more than she could take. They were even more surprised to discover their names at the head table than Christine was. As they found their places, they began waving over their friends from the chess, the math, the A-V, and the French clubs to join them.

Christine was losing the battle—she was about to fly apart. Storming back to the Zoo Crew table, she pointed accusingly at Jim Anderson with a brightly colored acrylic nail.

"I know you did this!" she hissed at him. "You've ruined the party."

Jim's face fell, and his bottom lip began to quiver. "What? I've ruin the party? Oh no!"

He threw his head down on the table and sobbed so loudly that everyone in the gym turned to see what was going on. A roar of laughter rolled across the gym. Levi was smiling so broadly, his face was beginning to hurt.

On the verge of tears, Christine went to the very back tables where the in-crowd was sitting and began apologizing profusely.

"I know it was the Zoo that did this," she said, pointing at the center table. "Those jerks will never grow up! They're animals!"

Hence the name, Zoo Crew, Levi thought. If you remember, my dear Christine, it was you who first called us that. You got a big laugh out of it at our expense—probably the only funny thing you've ever said.

But instead of taking it as the insult it was intended to be, the group had adopted the name as their own.

"Don't worry about it," said Al Harris, the class president. "This is fine, Christine. It's kinda funny actually."

Christine's eyes nearly popped out of her head. "Don't worry about it?" she said, her voice rising just to the edge of hysteria. "Don't worry about it? It's not you up there at the head table eating dinner with Smelly Ellie and Doobie Duane!"

That was almost too much for Levi. With tears were running down the sides of his face, he burst out laughing. Levi was enjoying this more than anything he'd seen in years. Payback is hell, Christine, he thought.

Suddenly, he was aware that somebody was standing behind him, but before he could turn to see who it was, she whispered just loud enough for him to hear, "What did you just do?"

Levi knew the voice well.

Tori . . .

18

"Well, are you just going to stand there looking at me with your mouth hanging open?" Tori said with a wide grin across her face. Levi's expression made her decision to come to the reunion worth it.

Levi couldn't believe it. Tori looked stunning, from her dazzling green eyes to her kinky blonde hair. She certainly wore her age well. The black jeans, boots, and blouse accentuated all her best physical attributes brilliantly.

"Sorry," Levi said. "I just thought you'd be old and gray and fat. But you look like you just stepped out of the yearbook."

Tori laughed. "Well, I have to admit, I thought the reason you wear that Panama hat on your book covers is because you're bald."

Levi ran his fingers through his hair. "Money can't buy you love, but it can buy hair."

"Yeah, that's nice," Tori said, reaching up to touch his hair at the temples. "Is that William Shatner's old hair piece?"

Levi laughed out loud. "I've sure missed you, Tori."

"I've missed you too, jackass."

She put her arms around his neck, and they hugged. When they were finished, she looked at the chaos in the gymnasium, shaking her head.

"You want to explain one thing to me?" she asked.

"Just one?" Levi said. "There's a lot going on here."

"Yeah, there is, but I have just one question. Why does Christine White have dollar bills sticking out of her dress?" she asked.

"Well, Tori, the Zoo Crew hasn't changed very much either."

"Ah," she nodded knowingly. "Jerry?"

"Of course," Levi said with a nod.

"So are we going to lean against the gym wall all night watching the Christine White Show, or are we going to have a seat eventually?"

"Let's go sit down," Levi said.

"Now I'm not accusing you of anything, Levi, but you don't happen to know where we're sitting, do you?"

"Wherever we want," Levi said with a broad smile.

He reached into his shirt pocket and pulled out two place markers. One read Levi Garvey and the other Tori Buchanan.

"You're a very bad man," Tori said.

"I just can't help myself."

"Oh, look! I think I see a couple empty chairs at the Zoo Crew table," Tori said with mock surprise.

When she pointed, Levi noticed there was no ring on her finger. "How fortuitous! Will you join me?" he said, bowing formally and offering his arm to her.

"It would be my pleasure, Mr. Garvey," she said, taking his arm.

Tori set an empty beer can on the beer-a-mid in the center of the table.

"The good thing about this," she said, "is that if we keep drinking, I won't be able to see Jerry in another hour."

"Oh, nice," Jerry said. "I know why you came here tonight, Tori. You knew I was coming, and you just couldn't resist seeing me again."

"Yeah," Tori grinned. "It was sure nice of the Illinois Department of Corrections to give you a furlough so you could attend."

"Well, they made me come with Alan here," Jerry said, elbowing Alan Haig.

Levi put an empty on the pyramid. "Oh, that's right, Alan. I heard that you're a police officer now."

Alan had been a quiet, soft-spoken kid in school, and he'd seemed the same this evening. But when the attention turned on him, he seemed to puff up right in front of Levi.

"I am," Alan said. "Right here in Twin Rivers. I'm Doug's number two man."

"Where is Doug?" Levi asked suddenly. "He said he was coming."

"He's probably writing some old lady a ticket for an overdue library book," Jerry said loudly.

The Zoo Crew burst in raucous laughter again—everyone, that is, except Alan whose face had gone hard.

"You don't even have respect for the law," he said, looking around the table with eyes flashing.

He started to rise from his chair, but a chorus of apologies stopped him.

"I'm sorry, Alan," Jerry said. "Sometimes my mouth has a tendency to run."

"Sometimes?" Alan said as the hint of a smile crossed his lips.

The Zoo Crew table erupted in laughter again.

Tori had been looking at Levi with a strange look on her face. "Did you say you've talked to Doug?"

"Yeah," Levi remarked. "He's mellowed. We've had coffee a few times during the last couple days."

Tori glanced around the table. Jerry looked surprised as he took a long sip of beer, and his eyes darted between Tori and Levi. Jim said nothing. The table was suddenly quiet.

"What?" Levi said when he realized the conversation had just died.

Jim Anderson looked at him sternly. "You're playing with fire there, Levi. Doug has not changed, and if he's being nice to you, there's a reason. I apologize for saying this, Alan, since I know you two have been friends a long time and you work together, but the fact is Doug Malone is still a complete asshole."

"I agree," Tori said angrily. "I mean didn't you learn your lesson after all those times he beat the snot out of you? How stupid can you be? You should stay away from him!"

"Stay away from who?" a voice said from behind her. Doug Malone was standing there dressed in his police uniform.

"You, Doug," Tori said sharply.

Doug smiled, apparently not offended in the least. He walked around the table until he saw his place card, then sat opposite her.

Tori looked at Levi incredulously. It was a look that clearly said, "You put him at our table?"

"I know there's some bad blood between us," Doug said, "but if Levi and I can put it behind us, I was hoping all of us could."

The table was dead quiet.

Then Jim Anderson leaned over to reach inside the cooler beside the table. "You want a beer, Doug?"

"Sure," he said, reaching over to take it.

"Are you shitting me? You gutless wonders." Tori's eyes flashed angrily at Jim Anderson as she pushed her chair back from the table. "I saw Lisa Paine earlier. I think I'll go say hello to her. Enjoy yourselves," she said sarcastically to everyone at the table.

19

Tori finally returned to the table when the meal was served, but she didn't have much to contribute to the conversation. She neither looked at nor spoke to Doug. As soon as she finished eating, Tori left the table again. Levi thought she'd gone to the restroom, but when she didn't return, he went looking for her.

He found her staring at one of the posters from the yearbook, a picture of a very pretty girl with dark hair, dark eyes, dimpled cheeks, and a voluptuous figure. Levi recognized the girl, but he'd forgotten all about her. It took him a minute to even remember her name.

"Hey, isn't that Mel?" he said.

"Her name is Melissa," Tori said. "Melissa Sinclair."

"Oh, yeah. She was so quiet and shy—always hanging around the Zoo Crew but not quite one of us. Didn't she go out with Jerry for a while?"

Tori nodded. "What do you remember about her?"

Levi thought for a minute. "Not much of anything."

Tori looked at him. "Back when I was in grade school in Calloway, before we moved to Twin Rivers, I went to school with her. I was terrible to her. I was almost as bad to her as Doug Malone was to you."

"I can't imagine that. What'd you do? Beat her up all the time?" Levi said, grinning.

"It's not funny, Levi," Tori said. "She was that girl with the thick glasses, who walked around all tense and clutching herself like she was afraid of her own shadow. She wore the same white sweater to school every single day—summer and winter. So, of course, the other girls started teasing her."

Levi knew something was bothering her, so he was careful about what he said. "Every class had a girl like that."

"I don't know why, but I took on the role of head bully. I used to tease her about her glasses and about wearing the same sweater everyday. I made fun of her hair. I used to make her cry just about every day."

"That doesn't sound like you. Why would you do that?" Levi said.

Tori shrugged. "I wasn't too far away from being her myself. You know my situation growing up."

"I do," Levi said. They'd talked often about her mother dying when she was little, about her dad's spiraling alcohol problem, about the fact there was never much money.

Tori sighed, "I guess at that age I thought it was better to focus the attention on somebody else—to keep it off me."

"We all did that at one time or another," Levi said. "Kids are terrible to each other."

"She was one of the first girls in our class to begin to develop."

Levi looked at her blankly.

Tori looked at him as if he were stupid. "She started getting her boobies, you moron."

"Oh," Levi said, suppressing a grin. "Right. Boobies."

"I started calling her Raisinette, and it stuck," Tori said regretfully.

Levi snickered. "That's pretty mean, Tori. Let me guess, she was all nipple and no—"

"You know, Levi, sometimes you can be a real ass," Tori said. "I'm trying to tell you something serious, and you're making jokes."

"Come on, Tori," Levi said. "It was a long time ago. She obviously grew out of it. I mean, look at her. She was beautiful—a real hottie. And, by the way, those aren't exactly raisins in that picture. In fact, those are more in the melon range. I'll bet she found a nice man, got married, and had a bunch of kids. She's probably happy now and has forgotten all about those difficult school years."

Tori looked at him and shrugged. "I was thinking about her earlier. I was looking through our old yearbooks before I left. You know, she was in just about every picture of the Zoo Crew in all four yearbooks. Where we were, she was."

Levi nodded. "She was always around us, I do remember that. Obviously, she forgave you. She got over it, so why haven't you?"

Something was still eating at Tori. "She was always around us, right? But can you tell me one single thing about her? Her favorite candy bar, for instance?"

Levi started to answer her, then stopped and shook his head.

"What's mine?"

"Almond Joy!"

"Jim's?"

"Snickers"

"And you went for peanut M&M's every time," Tori said.

"Still do."

Tori shook her head. "I bet I could name the favorite candy bar of every one of our friends from high school and about a hundred other things about them—their favorite car, rock band, TV show."

"I see where you're going with this, Tori," Levi said. "But she was very quiet. She didn't share much. Actually, she didn't share anything."

"You dated just about every hottie in this school. Did you ever go out with her?"

Levi looked at the picture. "No."

"She was always around us, so why not? She was pretty. She had those melons you seemed to like."

Levi smiled . "I remember noticing those—I mean her. I even talked to her a few times. Well, I tried to talk to her a few times, but I got nothing back. She didn't have any personality. She was a blank."

Tori was silent.

"I wonder what ever happened to her," Levi said, looking at the poster.

"Was there a place card for her?" Tori asked.

Levi thought for a minute, then shrugged. "Don't get mad, Tori, but I don't think I would've recognized her name earlier."

"Where would you've put her?" Tori asked.

Levi sighed. Suddenly, his experiment in social justice didn't seem nearly as funny. "If I didn't recognize the name, I'd have put her at the head table."

Tori looked over at the head table. "I don't think she's here, but I think I'll go ask somebody."

Tori walked towards the head table. Levi stood for a minute, looking at the picture. Something about Melissa Sinclair had grabbed his attention. Strange how you can completely forget about somebody you saw every day, Levi thought.

Something in the back of his mind sizzled, something he hadn't felt in a long time. It was an idea, ripe with potential. I wonder what ever happened to Melissa Sinclair? he thought.

Suddenly a story began to form in his mind. He knew he had something. He just had to think about it—let it perk a little while. But he knew if he could build a story to answer that simple question, he just might be well on his way to his next novel. It could be as simple as that.

The smile he'd been wearing all evening got even wider.

* * *

Doug Malone had been watching Levi and Tori standing in front of the poster. He didn't like that at all. It was the worst possible scenario. The way Levi and Tori had fallen back into step with each other was one thing, but now they were talking about Mel.

Melissa Sinclair and her junkie mom was an uncomfortable subject for him. What had gone on at the Sinclair house so many years ago was something he didn't want anyone to know about. Sweat popped out on his brow. Tori already knew something about it, but she probably didn't even realize it. And Levi wouldn't be in town long.

Twenty-five years had passed. What could they possibly learn at this point about something that had happened so long ago? I've got nothing to worry about, he thought. He wiped the sweat off his brow with the back of his hand, drained his beer, and walked to the bar for something stronger.

As Alan watched Doug watching Tori and Levi, his stomach knotted. He knew Doug well enough to recognize that look on his face. Doug's mask had come off, and his real face was showing—and it looked like a thundercloud. The reunion no longer felt like a fun evening full of reminiscence. Alan had a bad feeling that Doug and Levi's relationship was about to fall back to what it had been like so many years before.

Levi and Tori returned to the Zoo Crew table, where their friends were having a great time. Doug had gone off to talk with his old football friends at another table. But Doug eventually returned, obviously drunk, his eyes bloodshot. He sat sullenly, listening to the Zoo Crew chatter. His few contributions had been sarcastic. Jerry calling him "Doug the Slug" hadn't improved his mood at all.

At one point, Christine White flitted over with a camera, wanting a picture of Levi. Doug rolled his eyes and scoffed.

"Hey, Christine," Jerry said, balancing a beer can on his head, "take one of me."

But Jerry no longer existed in Christine's world. She never gave him a glance as she took pictures of Levi and Tori.

Jim said, "Oh, I see. The only way we're getting a picture taken is if Levi is in it."

Jerry laughed. "No, I don't think she'd take a picture of us even if Levi was in it. Now she might take a picture of Levi and the water fountain."

"Or Levi and the fire extinguisher," Jim suggested.

Imitating Christine's voice, Jerry held out his hands as if they were a photo album and said, "And here is the famous author Levi Garvey at *our* class reunion, sitting on the toilet."

Grinning, Levi looked at Christine. "Do you mind taking a few of the table? They'll never shut up if you don't."

She held the camera off to the side in Jerry and Jim's general direction, snapping off two or three without aiming.

"Oh I'm sure those shots will be great!" Jim said. "Can I get copies of those?"

Christine walked away, flipping them off as she went.

"I just don't get it," Jerry said. "What did we do?"

"Maybe it was shoving money down her dress earlier?" Tori called over to him. As she had predicted earlier, the beer-a-mid had blocked her view of Jerry over an hour ago.

"Who said that?" Jerry said, looking all around. "Did you hear a voice? It sounded kinda like a bitchy angel."

"Bunch of damned morons," Doug muttered.

He kicked the edge of the table violently. The entire beer can structure fell with a clatter, and beer cans bounced across the gym floor. The noise stopped everything in the gym as everyone turned around to see what had happened. Doug leaned back with a satisfied sneer on his face.

"Ah," Jerry said, looking at Tori across the table. "It *was* a bitchy angel. I forgot you were over there, Tori. Thank you, Doug.

You cleared that up nicely. But now we have to start all over again."

He placed an empty can at the center of the table. Jim handed him a full one from the cooler.

Doug glared at Jerry, and Jerry shut up. There was a long uncomfortable silence. Finally, Doug leaned forward in his chair and polished off his drink.

He looked Levi in the eye. "So Levi—when are you leaving?"

Tori glanced at Levi. Surely he could see Doug now—the Doug the rest of them saw.

In truth, Levi had never fallen for Doug's act.

"Is this the old 'this town isn't big enough for the two of us' bit, Sheriff?" Levi said.

Doug smiled. "It's Chief, and I'm just curious," he said with a bit of a slur. "We've been hearing all night all about these losers and their pathetic lives but not a word from our brilliant celebrity. So what's next for the great writer?"

"I don't know yet," Levi said. "I'd planned on staying for a week or ten days. I've got some work to do on the house yet. When I get all that work done, I'll head back to Savannah."

Doug nodded.

"Unless I decide to stay here permanently," Levi added nonchalantly.

Doug's eyes narrowed. "Why would you want to live here?"

"It's my home."

Tori wasn't sure if Levi was serious, but she recognized that he was challenging Doug, just as she'd seen him do so many times before. She tried to look calm, but her heart was beating wildly in her chest.

"It's not your home anymore," Doug said, his tone hard. "I mean, what do you have here? A drunk uncle? An old house? A beater truck?" He waved drunkenly toward Jim and Jerry. "Hell, even your little buddies here, dumb and dumber, don't live in Twin Rivers anymore."

"Hey," Jerry said, lurching wobbly to his feet, "I resemble that remark."

"Shut up, Jerry," Tori said tersely. Jerry plopped down.

Levi looked Doug square in the eye. "I don't mean to be rude, Doug, but it's not your decision. It's mine. And I'll make it."

"You know, Levi, that's just like you." His voice boomed across the gym, and all eyes turned to the center table again. "You're either too stupid, too arrogant, or too selfish to see what coming here might do to this quiet town. You think having a famous author here won't change that? You think the press won't find you here? You think your creepy little fans won't show up here looking for you?"

Levi chuckled. "Well, I think that would be a problem for the police department, Doug."

Doug lunged forward. He grabbed the edge of the table and flipped it. Jerry and Jim were barely able to scramble out of the way as it crashed over. Doug loomed over Levi, who was sitting calmly in his chair, looking up at him with a bemused smile, still holding his beer.

"Are you going hit me, Doug?" Levi asked. "Would that be a wise choice, considering you're drunk and in your uniform with a gym full of witnesses?"

Doug's hands were clenched so tightly Levi didn't think there was any way to avoid a beating. But he'd been hit by Doug before.

"Now that would sure bring the press," Levi said, continuing to taunt Doug. "I can see the headlines—'Local Police Chief Strikes Famous Author.' That would definitely make the national news."

Fear flashed across Doug's face. His hands relaxed a little bit. Levi stood up slowly and paced around Doug.

"Of course, with all the media attention, I'd have to press charges against you," Levi said, as if he were picturing it all in his head and just relaying the facts. "The town would be horribly embarrassed, and you'd get fired for sure."

Doug took a deep breath. He looked around. Everyone in the

gym was watching with rapt attention. Levi stopped pacing and stood right in front of him, his eyes sparkling with amusement. He knew he'd won.

But Doug leaned in closer to Levi, "You have no idea who you're screwing with, Garvey."

Levi laughed. "Actually, I do. I've dealt with you many times before. However, you've never had to deal with me. Things have changed, Doug. That's what you should consider before you get in my face again."

Doug stepped away from the mess in the center of the gym. Levi was right about one thing. He could get fired for this little scene. He flashed one last angry stare toward Levi before storming out of the gym.

20

Tori glanced at Levi. He'd been silent for a long time, looking out over Kingery Pond from the overlook, a strange smile on his face. He was wearing his goofy Panama hat which he'd gotten when they'd stopped at the house to drop off her car and get beer. They were sitting on Old Blue's tailgate as they had so many times before. The sky was clear with stars and a quarter moon making it bright enough to read.

"You're fun to talk to, Levi," Tori remarked.

"I was just thinking about where I was just a week ago."

"In Savannah," she said.

"No, I meant more . . . emotionally," he said, glancing at her.

She didn't say anything.

"I've been having a mid-life crisis, Tori. I didn't know it until recently, and I guess I'm not the only one since it was such a common theme at our table tonight. A week ago, I thought my life was over. I'm on the edge of losing everything I have—the life I know, the money, the house on Pulaski Square, the celebrity.

"A week ago, my stomach was doing flips every time I thought about anything changing from the way it's been for the last ten years or so. I loved my life. The only thing that scared me worse than losing the life I've known was the idea of trying to save it by writing another book. The creative well was empty."

"Past tense?" Tori remarked.

"You never miss anything, do you? I wasn't kidding tonight," Levi said flatly. "I'm staying. The idea of going back to that life now fills me with the same sense of dread I had a week ago at the thought of leaving it."

"And the book?" Tori said.

"I've got a couple of ideas," Levi said. "I've got to find a new voice in my writing. All three of my books are just variations on the exact same theme. But Twin Rivers is ripe with ideas. I've experienced more raw emotion in the last few days than I have in the last ten years. I think I've isolated myself from who I really am over the years, but since I've been back, I've found my muse again. I don't think my next novel is going to come out of this place—I think my next ten novels will."

"And Doug?" Tori said. "You've got a real problem there."

"Ah, screw Doug. I'm more afraid of what Christine is going to do to me for busting her party up before ten o'clock. They never even got a chance to dance tonight."

Tori laughed. "Doug flipping a table will pretty much end a party. But you're right. I'd be watching out for Christine. She's probably pretty pissed off that she didn't get to pull out her old dance moves. I bet she's been practicing that Molly Ringwald dance from *The Breakfast Club* for a month."

Levi laughed.

After Doug and Levi's confrontation, everyone had begun leaving the reunion in droves. Within a few minutes, the gym was empty. Jim and Jerry were the last to leave. They'd hung around to steal all the remaining beer from the bar.

Levi looked out over Kingery Pond and shook his head.

"What?" Tori asked.

"You know, this place isn't exactly the way I remembered it."

"Yeah," Tori said. "It's a lovely view from up here on the overlook. Gorgeous moldy pond below with the spooky dead center, ringed with dead trees along the edges. And don't forget the fragrant fresh breeze blowing off the water."

"I'd forgotten about the smell. It kind of burns your nose," Levi remarked. "Was it always that strong?"

"What? The fragrance of old jock strap marinated in raw sewage?"

"No question. It's a romantic spot," Levi said with a chuckle. "I used to bring dates up here."

"Oh, Levi! Did we come up here for romance?" Tori said, reaching over to take his hand.

Levi pulled his hand back. "In front of Rosco?" he said, cocking his thumb toward the snoring mass in the bed of the truck. "What's wrong with you?"

"Well, what are we going to do then?" she said. She held up her empty beer can and shook it. "I drank the last beer."

"Oh, Tori," Levi said sternly. "I used to have such respect for you. I only got two of those."

"Like hell," Tori said. "As always, you had four, and I only got two. If I hadn't grabbed this one when I did, you'd have had it, too."

He grinned broadly, "I've got more beer at the house."

Tori nodded and tossed the empty into the cooler. After they slid off the tailgate, Levi closed and latched it. Levi started for the driver's door, but Tori remained at the tailgate.

"You know, Levi, you never let me drive Old Blue," she remarked.

She'd bugged him a hundred times—begging him to let her drive his truck just once—but he'd always refused. He paused before reaching into his pocket. He tossed the keys to her, walked around the hood, and climbed in the passenger door.

Tori was stunned. She walked to the driver's door, climbed in, and pulled the door shut. She sat for a moment, looking at the white steering wheel in disbelief. She glanced at Levi. He nodded. But she shook her head, opened the door, and walked around the hood. Levi slid across the seat behind the steering wheel as Tori climbed into the passenger side.

"I can't believe you were going to let me drive Old Blue," Tori said, holding the keys out to him.

Levi laughed. "Those are the keys to my rental car," he said, fishing the truck keys out of his shirt pocket.

She looked down at the keys, then at him coldly. "You ass."

Levi reached down and fired up Old Blue, a smug smile on his face.

"I'm keeping these," Tori said. "I hope you bought the extra insurance on that rental car."

21

Doug Malone had gone back to his office in the Twin Rivers Police Department. He had the place to himself. He was leaning back in his chair, drink in hand, with his feet up on his desk, his Glock 9mm sitting on the desk next to a half-empty bottle of Wild Turkey. The only light on in the office was a green-shaded banker's lamp on the corner of the desk. He'd been drunk earlier at the reunion, but now he was completely loaded. He was still seething over how easily Levi Garvey had made him look like a fool. Levi knew exactly how to punch his buttons to get a reaction.

Doug drained his glass. He'd relived the experience over and over again—the way Levi had just sat with that smug smile on his face after Doug flipped that table, the way he'd slowly gotten up to lecture him like a school boy as he circled him, how he'd laid the whole thing out for Doug while he pointed out to everyone at the reunion that Doug had started it. Levi had come off as the calm voice of reason.

The story will be all over town tomorrow, Doug thought

"That son of a bitch," he said tightly. He hurled the glass against the far wall. It exploded.

And he was right, Doug thought. That's the part that burns my ass. I can't lay a finger on him and keep this badge.

Doug reached for the bottle and took a long pull.

Levi had to go. There was no question about that, but Doug would have to be smart about it. He'd have to be calm and think it through. He couldn't let Levi punch his buttons and gain control. The only way he could beat Levi was to be smarter than he was.

Doug thought back to high school. Levi would mouth off to him, and Doug would pound him to bits in front of everyone. But he'd get up every time, and his friends would surround him and look at Doug like he was dirt. Doug always wound up looking like the ass. He just couldn't beat somebody who refused to be defeated.

Doug had been clenching his jaw so tightly for so long, his face was beginning to hurt. He rubbed his chin and worked his jaw back and forth with his hand.

He thought, what if he'd done the same thing to me? What if one night Levi finally got fed up with me and beat the hell out of me?

In a fit of rage, Doug's shot his foot out. The banker's lamp flew off the desk and shattered against the wall. The chair creaked loudly as he got up. Not realizing how drunk he was, he nearly fell. He caught himself on the edge of the desk and then made his way to the window. He looked through the blinds at the diner which Harv and April had just closed down for the evening. Harv was locking the door as April walked to the car and got in the passenger side.

I'll tell you exactly what would've happened, he thought. He'd have been hailed the hero of the high school. The town might've even had a parade in his honor. The Mayor would've declared it Levi Garvey Day.

With a sigh, Doug raised the bottle for another slug, weaving and nearly falling. He leaned heavily against the file cabinet and took a long drink.

More thoughts ran through his alcohol-soaked brain. How do you defeat that? I can't scare him. I can't intimidate him. But I sure can't have him living in Twin Rivers. He's gunning for me. He'll have this town behind him. Hell, he already does.

Doug thought of the snappy remarks April Jenkins had made in the last few days. She wouldn't have done that if Levi hadn't been there. Something about Levi Garvey brought strength out in people.

Jerry had called him "Doug the Slug" tonight. He sure as hell wouldn't have done that if Levi Garvey hadn't been sitting there. Doug had flipped the table, and nobody had run. Nobody had sneaked out of the gym. They'd stood where they were, and they'd looked to Levi. They knew Levi would protect them—with his face if necessary.

Doug's head was pounding. Suddenly, a wicked smiled crossed his face. He set the bottle on the edge of the desk.

Maybe there's a way I can start pushing Levi's buttons, he thought. Maybe there's a way I can convince him his mansion in Georgia and his juicy little girlfriend and his celebrity lifestyle are much more attractive than living here in the sticks. Maybe, if I'm patient and smart about it, I can get Levi to snap. Maybe I can get him to come after me. That would be a violation of the law. I can arrest someone for coming after an officer of the law. Of course, the town would side with Levi, but would the rest of the world when they found out?

Doug laughed.

That's how I'll get him out of here, he thought. He ran here because that last book of his was crap. People are talking bad about his royal highness, and he just can't take that. That's exactly the way I'll send him packing back to Georgia. I'll get the anointed one to embarrass himself here, too. Better to be embarrassed in front of strangers in Savannah than in front of your friends in Twin Rivers.

Doug chuckled. "And when he snaps, and he will, I'll bring the entire world to his doorstep," he said aloud to the empty office.

22

"Watch where you step," Levi cautioned as he walked along the edges of the porch steps.

Rosco shot up the opposite side. Tori followed him onto the porch, then turned back to look down at the broken stairs.

"I hope those steps are on your repair list."

Levi unlocked the door, reached in, and flipped on the porch light.

"They are. Uncle Ed knows a guy. I'm not much of a carpenter."

"They wouldn't be very hard to fix," Tori remarked. "I could rebuild them in an afternoon."

"Really?"

"Sure, I was born with a claw hammer in my hand. Remember, my dad was a contractor. There are a few things he taught me."

"I guess I didn't remember that," Levi said. "I mean I knew your dad worked some construction."

"When he wasn't drunk, you mean. Actually, I love working with my hands. There are few things I've enjoyed more in the last several years than restoring and renovating the Comet Theatre."

"What? The Comet is still around?"

"You haven't seen it? It's right up the street from Harv's. It's kinda hard to miss," she said, shaking her head.

"I know where it is, Tori," Levi growled. "I guess I didn't notice it. Maybe you've forgotten, but I'm a man. I can't find the ketchup in the refrigerator either."

"Don't make any plans for Wednesday night," she said. "The Comet shows classic movies two nights a week in the summers—Wednesdays and Saturdays."

"I figured it'd been torn down," Levi said. "I mean it was a mess back in the 70s and 80s. I can't believe somebody bought it."

"Actually, I bought it," Tori said. "Most people in town thought I was nuts. They thought it was a hopeless cause. I did most of the restoration myself over three years. Your Uncle Ed would drop by some evenings when I was working and help me. He also suggested contractors for the parts I couldn't do myself, like carpeting and upholstering."

"That sounds like Uncle Ed," Levi said.

"When I finally got it done, I sold it back to the town. I had no desire to run a movie theater. And it's been a great success story for the town. It paid for itself the first year. Almost every show is a sell-out. People come from miles around to see classic movies in a classic theatre. The money has been used for several community improvement projects. They even bought computers for the grade school and that new electronic billboard at the high school. There's talk about restoring the Twin Rivers Library next."

"I'll be damned," Levi said. "This town has been full of surprises since I got home. I wonder what they're showing Wednesday?"

Tori smiled broadly, remembering the ad she'd seen in the *Gazette*.

"What?" Levi said.

"Oh, Levi, you sure picked a good time to come back home."

"What is it?"

"One of your favorites," she teased. She began humming a

melody. "Dum da dum daaaa . . . dum da dum . . . dum da dum da . . . dum da DUM DA DA!"

"*Raiders of the Lost Ark*? Are you kidding me? On the big screen?"

Tori nodded.

"Oh, we'll be there, Tori. I'll buy the popcorn," he said with a grin.

They walked into the house. Tori stopped to look around. She hadn't come in when they'd dropped by earlier.

"Wow, this place looks exactly the same," she said.

"Don't be fooled by appearances. Grandma updated a few things. Come into the kitchen," he said.

She followed him down the narrow hall. When he flipped on the light, she gasped, "Whoa, Lucille!"

The kitchen had all new appliances, under-counter lighting, and an island in the middle that, while a modern addition, looked as if it had been original to the house. Tori sat at one of the new stools at the island. Levi went to the fridge and brought over two beers.

"This is beautiful," she remarked. "Are those new cabinets too?"

Levi shrugged. "I don't know. Everything looks like it belongs here. I don't know who she had remodel this kitchen, but it sure is hard to tell what's new and what was original to the house. It's the same story with the bathrooms. She wanted to keep it original, but I think she also wanted a few modern conveniences she didn't have before."

"That's exactly what I was shooting for at the Comet Theatre."

She reached over the counter and grabbed a box which was sitting on it.

"What's this?" she said, opening the box.

"Those are fiber bars," Levi said, looking embarrassed.

"Fiber bars?"

"I had to go grocery shopping, and it seemed like a good idea at the time. I haven't been grocery shopping in ten years, and I had no idea what I was doing. Anyway, I saw those, and I figure, at *our* age, you can't get too much fiber," he said defensively. "And they taste great, they've got only a hundred calories each, and they fill you up. Those are chocolate chip."

Tori chuckled at how defensive he was. "Okay . . . grandpa. Don't get your colon in a twist."

Levi glared at her.

"I'm kidding," she said with a grin. "I've been watching my diet, too. I eat bananas now."

Levi reached over the island, snatched the box out of her hand, and put it in a cabinet.

"The thing with those fiber bars I didn't know is they give you terrible gas. I've come to think of them as fart bars."

Tori laughed aloud. "Weren't there a few missing from that box?"

"Yeah, unfortunately. If you eat two of them for breakfast and then spend a morning climbing up and down a ladder, scraping paint off an old house, you'll find that you can play 'Stars and Stripes Forever' with your butt by noon."

Tori laughed so hard, she nearly fell off her stool.

"But don't worry," Levi said. "Grandma updated the plumbing in this house, too. Thank God!"

Levi motioned to her, and they walked back up the hall. Tori was still laughing. He turned into the library and flipped on the light. Tori flopped down in an old wing-back chair she'd sat in many times years before.

"I always loved this room," she remarked.

"Me, too. The fireplace, the library shelves with the rolling ladder, the old roll-top desk, and, of course, the little alcove," he said, pointing.

He was talking about the small round room in the corner that was actually the first floor turret room of the house. The alcove was hidden in darkness.

"They went to so much effort to build those stylized turrets during the Victorian era," she remarked. "They looked great on the outside, but they weren't very useful inside. They didn't offer much usable space."

"In the winter, it's the warmest room in the house because of the south light that comes in through the tall windows," Levi said.

He reached around the corner and flipped on a light. There was a reading chair in the center of the little room with a thick afghan across the back of it. "I don't know how many hours I spent in that chair reading during the winter when I was a kid. It was one of my favorite places in this house. Grandma never changed a thing in here—she knew it was perfect as is."

Levi went to the stereo, which was on the library shelves near the fireplace, flipped it on, and looked for a radio station. It was just after midnight. He figured he and Tori would catch up. They both talked best with a little background 80s metal.

Behind him, Tori said, "I don't know why you're being so shy. Why don't you just come over here and give me a kiss? I know you want to."

Levi stood straight up. Static hissed out of the speakers of the stereo.

Are you kidding me? he thought. Of course I do! So this is how it finally happens?

Gathering up his courage, he turned to her.

Rosco's paws were up on her lap, and he was licking Tori's face.

"See, I'm not going to bite you," Tori said as she scratched his ears and kissed his nose. "What a sweet dog, Levi. I didn't think he liked me. He's been giving me the evil eye all night."

Levi sighed.

"Having problems with the radio? Try 106.7—they play classic metal after midnight," she said.

Levi turned back around and dialed in the channel. When he faced Tori again, Rosco was lying across her lap in the chair as she rubbed him behind his ears. He glared at the dog. When Rosco saw him, his ears went flat as he received the message: I never liked you, Rosco.

"Hey, while you're up," Tori said, shaking her beer can.

Levi took it and headed to the kitchen for another.

"I was married for ten years," Tori said. She was gently stroking Rosco, who was asleep in her lap.

"What happened?" Levi asked.

"We met as freshmen at Purdue. We dated for a year and seemed to want the same things in life, so we got married," Tori said. "The plan was to graduate from college, get that great job, the house, and then maybe we'd one day have a family."

"And?" Levi asked.

"We both graduated in '89. I got the great job and supported us both. I worked in the accounting department of a big insurance company headquarters in Bloomington and later became the finance manager. I thought he'd eventually find something, but he had trouble keeping a job. This went on for a couple years. He'd get a job and brag about how well he was doing even though his paychecks didn't show it. He would tell me about all the possibilities of a promotion he was being offered. Then one day, he'd come home and tell me he'd quit—how he'd decided it wasn't what he wanted to do with his life. I was so blind. It was right there in front of me, and I just couldn't see it. Either that, or I just couldn't accept it."

"What did he want to do with his life?" Levi said.

"Same thing my father did," Tori said. Her eyes were clouding up. "I can't believe I'm telling you this. I can't believe I'm telling anybody this."

Levi said nothing. The silence was long before she continued.

"I came home one day early, and he was passed out on the couch in his underwear. As usual, there was an empty bottle on the coffee table and another half-empty one in his hand. I suddenly realized I'd married my father," Tori said coldly. "But I couldn't seem to divorce him. The last five years of the marriage, he never worked. He was rarely sober. Then one day I realized I was helping him kill himself."

"So you divorced him," Levi said.

Tori nodded. "I filed in '97. Soon after, I was offered the bank president job at the First National Bank of Calloway, so I moved back home. I bought a nice little three-bedroom house on Hillsdale Avenue. I'd never worked a nine to five job, so I had a lot of free time to pursue my interests. It was the first time I'd ever felt so completely free.

"But that didn't last long. My ex showed up in Calloway not long after I got back. He got this awful apartment over a little grocery store, and for some reason, I couldn't stop sending him money. I was making a very good living, and I guess I was feeling guilty. I felt like if I hadn't supported him all those years, if he'd ever had to stand up on his own two feet, maybe he wouldn't have become like that."

"Bullshit," Levi said. "You can't blame yourself for that."

"Six months later," Tori said, "he disappeared. He just vanished. It was winter, and he'd said several times how he just couldn't deal with the Midwest winters anymore. I hoped maybe he'd just picked up and moved somewhere to make a new life for himself—somewhere warm.

"Six weeks later, they found his car down at the bottom of a gulley off a back-road shortcut he used to take when he was coming home from his favorite tavern. It was his drunk route—the one he would take when he was drunk to avoid the police. They figure he passed out, went off the road, and froze to death."

Levi never said anything.

"I was a real mess. I needed something to occupy my time. When I saw that Twin Rivers was planning to rip down the Comet Theatre, I knew what I wanted to do. I bought it for back-taxes from the county and worked on it evenings and weekends for over three years. I finished it in 2002 and sold it back to the town. It had served its purpose well. It had taken me back to a happier time, it kept my mind occupied, and all the time alone helped me work a few things out and see my life clearly for the very first time."

Levi smiled. "I've been learning a little something about work therapy myself lately."

"That was a pretty awful story, huh?" Tori said grimly. "Of course, you've heard some of my awful stories before."

Levi nodded. "As awful as that story was, at least you felt something for someone once in your life. At least you made a commitment and tried to make good on it. I've never been able to do either one."

Tori smiled. "I've seen some of your distractions over the years in the gossip magazines at the grocery store check-out."

"And all of them were as empty-headed as they were beautiful," Levi snorted. "I don't like to be alone, but I've learned that sometimes you feel loneliness the most intensely when you're with somebody that you don't understand and who doesn't understand you. You pay a heavy price for keeping people at arm's length."

"We're not that much different," Tori said.

Levi looked at her questioningly.

Tori smiled. "You're incapable of letting people in, and I can't seem to let them go."

"We're a mess," Levi said with a chuckle.

Levi woke up suddenly. He was still on the settee in the library. He wasn't sure when he'd fallen asleep. They'd talked for hours. He glanced over at Tori a few feet away. She was asleep in the wing-back chair with Rosco still on her lap. He glanced at his watch—3:30.

Ah crap, is that 4:30 Illinois time or 2:30? he thought.

It didn't matter. He got up to cover Tori with an afghan. He pulled the blanket off the back of the settee for himself. As he lay back down, he couldn't stop looking at Tori. He couldn't believe she was here. He couldn't believe she wasn't married. He couldn't believe she wasn't old, fat, and gray. He smiled when he saw the loose spiral of hair hanging in front of her face. He fell back to sleep watching Tori sleep.

23

"So what's the verdict?" Levi called down from the porch roof. He had a paintbrush in his hand.

Tori put one hand over her eyes to shade against the sun as she looked up. She had a crowbar in her other hand. She was wearing a pair of old bib overalls she'd found in the farm closet and his grandmother's beat up Chicago Cubs baseball cap—the one she'd always worn when she gardened. It was already getting hot. Tori glistened with sweat, and tendrils of her kinky blonde hair, which had escaped from under her hat, clung to her forehead and the nape of her neck. Pieces of the old porch steps were lying all over the sidewalk and the yard.

"Piece of cake," she said. "The stringers are solid. I just need to replace the risers and treads."

Levi grinned. "So why did you have to dismantle the whole thing?"

She looked at him coldly. "You want to do this, Levi?"

"Nope," he said with a shake of his head.

"I'm going to need some L-brackets and deck screws. I didn't find any in the carriage house. But there's plenty of lumber in the loft," she said.

Levi nodded.

"Well?" Tori said with her hand on her hip.

"What?" Levi asked.

She enunciated very slowly and carefully. "I'm going to need some L-brackets and deck screws. The hardware store in Twin Rivers closes at noon on Sundays. It's 11:15."

"Ah, got it. You know, you get a little pissy when you're working on a project," Levi said.

He laid his brush across the top of the paint can and started down the ladder.

"You're going to think pissy when I clunk you with this crowbar," she remarked.

They'd been going back and forth all morning. Levi had enjoyed every minute of it. It was amazing just how fast they'd fallen back into sync with each other. Of course, Tori had started it that morning. When Levi woke to the sound of banging outside, he sat up on the settee and found that Tori had made him breakfast. There were a couple fart bars lying in his lap. Nice one, Tori, he'd thought.

When Levi reached the bottom of the ladder, he stopped and looked around for Rosco who'd disappeared. "Wanna go for a ride?" he yelled.

They heard some commotion under the porch before Rosco popped out through the hole where the porch steps had been. He was covered from head to toe in cobwebs that had been accumulating under there for decades.

Tori laughed at Rosco, who looked as if he were wearing a wedding dress. She went down on one knee to pick off the cobwebs. Levi shook his head, walked over to Old Blue, opened the door, and stood impatiently for several minutes while Tori cleaned up the dog.

"They close at noon!" he reminded her.

Rosco finally leaped in—cobweb free.

"You keep this up, Rosco, and you're going to be riding in the bed."

"Hey," Tori called. "Get me a pop, too—would you?"

"There's root beer in the fridge," he called back.

She shot him a look.

He corrected his oversight. "But you'd like a Mountain Dew, wouldn't you? Maybe an Almond Joy as well?"

"Thank you," she said, smiling.

As he backed down the driveway, he rolled down the window.

"While I'm gone, you want to get this mess cleaned up? I mean, jeez, Tori, I don't live in a trailer park, you know."

She reacted quickly, reaching down to scoop up a piece of 2x4 off the ground and running a few steps towards him. He floored the accelerator and backed quickly down the driveway and into the road.

Levi was fiddling with the radio as he drove up Elm Street, unable to find any music. He remembered arguing with Uncle Ed about the radio when they were restoring Old Blue. Ed had thought they should pop in a nice AM/FM radio with a cassette player and some "kick ass" speakers behind the seat. That meant either cutting a bigger hole in the console to accommodate it or mounting it under the dashboard. Neither choice was acceptable to Levi. He'd insisted they stay true to the original truck, which meant an AM radio. It hadn't been an easy task finding an original radio that still worked even then. It was amazing it still worked now—fifty years after it was made. As surprising as that was, he was beginning to regret that decision now.

Levi sighed. "You know, Rosco, when I was a kid, they used to play music on AM radio. Now AM radio is all talk. Even WLS out of Chicago has caved in to talk radio. You've got your choice now on AM—either Rush Limbaugh, Glenn Beck, or Sean Hannity."

Levi snapped the radio off and turned down Main Street beside the grade school. He'd just clutched the three on the tree into second gear when he heard the siren. When he glanced in the mirror, he saw red lights flashing inches off his bumper.

"Are you kidding me?" Levi muttered as he pulled over.

Doug walked to the window. He looked like hell.

"Wow, Doug," Levi grinned. "I can't believe you caught up with me! What have you got under the hood of that cop car?"

Doug glowered over him. "License, registration, and proof of insurance."

"Right," Levi said.

He pulled his license out of his wallet and handed it to him. He reached over the seat to the glove box for the registration card. There was a mess of papers in the glove box—twenty years of vehicle registration cards and insurance cards Uncle Ed had shoved in there. Levi thumbed through them.

"Here's the registration, but the last insurance card I have expired last month. I'm sure Uncle Ed just forgot to—"

"Just give them to me," Doug said, snatching the documents out of his hand.

Levi sat, waiting for Doug to finish examining the documents. He was taking a long time.

"Uh, I'm trying to get to the hardware store before it closes at—"

"Do you know why I stopped you, Mr. Garvey," Doug said. His eyes were bloodshot, and a thick film of sweat covered his face.

Levi sighed. "Why don't you just tell me, Doug," he said shortly.

"Have any idea how fast you were going back there in front of the grade school?"

Levi shrugged. "I don't know, Doug. I'd just kicked Old Blue from walk gear up into jog. I was just about to punch it into trot when you got me. I'm thinking maybe thirty at best?"

"I clocked you at forty-eight miles an hour in a thirty, *and* it's a school zone," Doug said.

"There's no way," Levi said with a laugh. "You'd better go back and give Mr. Collins a ticket, too. I'm pretty sure he passed me on his riding lawn mower. And it's summertime, Doug. There's no school in session."

But Doug was gone from beside the window. He was back in his car.

Levi looked over at Rosco, who was lying with his head down on the seat and looking at Levi with his big brown eyes. Levi glanced at his watch.

"We don't get back with brackets and that other thing Tori wanted, we're going to be in deep ka-ka. Crap, what was the other thing she said she needed?"

Doug walked back to the window and handed his documents back.

"I'm afraid I've had to write you a citation. I'm going to give you your license back, but you need to pay the ticket within thirty days or appear before the judge on the date on the ticket," he said, handing a clipboard to Levi. "I'll need your signature on this."

Levi looked at the ticket. "$350 dollars?" he exclaimed.

Doug nodded. "Speed in excess of ten miles an hour over the posted limit—and in a school zone. You had no proof of insurance, and you're not wearing a seatbelt. There's a seatbelt law here in Illinois, Mr. Garvey."

"This truck doesn't have any seatbelts," Levi snapped. "It doesn't have any airbags either—unless you count the great big one outside of it writing me a ticket."

"You can take that up with the judge," Doug said, smiling at him, "in three weeks."

"And what the hell is this? A safety violation?"

"Broken tail-light," Doug remarked off-handedly.

"I don't have a broken tail-light," Levi said.

Doug sauntered back to the rear of the truck, pulled out his Glock, and smashed the tail-light with the butt of his gun.

Furious, Levi swung the door of his truck open and started to step out.

Doug put his hand up. "I didn't ask you to get out of your vehicle, Mr. Garvey," he said officially.

"Doug, God damnit! This is bullshit!" Levi said, pointing at him.

"Get back in your vehicle," Doug said, standing at the rear of the truck. He still had the Glock in his hand. "I'm not going to ask you again."

Levi knew he was on dangerous ground. For a moment, he stared at Doug, who had a strange smile on his face. When Levi realized Doug was hoping he wouldn't comply with his request, he got back into the truck and slammed the door.

Doug smirked. He could see Levi looking at him in the side mirror. He walked back to the window, dragging his ring down the paint job as he returned. He could see the look of fury on Levi's face. During all those years in school, he'd never gotten to Levi, but he knew he had him now. It was so easy. He'd finally figured it out. Levi was livid—he was right on the edge.

Doug put his elbows on the window sill and leaned into the truck.

"You going to sign that ticket, Mr. Garvey? Or am I going to have to impound this truck? Of course, we're not responsible for any damage that might happen to it while it's in the impound yard."

Levi was beyond words. He picked the clipboard up from the floor where it'd fallen. As he leaned over, he heard a strange rumbling sound. Rosco's head was down on the seat, but his eyes were open, his ears were up, and his teeth were bared. Levi couldn't believe what he was hearing. Rosco was growling—Rosco was growling at Doug.

After Levi signed the ticket, he handed the clipboard back to Doug, who was still leaning in the window.

"Thank you, sir," Doug said.

Levi stared straight ahead through the windshield. He couldn't remember ever being so angry.

"Nice dog, by the way," Doug said with a sneer. "Kind of a lazy, sleepy, stupid-looking dog, but dogs often take on the attributes of their masters."

Levi turned to look Doug in the eye and said, "He's in training."

Doug snorted. "What could a useless animal like that be good for?"

"He wants to be a Twin Rivers police dog," Levi said with a forced grin.

Anger flashing in his eyes, Doug started to lean farther in the window. The second Doug moved towards Levi, Rosco jumped onto Levi's lap. He snapped his jaw a couple times, showing Doug a mouthful of sharp teeth, and growled loudly just inches from his face.

Rosco stopped Doug in his tracks. As he backed up slowly, he ripped a copy of the ticket off the clipboard, but when he started to reach into the truck to hand the ticket to Levi, the tenor of Rosco's growling increased, and he snapped his teeth menacingly a couple more times. Doug jerked his hand back. Reaching out the window, Levi snatched the ticket out of his hand.

"Enjoy your stay in Twin Rivers, Mr. Garvey. Be sure you watch your speed. And by the way, we have a very strict leash law here in Twin Rivers as well as an ordinance about vicious breeds."

As Doug walked back to the patrol car, he raked Old Blue down the side again, this time with the metal part of his clipboard. Levi sat behind the steering wheel with his eyes clenched tightly closed, listening to the sound of the clipboard against Old Blue's paint and Doug's laughter.

Doug pulled around Old Blue in his cruiser, honked his horn twice, and waved politely. He was still laughing.

Levi reached down, fired up the truck, and revved the engine.

"You want to write somebody a ticket today, Doug?" he said.

He had visions of ramming Doug's cruiser as Doug had rammed Old Blue with The Reaper two-and-a-half decades before. When he reached for the gear handle on the column with a shaking hand and pushed in the clutch, Rosco barked. Levi glanced at Rosco—his hand about to throw the truck into gear. Rosco whined, climbed onto his lap, and started licking his face. Levi's foot came off the accelerator, and he released the clutch.

"That son of a bitch," he said between clenched teeth as Rosco licked his face.

Anger fell away as he tried to dislodge Rosco from his lap. But Rosco wouldn't get off. Rosco had never acted like this before. He was licking Levi to happy.

"Get off me, you stupid damned mutt," he said, laughing as he tried to escape the tongue. "I get it! I get it! You're right, Rosco. That's exactly what he wants me to do."

Levi sat there for a couple minutes as the angry thoughts slowly subsided. When he glanced at his watch, he realized the hardware store was closed.

"Let's go up to the gas station and at least get Tori a soda," Levi said. "And I'm thinking you might deserve a couple of those beef jerky sticks you like."

Rosco climbed up in the passenger seat window and stuck his head out the window. Levi nearly went around the block to turn around but then decided differently.

"What the hell," he said to Rosco, "there's no law in Twin Rivers."

Levi did an illegal U-turn right in front of the grade school. It felt good.

24

"Well, how bad is it?" Tori said, walking into the carriage house with a sack from the home improvement store in Calloway in her hand.

Levi was standing a few feet from Old Blue, staring intently at the driver's side of the truck with a buffer in his hand.

"I don't know. What do you think?"

Tori set the sack on the workbench and walked over to the side of the truck. She squatted down and looked carefully. When Levi had returned from his encounter with Doug, the side of the truck had looked pretty bad. The ugly scratches and the look on Levi's face had made her wince.

"I don't see anything at all now. The scratches buffed out."

"But you can still *feel* the scratches," he said angrily, rubbing his hand down the side. "Good thing we put on several layers of clear coat. He didn't get down to the paint."

Tori felt the side of the truck very carefully. It felt perfectly smooth to her, but she knew better than to say anything. She walked to the back of the truck.

"Oh, good, you had a spare tail light."

"We've got quite a collection of spare parts," Levi said, pointing to the cabinets along the back of the carriage house. "I found a drawer that had several tail light lenses in it. Did you get your brackets?

"I did," she said. "I got you some better paintbrushes, too."

"Thanks."

Neither of them spoke for a moment. When Levi looked at Tori, he noticed the troubled look on her face. He knew what she was thinking.

"I know," he said harshly. "Something really weird happened today, didn't it?"

Tori nodded.

"Doug got to me. He's never done that before. He's always been so predictable, but today he was different. He knew exactly what he was doing."

"I've never seen you so angry," Tori said. "In the thirty plus years we've known each other, I've never seen you so completely unglued."

Levi put the buffer on the workbench, then jumped up, and sat on the edge.

"Well, usually, I'm the puppet master, and he's the puppet. Today, he was pulling the strings. What the hell is his game?"

"I don't know for sure," Tori said, "but I've got a theory."

"Tell me."

Tori jumped up on the workbench next to him.

"Everyone in this town is afraid of Doug Malone. Of course, they won't admit it, but they are. They give him a wide berth. Doug loves being the big man on campus. It's all he has if you think about it."

"You're right," Levi said. "It's kind of sad really."

"Levi, I'm worried about you," Tori admitted. "Doug's coming after you because he sees you as a threat. You've never been afraid of him. You're the only person he's ever encountered in his life that he can't intimidate."

"He's probably done a lot of thinking about me since last night,"

Levi said. "He's realized just how easy it was for me to push his buttons."

"And he saw how well it worked," Tori added. "You got him so worked up, he put his job at risk, the one thing he has that means anything to him."

Levi nodded.

"And there's something else, too," Tori said. "I think the thing that worries Doug the most is that you have a lot of friends here. You're also a famous writer and a wealthy man who has gained a lot of respect in the world outside of Twin Rivers."

"If he ever tangled with me, my name carries enough weight. . ."

Levi's voice trailed off into silence, but Tori finished the thought.

"You could take his badge," she said.

Levi thought for a few minutes. "So instead of just reacting, like he's always done, Doug sat down and thought this through. Now he's trying to push my buttons, and I must admit, he did a pretty good job of it. I could have easily hit him today."

"And you could have easily gone to jail," Tori agreed. "Doug's probably kicking himself for that mistake right now."

"Yup," Levi said with a nod. "If he hadn't still had that gun in his hand after knocking out my tail light, I would've punched him right in the mouth."

"And I'd be bailing you out right now," Tori said, trying to smile, but the worry was apparent.

"Assuming I could even get bail, me being a man of means with no particular ties to the community. And I'd be going to court for assaulting an officer, which is a very serious crime," Levi said, looking at her blankly.

"Just realized how close you came to screwing up, didn't you?" Tori said.

"Yeah, if I'd done that, it would get out. That's tabloid fodder," Levi admitted.

They sat quietly for a couple minutes as Levi thought about just how damaging it would be to his reputation to be charged with a felony and to have his face plastered all over the checkout newsstands.

Levi shook his head. "You know, there's got to be more to all this than what we've already said."

"You're giving Doug too much credit," Tori said. "He's very two-dimensional. He's all brawn and no brains."

"And yet, he nearly got the better of me today with his brain not his brawn," Levi pointed out. "No, Tori, I don't think I've been giving Doug enough credit."

"What else could there be?"

"I don't know," Levi said, looking across the carriage house. "But I think I'm missing something."

Tori smiled and put her hand on his shoulder. "You're thinking like a writer—plot twists and motives. Isn't it much more likely that Doug Malone is just an asshole—always has been and always will be?"

Levi looked at her and laughed.

"That does have a ring of truth to it."

"If you're about done buffing scratches only you can see, you've got a lot of painting to do, and I've got some porch steps to work on."

"You know the amazing part of today?" Levi asked.

Tori shook her head.

"Rosco," he said.

Rosco heard his name and trotted over from where he'd been sleeping on a tarp.

"This worthless dog protected me today," he said, stroking Rosco's head. "Rosco the Lethargic leaped to my defense, and as a reward, he earned several delicious meat snacks from Hillbilly Bob's Convenience Store. He acted much more like Rosco the Big Sweetie than Rosco the Lethargic today."

"Rosco the Big Sweetie was a little more aggressive?" Tori asked.

Levi nodded. "You never had to worry about walking into any

situation if you had Rosco the Big Sweetie with you. That dog was alert and ready to go 24/7. This Rosco—well, this one is pretty much asleep 24/7."

Tori laughed. She slid off the bench, stroked Rosco on the head, and walked up the wooden steps into the loft of the carriage house. She began pulling out lengths of 2x6.

Levi dug the new brushes out of the bag and began walking to the carriage house doors. He stopped to look back at Old Blue. He cocked his head to one side, looking at the driver's side. Then he dropped down on one knee and looked again, raising and lowering his head to catch the side of the truck in different light. Tori peered down from the loft.

"You're obsessive,"she yelled. "There's nothing there, Levi. No damage done. Forget about it."

Sighing, he stood up and said, "You're right. Got to forget about it and move on. But I'm going to tell you one thing right now, Tori. I don't know what it was I ever did to make Doug hate me, but I'll be damned if he gets the better of me. I'm not going to be run out of this town by Doug Malone. That I can promise you."

Levi turned and walked through the doors. Tori stood in the loft above looking down at the floor of the carriage house. She knew what it was, but she'd never told him. Eventually, she'd have to tell, but she just didn't know how to explain that she was the reason for all those black eyes and bruised ribs years ago.

Doug thinks you know, she thought. Doug believes you can hurt him. What he doesn't know is I never told you.

25

The bell over the door jangled. Silence fell across the nearly-full diner as it always did when Doug Malone entered. When he turned to walk to the coffee counter, the various conversations began again but more quietly than before.

Doug sat on the first stool. April ignored him.

"Can I have a cup of coffee?" he snapped.

April turned. Before she could say anything, Harv stepped between them, pulled a cup from under the counter, and placed it in front of Doug.

"Of course, you can," Harv said, reaching for the pot.

Doug lifted the lid off a glass-domed pastry display on the counter and helped himself to a glazed donut as Harv filled his cup. As soon as Harv walked away, April slapped a green ticket on the counter. Doug looked at her evenly with his bloodshot eyes. Her gaze on him never shifted. Finally, he spun around and looked at the customers in the diner.

"Busy today," he commented.

"Yeah, there was a big farm auction at the old Walken place this morning," Harv replied. "We've had a pretty good day so far. We were packed full for both breakfast and lunch."

Doug nodded and turned back around. "Been pretty busy today myself," he remarked loudly enough for all to hear. "I wrote Levi Garvey a hell of a ticket earlier."

"Really," April snorted.

"He had that old truck really rolling," Doug said with a chuckle. "Got him for doin' forty-eight in a thirty over by the grade school. Went ripping around the corner of Elm. I pulled him over at Main and Oak Street. He argued with me, of course."

April and Harv glanced at each other. Harv gave her a silent warning glance that said, "Don't antagonize him."

"That's the problem with these out-of-towners," Doug continued. "They come in here thinking they can do whatever they want. It's just arrogance. I had him dead to rights. He was speeding, had a broken tail light, no proof of insurance, and no seat belt."

April laughed.

"What?" Doug said sharply.

Harv glared at her.

"Oh, nothing. I'm just trying to imagine Levi getting his truck up to that speed in less than two blocks. Even if he could, which I doubt, I just can't see him abusing Old Blue like that. He loves that old truck."

"Are you questioning me, April?" Doug shot back. "He's got money now. He could buy ten trucks just like that old piece of crap if he wanted to."

"Well, I'm sure you did your duty," Harv remarked, shooting an angry look at April as he walked to the register to ring up a ticket for a customer. "That's pretty fast to be going in a residential area."

"Of course, that truck *is* insured," Lee Miller, the local agent, said as he paid his ticket. "Ed Garvey has carried liability insurance on it for as long as I can remember."

"Then why didn't you send him the proof of insurance card the law requires?" Doug growled as he spun around on his stool to face him. The diner went silent.

"I'm sure I did," Lee said nervously.

"Then he should've had it. He didn't, so how is a law enforcement officer to know he hasn't let the insurance lapse? I don't make the laws. I just enforce them."

Lee shrugged, "Well, if you'd called me, I could've told you. You've called me before when you've made a traffic stop. You have my number since I insure your house and your—"

Doug's glare shut him up. Lee stuffed his wallet back into his pocket and beat a hasty retreat as Doug smirked.

Then Doug spun around on his stool to face the whole diner. "That's the problem with Levi Garvey," he announced. "This town just doesn't understand how having him here is a problem. Levi is up there on his pedestal, looking down his nose at us unsophisticated hicks, and he doesn't think anybody else matters but him. He believes the most important date in history was the day of his birth. I've known him for a long time, and I saw that in him before anybody else did. Now that he's the famous writer, he knows he can do what he wants when he wants and pay his way out of anything he gets himself into. He's going to *use* this town to advance his career."

Doug paused as he surveyed the customers. No one moved. No one spoke.

"If he decides to live here permanently, this whole town had better get used to the idea that our community is going to be under a microscope. He'll be sitting up there writing his books in the Garvey house, and he will bring the whole world into our town to show everyone what a normal guy he is.

"You people will be nothing more than extras in the stage play he's going to be putting on here—window dressing for the *Levi Garvey Show*. I mean seriously, how many times have you seen him interviewed from his Savannah mansion talking about his "normal quiet life," using those hicks in Savannah the same way? How many times has he gone on talk shows and talked about his small town beginnings? Makes me want to puke the way he uses the fact he grew up here to sell his books. As if he's been back here even once in the last twenty years."

Doug rose and began to pace back and forth in front of the coffee counter.

"It won't be long before he'll have Oprah sitting on his front porch interviewing him. He'll bring her down here to eat one of Harv's famous cheeseburgers. April here will serve Oprah a piece of Levi's favorite chocolate pie and tell her all about the pretty girls he used to date and how clever he was and how she always knew he was destined to do something important. Then Oprah will talk to all of you about how you know Levi. When that show airs, the whole world will have a chance to laugh at us stupid country bumpkins and how the most important thing in our lives is the fact we know such an important celebrity—Levi Garvey."

Doug laughed—a laugh devoid of humor.

"I'd bet even Harv will point out the picture mounted on his wall of fame. You folks are gullible. You're buying into the whole thing. Give it a couple years, then tell me I'm not right," Doug challenged as he walked to the door. "Two years of stalker fans showing up out of the blue and interviews and the media circus that will show up every time he publishes a book—two years of that and you'll all see it the way I do. You'll be sick of it. Levi Garvey is going to wind up using all of you, and you're too stupid to realize it."

With that, Doug stomped out.

The diner was dead quiet. Nobody moved or said anything. April feared that Doug had made a convincing argument to the crowd in the diner.

Finally, Lawrence Tidwell at the farmers' table broke the silence. "When Oprah shows up, I'm going to tell her about how I fired Levi as a bean walker. At thirteen, Levi was one lazy damned kid."

Nobody said anything, but a few people smiled.

Norm Bagley spoke up next. "I'm going to tell her about the time

I caught Levi and Doug Malone stealing candy bars from my pharmacy." He chuckled. "I had those two little criminals sweeping and moving stock in my storeroom for two weeks under the threat that I would tell their folks about it. Best bargain I ever got in forty years for sixty cents worth of merchandise."

A few people laughed.

April said, "I think somebody ought to tell the story about how Levi and Jim Anderson put the *FOR SALE BY OWNER* sign on the Twin Rivers city limits signpost with the mayor's phone number on it."

Harv added, "Or how he was the prime suspect when somebody put a polka dot bikini on the statue of Lady Liberty on top of the War Memorial in the park one Halloween night."

Laughter exploded throughout the diner.

April smiled, a smile of great relief. Nobody was buying what Doug was selling. She snatched the green ticket off the counter and stuffed it into the box under the register.

26

Tori was driving her Impala down Main Street when she saw Levi's truck parked in front of Harv's. She glanced at the clock on the car dash—it was well past the noon hour. She wondered why he wasn't painting the house. Maybe April made pies again, she thought.

She pulled in next to his truck. The place was nearly empty after lunch. She spotted Levi in a booth on the far wall, staring at a laptop screen and sipping coffee. He was wearing his goofy Panama hat and reading glasses—she'd never seen the glasses before. She quickly crossed the diner and plopped into the booth opposite him.

"Hey," she announced.

Levi jumped, spilling coffee down the front of his shirt.

"Damn it, Tori. What the hell is wrong with you?" he said, pulling napkins out of the dispenser and wiping the front of his shirt.

Tori couldn't quit grinning. "Sorry, Levi. You're awfully jumpy today."

Levi scowled at her over the top of his glasses. Suddenly realizing he was wearing them, he took them off and stuffed them into his shirt pocket.

"Don't you have somewhere to be? A job or something?"

"Actually, I decided to do something I've never done before."

"What's that?"

"Take a vacation," she said beaming. "I thought I'd help you fix up the house this week."

"I am so blessed with the friends I've made in life," Levi said sarcastically.

April appeared at the table.

"Can I get you something, Tori?"

"Coffee, thanks."

April nodded and headed to the counter.

"So what are you so focused on, Levi?"

When Tori raised up from the booth seat to peek at his computer screen, he snapped the lid closed.

"So who pissed in your Wheaties this morning?" she said.

April returned and slid a coffee cup in front of Tori.

"Oh, Levi's in a real mood today. He kicked a paint bucket over this morning—all down the shingles on the porch roof."

Levi's eyes shot daggers at April.

"So we'll need some new shingles?" Tori said with a grin.

"Yes, of course we'll need some damned shingles," Levi huffed. "I hope everyone is having a good time at my expense today."

April nodded. "I'm having fun. How about you, Tori?" she said.

"Yes, I'm having fun, too."

April laughed as she walked away from the table.

"So, really, what are you working on?" Tori asked.

Levi shrugged. "It's not much yet, just an idea I've been toying with."

"A book?"

"Too early to tell," Levi said. "I got this idea the other night at the reunion—an idea about Melissa Sinclair."

Tori's smile faded ever so slightly, but Levi noticed.

"See, you don't like the idea already."

"No, tell me," she said.

Levi thought for a moment about how to put the idea into words.

"I can't stop wondering how somebody disappears, and nobody notices," he said. "I know you asked several people at the reunion about her. Nobody knew anything. Nobody has seen her since graduation. I even asked Harv and April about her since she was in here with us a million times, but neither one of them remembered her—until I pointed her out in the picture up there."

Tori hadn't noticed the picture hanging over the booth when she sat down. It was a black and white photo of a group of high school kids standing at the curb in front of the diner with a row of cars and pickups behind them.

"Oh my God, would you look at that," Tori said, leaning towards the picture. "That's all of us—the Zoo Crew. There's me, you, Jerry, Jim, Alan Haig, Tammy, Vince, Lisa, Robin, Kathy, Jeff, John Richardson, and Mel—I mean Melissa."

Tori had been smiling broadly as she looked at the picture, but suddenly the smile disappeared.

"You know something, Levi?"

"What?"

"You wonder why the hell Doug Malone used to beat the shit out of you all the time?" she said, tapping on the glass covering the photo.

It was Levi's turn to smile when he saw what she was pointing at.

"Doug was more anal about his truck than you were about Old Blue," she said. "And there you are, standing in front of his truck with your cowboy boot up on his chrome bumper. You were just asking for Doug to come out of the diner and cremate you."

Levi grinned ruefully. "Actually, I think he did just that—a few seconds after this photo was taken."

Tori looked at the picture again, her face was serious. "That is weird, isn't it?" she said. "I keep wondering if Christine White hadn't printed that poster of Melissa Sinclair and hung it up at the reunion would I have even noticed she wasn't there?"

They sat quietly, looking at the picture for a moment.

"I think there's a story here," Levi finally said. "I can't quit thinking about where she is today and how she could have slipped away without anyone noticing and why she's never been back. Obviously, I have a rather unique perspective on the subject . . ." His voice trailed off.

"What kind of story would you write?" Tori asked.

Levi shrugged. "I've been trying to work that out. I'm working out a few angles on the story, but I think at its core it's a story about power. The most important lessons kids learn in high school are about power—who has it and who doesn't. You've got the in-crowd, and you've got the out-crowd. You've got the bullies and the bullied. But if you're very lucky, you figure out that you create your own power. I figured that out, and when I did, it made Doug Malone powerless over me. The Zoo Crew figured it out too, and the in-crowd no longer held power over them. I think Melissa's story is about her discovering she had power, too."

"I like it," Tori said, nodding.

"I need a lot more though. Harv remembered that Melissa and her mother, Sarah, rented that house over on Ash Street from Millie Burmeister. I don't know her, but I thought I'd go talk to her—see what she remembers about them, if anything."

"Sounds good," she said as a sly smile crossed her face.

"What?"

"While you're doing that, I'll go get some shingles," Tori said. "I can't remember though—are those shingles black or dark gray?"

"Actually," April interrupted as she walked by with coffee for another customer, "they're black and white striped."

Tori and April exploded into laughter. Levi glared at them as he collected his computer and slid out of the booth. They were still laughing as the bell jangled over the door behind him.

27

As Levi rounded the corner of Ash Street, he realized the house Melissa Sinclair had lived in during high school was gone. In its place was a well-tended lot with a few shade trees. Harv had told him that Millie Burmeister, the former landlady, lived right across the street. Levi pulled his truck into the driveway of the meticulously maintained brick home. An old woman was tending one of several large planters on either side of the porch steps. Levi got out of the truck and walked up to the bottom of the steps.

"Miss Burmeister?" he said gently, not wanting to startle her.

"It's Missus," she corrected him, standing upright and slowly turning toward him. "Although my Charlie has been gone for many years, I'm still Mrs. Burmeister."

She couldn't be more than five feet tall. Her face was deeply lined with wrinkles, and long strands of snow-white hair that had escaped from a bun were hanging around her face. She peered at him curiously from the top of the steps with eyes that were such a pale blue they looked ash gray.

Levi thought he recognized her. "Mrs. B?" he asked.

When she smiled, a thousand tiny wrinkles erupted on her face.

"Now let me see," she said looking him up and down. "Don't tell me. I'll get it. Take off your hat."

Levi complied immediately.

"Hmmm," she said as she regarded him. "You were a lot shorter the last time I saw you." She rubbed her chin as she tried to see the boy the man before her had once been. Suddenly, she smiled broadly. "Mr. Garvey."

"Well, Mrs. B, truth be known, you seemed a lot taller last time I saw you," Levi retorted.

She cackled loudly and waved him up onto the porch.

"So what brings you here, Levi. Don't tell me you've decided to return that library book you borrowed three decades ago."

Levi remembered her well since he'd spent a lot of time in the Twin Rivers Library as a boy. Mrs. B., the librarian, had seemed old then. Now she was absolutely ancient.

"No, ma'am. So far as I know, I paid all my fines years ago."

"Tell me something, Levi," Mrs. B. said, looking past him toward the lawn. "Is that your dog pooping in my gladiolas?"

"Rosco!" Levi shouted.

Smiling, she took a seat in a white wicker chair and motioned for him to take the other one. It creaked loudly as he sat down. Rosco trotted up the porch steps and sat at his feet.

"So what can I do for the famous author?"

"Well, I'm researching an idea I had about a girl I went to high school with, Melissa Sinclair."

When he shifted in his chair, it protested loudly. He envisioned it collapsing into splinters, so he sat very still.

Mrs. B. thought for a moment before the memory returned. "Oh, yes. I do remember her. Her mother, Sarah, rented my house across the street. They lived there about three years, I think."

"That's right," Levi said. "What can you tell me about them? Anything you know would sure help me work my story out. And, of course, I'll never repeat anything you tell me. I'm just researching to write fiction."

"I don't like to talk about people," she said, looking at him squarely, her weathered face dark and brooding.

"I understand, but it's just fiction. By the time I get done with what I find out, it probably won't seem anything like the real story."

Mrs. B. thought for a few moments, then sighed.

"That poor girl, Melissa. Her mother had a lot of problems. I think she was one of those flower girls that never really came back from Woodstock. She was that generation. Do you know what I mean by that, Levi?"

Always the teacher, she was testing him as she so often had at the library when he was a boy.

"Drugs?"

Mrs. B. nodded.

"How did you meet Sarah?"

Mrs. B. chuckled. "Well, the patron saint of lost causes here in Twin Rivers came to see me about her."

Levi looked puzzled.

"Your Uncle Ed."

"Really?"

She nodded. "He told me the honest truth about her—everything he knew. He didn't hide anything. She'd been working at the Beer Chaser as a waitress—that's how Ed knew her. Ed found out she'd been evicted from her place in Calloway. There wasn't anyplace for her to go, so he was concerned about what was going to happen to her and, more importantly, her teenage daughter."

Levi smiled. That sure sounded like his Uncle Ed.

"My rental house was really old. It was old when my husband and I bought it after we married in the mid-40s. Then we lived in that house for twenty years before buying this one. Instead of selling it, we rented it out. By the time Sarah came along, the house was in very bad shape. My Charlie had died in 1980, and I just wasn't sure what to do with it. I was worried that it wasn't safe to rent, to be honest with you, and I was seriously thinking about just having it torn down. Ed knew that because I'd talked to him about it. Ed knows people, and I'd asked him if he knew anybody who'd tear it down for me for a reasonable price."

"So Uncle Ed talked you into renting to her instead of tearing it down," Levi said.

Mrs. B. nodded. "He did more than that. He had a couple of friends do a little work on it to make sure it was safe to rent—I never got a bill for that work even though I asked Ed about it several times. He also promised to cover her rent if she failed to do so. He felt like Sarah was trying to pull her life together, so he wanted to help her and hopefully Melissa in the process."

"And you agreed," Levi said.

"I've always been a soft touch. But Ed seemed to be right. For the first year or so, Sarah walked over here the first of every month with the rent. Never failed. She seemed to have it together. She was a pretty woman in her late thirties. She was always clean, and I never got the impression she was using drugs although Ed had told me she'd had problems with them in the past. I began to think she'd finally put that behind her. Since I knew there wasn't much money to spare and she was barely making ends meet, I felt pretty good about giving her a chance."

"But—" Levi said.

"But that changed," Mrs. B. said, her lips tight. "I think Melissa was a junior in high school when things changed. The rent quit showing up. I'd have to go find Sarah, and there was always an excuse why she didn't have it. She looked terrible. It wasn't hard to see what the problem really was. I think working at that tavern was a bad place for her to be, especially considering the problems she'd had in the past."

"She'd started using drugs again," Levi said.

Mrs. B. nodded. "I'd appreciate it if you'd keep this to yourself, but she got fired from the Beer Chaser. Ed came to see me again when that happened. He thought I needed to know. There was some money missing from the tavern, he said. She'd probably taken it to support her habit was his guess. He offered to help evict her since he felt bad for putting me in a bad position. I told him we'd just wait and see what happened.

"It wasn't long after she got fired that there was suddenly a lot going on across the street—cars coming and going at all times of the day and night. There were a couple fights outside between this guy or that. It was getting to be a real problem. The police were over there often."

"What do you think was going on across the street?" Levi said.

Mrs. B. shook her head. "I don't know for sure."

"But you had an idea, didn't you?" Levi pressed.

Mrs. B. nodded. "I don't like to speculate, but you can probably guess."

"Selling drugs?" Levi suggested.

"I don't think so. I think she was so into using drugs that she'd never sell them no matter how much she had."

"You don't think she was. . ." Levi paused. It was hard to say what he was thinking to this lovely, wizened old woman.

"Hooking?" Mrs. B. said.

Levi nodded.

"Sure," Mrs. B. said flatly. "I may be an old woman, Levi, but that kind of thing has been going on since the Bible was written. That's exactly what I think she was doing. Chief Craig came and saw me once. He thought that's what was going on over there, too."

"And Melissa was living there while all that was going on?"

Mrs. B. nodded slowly. There was pain in her eyes.

Suddenly, an upsetting thought crossed Levi's mind. "You don't think Sarah Sinclair was so deep into drugs that she would use her own daughter to get money, do you?"

Mrs. B. sighed. "The thought never crossed my mind back then. If it had, I would've reported it. I didn't know much about drugs then and the lengths people would go to get them. I've learned a lot of horrible things since. Right now, Levi, I just don't know the answer to that question."

They sat quietly for a time, neither saying anything.

"What time is it, Levi?"

Levi glanced at his watch and shook his head. "I'm not sure. It's either 2:30 or 4:30 Illinois time."

"You like margaritas?"

Levi looked at her in amazement.

Mrs. B. shrugged. "I find the best thing for my arthritis is to keep my blood thin. I usually enjoy a couple of margaritas in the afternoon—but not on the front porch. I don't want the neighbors talking. Would you care to join me around back on the patio? I'll tell you the rest of this story."

Levi nodded.

It was a beautiful day for a drive around Twin Rivers. The locals often claimed that in the summertime, one could drive from one side of Twin Rivers to the other and never see blue sky. Most of the neighborhood streets were completely canopied by old shade trees. In the fall, the leaves would fall so thick it was hard to tell where the edges of the streets were.

The streets themselves were named for those old, established shade trees: Elm, Maple, Oak, Ash, Poplar, Walnut, and Sycamore. The tree streets ran east and west, and the President streets ran north and south: Washington, Jefferson, Polk, Jackson, McKinley, and Lincoln. Main Street ran right down the center of town. It was all very orderly and very Midwestern.

Chief Malone was patrolling the streets in his cruiser, the part of his job he most enjoyed. He was leaning back in his seat, his flat-brimmed hat low over his eyes and his air conditioning vents aimed to blow right in his face. As he patrolled up Main Street, his eyes shot left and right up the residential streets as he crossed each intersection—an action that was habitual. It was a quiet afternoon. There weren't many kids out, and other than the occasional gardener, there weren't many adults outside either. As he crossed the Ash Street intersection, his eyes automatically glanced left and right.

He was well past the intersection when he suddenly jerked upright and locked up his brakes. Something seemed out of place. He sat for a moment with his hands tightly gripping the steering wheel and what felt like a hot wire twisting in his stomach. He thought about driving on, but the twisting wire wouldn't let him go. He knew what he'd thought he'd seen, and he had to go back and look again. Glancing in his rearview mirror, he saw he was alone on the road. He did a quick U-turn and returned to the intersection. His mouth was dry.

Parked in the driveway of the brick house on the corner was a familiar blue truck. He turned down Ash Street and drove by very slowly. Sweat popped out on his forehead. Levi Garvey's truck was parked at Mrs. B.'s house. There was nobody on the porch or anywhere in sight. He drove well past the house before turning around in a driveway to make a second pass. His heart was thumping in his chest as he rolled to a stop at the end of Mrs. B.'s driveway.

What the hell is he doing here? he thought. Surely, he didn't stop to say hello to the old crow. He's up to something.

When Doug glanced across the street at the empty lot on the other corner, a wave of nausea seized him. Levi couldn't know anything about what'd happened so many years before in the house that had once sat there, but Doug couldn't think of any other reason why Levi would be here.

His mind raced.

I've got to think of a way to get Levi Garvey to leave town, he thought. First he and Tori were standing in front of Melissa's picture at the reunion, talking, and now he's here. Levi's got to go. I've got to get him out of town.

* * *

Levi and Mrs. B. were sitting on the swing, both sipping margaritas. The backyard was at least ten degrees cooler, completely shaded by an old oak. There was a pitcher sitting on a table nearby. Rosco was in front of Mrs. B., looking at her with his ears up and his tongue hanging out. She'd been feeding him vanilla wafers when she thought Levi wasn't looking.

"So you were saying?" Levi said finally.

"Sarah pretty much stopped paying rent. I wasn't about to hit your uncle up for it, so I decided to serve her a legal notice of eviction. It's an ugly process. I felt sorry for Melissa, but I couldn't have that going on across the street. The town was buzzing with gossip about what was going on over there."

Levi nodded. He couldn't believe he hadn't heard the stories himself, but, of course, he'd learned just recently that the adults in Twin Rivers were very good at keeping things from their kids, like the fact Doug's father had committed suicide.

"When I starting that eviction process, it seemed to calm Sarah down a little bit since she realized she didn't have anyplace else to go. Some of the nonsense stopped, and she got a job at Hillbilly Bob's Convenience Store as a cashier."

"Yeah, I remember Melissa's mom working there when I was in high school."

Mrs. B. continued. "I think she was still using drugs because the rent payments continued to be a big problem. I'd get a little bit every once in awhile but nowhere near what she owed. Then Melissa came over and talked to me one day. She knew what was going on with the rent, which was very low, only $150 a month. Like I said, the house needed to be torn down, and I was trying to get enough out of it just to pay the taxes."

Mrs. B. took another sip of her drink. "Anyway, Melissa came to see me. She wanted to work for the rent because she wanted to graduate. That was her goal, and it seemed more important to her than anything else. She knew if they were evicted that was unlikely to happen.

"Melissa had an escape plan—one she'd been thinking about for a long time. She mentioned a school somewhere she wanted to go to. I know she'd already talked to the school. She was very sure she could get financial aid, and she planned to work as well. She couldn't depend on her mother—she said as much. I really respected that, of course. This was in the late summer of . . . what year did you hooligans graduate?"

Levi smiled. "1985."

"So she must've come to see me in August or September of 1984."

"And again, you were the soft touch," Levi said.

Mrs. B. smiled. "We were talking about maybe ten months. I wanted to give that girl a chance to graduate, and I wanted to give her the opportunity to put that escape plan into use. But I had decided right up front that Melissa was either going to be serious about it, or I wasn't going to consider it. But she proved herself very early on. She mowed here and across the street at the rental. That saved me money I was paying out at the time to a local man. She trimmed bushes. She painted. She scooped snow that winter. All that saved me money. She even shopped for me and cleaned my house. She worked for some of the neighbors, too, and paid every cent of the rent every month. She was desperate to keep a roof over her head until she had that diploma in her hand. Even with the things going on over there and the gossip around town, I wasn't about to evict them until Melissa had what she needed to make her big break. At the end of some months, I wound up writing her a check for the balance I owed her. She was a hard worker, and I never regretted giving her a chance."

Levi grinned.

"That's what you needed for that story, isn't it?" Mrs. B. said, looking at him knowingly. "You never really knew that girl, did you?"

Levi shook his head. "I'm ashamed to say as much time as she spent around me and my friends, none of us did. I had no idea she was that strong. You know, I'll bet she made it."

Mrs. B. nodded. "I'd bank on it. Poor girl. Nobody had ever paid much attention to her. She was so quiet I believed for a long time there wasn't much going on upstairs. But I sure learned differently. She was a thinker. She had it all worked out, and she wanted it so badly. I'll bet after she had that diploma she got as far away from her mother as she could and put that escape plan to work."

"Thanks, Mrs. B. That is just the story I needed to hear."

Levi stood up before realizing there was still one question he had.

"So when did Melissa make her break for it?" he said.

"Oh, you know, that's the weirdest part of the story."

Levi sat back down. "Weird? How?"

You guys graduated on a Saturday. I remember that because Melissa was supposed to grocery shop for me that next morning on Sunday. It was the first time she didn't show up."

"She was gone," Levi said with a smile.

"*They* were gone," Mrs. B. corrected.

"Both of them?"

"They didn't have a phone, so I went across the street to find Melissa, but I found the door key stuck in the outside lock. I knocked and peeked in the front windows, but it didn't seem like anybody was there. Finally, I went in. They were gone."

"The night of graduation, they left town?" Levi said.

"Yes, but they took only their clothes and some stuff from the bathroom vanity. The furniture was mine, so I expected to find that. But I didn't expect to find other things left behind, like dishes and pans and sheets and towels. They even left a load of clothes in the dryer."

"That is weird," Levi admitted.

"Maybe not. Maybe they were in a hurry," Mrs. B. said with a shrug. "You remember Chief Craig?"

"I sure do," Levi said, grinning. "He thought I had something to do with a bikini and the War Memorial statue one time."

"I never did figure out how you got up there," Mrs. B. remarked, looking at Levi with one eyebrow raised.

"Are you going to finish this story, Mrs. B.?" Levi said, smiling.

"So anyway, Chief Craig told me Sarah had some court cases coming up. She was looking at doing some jail time at the very least. The timing pretty much convicted her in his mind. I mean the daughter graduating the very day they both vanish in the night."

"And hopefully, Melissa made her escape from Sarah later on," Levi said.

"Of course, she did," Mrs. B. said resolutely.

Rising, Levi placed his glass on the table next to the pitcher.

"Thanks again, Mrs. B. This is good fodder for my story idea."

"Glad I could help," she said. "And, Levi, you need to stop by the library. There is the matter of a missing book we need to discuss."

"Huh?" Levi said, looking at her blankly.

"I think it was a Stephen King book. You never brought it back," she said. "I still work mornings at the library. Come in, and we'll work something out."

Levi smiled, but then he realized she wasn't kidding.

"Yes, ma'am, I'll come see you."

28

"I thought you were on vacation?" Regan Miller said from behind her cashier's station as Tori entered the First National Bank of Calloway.

"Just act like you never saw me," Tori said, smiling.

Quickly crossing the lobby, she walked into her office, shut the door behind her, and flipped the blinds closed.

Something had been bothering her ever since Levi had told her what Mrs. B had said about Melissa's escape plan, her plan to work her way through school. Tori couldn't stop wondering if Melissa had ever managed to put her escape plan into action or if she'd gotten stuck in her mother's sordid life. Tori knew she could spend months trying to find the school Melissa had attended, but as she'd sat in the drive-thru at Starbucks in Calloway, she'd suddenly had an idea. It was so simple if it worked, and it would answer her questions and put her mind to rest. All she needed was a phone number.

She pulled the phone book out of her desk drawer and looked up the number for Twin Rivers High School. She dialed the number on her cell phone. As it rang, she began to doubt her plan. He doesn't have to tell me, she thought. He probably won't tell me what I want to know.

"Yes, may I speak to Principal Weaver, please? This is Tori Buchanan."

She waited for what seemed like a long time before the familiar voice came on the phone. His hair might have thinned and turned gray, but the voice hadn't changed at all.

"Tori?"

"Hello, Mr. Weaver," she said.

"How are you? I haven't seen you since the grand reopening of the Comet Theatre. What was that? Five years ago?"

"I've been fine. In fact, I just visited the school last Saturday. It'd been a long time."

"Yeah," Weaver said with a chuckle. "I heard about that party you had here. That class of yours . . . let's just say I'm glad all of you graduated. We donated the aluminum beer cans to the local scout troop. You'll be glad to know they can all afford a college education now."

Tori laughed.

"But that's not why you called, is it?"

"I've got a strange question for you and maybe a strange request to make," Tori said.

"I can't imagine," he said as he chuckled again. "Wait a second. I'd better sit down."

"I was wondering. Does the high school keep track of who they send student transcripts to?"

"Oh sure," he said. "That's private information, and we can provide it only with the student's permission and to the schools the student indicates. Why? Have we made some kind of mistake?"

"No, not at all," Tori said. "This is where the strange request comes in."

"Okay," Weaver said cautiously. "What do you want to know, Tori. It's not like you to beat around the bush."

"Do you remember Melissa Sinclair—class of 1985?" Tori said.

There was a long pause. "I'm sorry, Tori. That name isn't ringing a bell with me," he said.

That didn't surprise Tori—it seemed like nobody remembered Melissa Sinclair.

"All I want to know is if the school sent her transcripts out anywhere," Tori said bluntly.

There was a long pause. "Tori, I think you know my problem with that. That's right on the edge of a breach of confidentiality."

"I know," Tori said. "I just need to know."

Weaver sighed. "And you'll want to know what school or schools, right?"

Tori knew she would, but realized asking that would be too much. "What if I said I was more interested only in how many schools you'd sent her transcript to?"

There was another long pause on Weaver's end. "Does this have anything to do with the bank?"

"Absolutely not," Tori said. "This is personal. I'll level with you, Mr. Weaver. She was a friend of mine back in high school. I lost track of her. She had a dream to go off to college to escape a very difficult home life. When I didn't see her at the reunion, I began to wonder if she'd ever . . ." Tori suddenly had a lump in her throat.

"I see." There was another long pause. "Hold on a second, Tori."

She heard the receiver clunk onto the desk and his door open. She waited a long time. Faintly, she could hear file cabinets rolling open and closed.

"Tori?" he said.

She knew by the tone of his voice what he was going to say.

"There were no transcript requests for Melissa A. Sinclair," he said apologetically.

Tori sighed. "What if she'd picked up a copy of it herself?" she said hopefully.

"We'd have a record of that, too," he said. "And actually she did get a copy. She asked for one at the beginning of her final semester, senior year. Probably curious about what it said. She may have even sent it out, but the college would still require a final transcript after graduation from the high school. But I could definitely see Melissa getting several schools interested in her. I'll tell you something about this young woman, Tori. She was a mediocre high school student, but her SAT scores were amazing—those scores alone would have given her a wide choice of just about any school she wanted to attend, and there's an excellent chance she could've gotten a full scholarship. I haven't seen scores like this very many times in my thirty year tenure. I can't believe I don't remember her."

"We're talking about Melissa Sinclair? Class of 1985?" Tori said dumbfounded. "You're sure?"

"Melissa A. Sinclair," Mr. Weaver replied evenly. "She was obviously a bored student, but her scores show she possessed a remarkable intellect."

"But there's no request for a final transcript from the college, so it's unlikely she ever made it," Tori said more to herself than to him.

"If we'd sent one, we'd have that school's transcript request on file. I'm sorry, Tori."

"Well, thank you, Mr. Weaver. I certainly appreciate it. I know I put you on the spot," she said.

"No problem, Tori. Good to hear from you."

Tori hung up. She'd known what the answer was before she called. She'd known it in her heart. Levi was looking for a story of strength and determination in the face of overwhelming odds. Levi wrote fiction. The reality was often much harder to take.

She decided not to tell Levi.

29

"Levi," Mrs. B. argued. "You signed it out April 4, 1985, and you never brought it back. That's a nickel a day for twenty-five years—give or take."

"$456? I don't even remember checking out *Christine*," Levi argued. "I mean I used to read Stephen King's books, but I don't remember reading that one."

"You probably didn't read it—because you *lost* it."

Mrs. B. looked up at him with her pale blue eyes from behind the librarian's desk. The dome of the Twin Rivers Carnegie Library loomed over her head.

"Of course, maybe we could work something out about the fine—you being a famous author and the kind of man *children* could be inspired by."

"What are we talking about here?" Levi replied cautiously.

This was one tough old bird, he decided.

"You work it off—$10 an hour," she said firmly. "We have a Young Author's program here. The *children*, ages 8-12, write stories for a contest right here at the library. You could work with them. You could teach them how to be creative in their writing. Then at the end, you could be one of the contest judges."

"You drive a hard bargain," Levi said with a smile.

"Of course, we could call the annual award the Levi Garvey Young Authors Award for—" She stopped to think, her brow furrowed.

"I'm sure you have an idea," Levi said, suppressing a chuckle.

"I think if you made a $500 donation towards the *children's* library fund, the library board would approve that."

"So I pay off my fine by working over forty-five hours at $10 an hour, *and* I make a $500 donation. That's what you want me to do to replace the $5.99 paperback book you say I checked out in the 1985?"

"Well, I thought you might also donate the trophy for the winner each year, too, and present it," Mrs. B. said as she smiled gently. "It would mean so much more to the *children*."

Levi sighed. He noticed how Mrs. B. was emphasizing the world *children* as she laid out her plan.

"Oh, you're good, Mrs. B. And the alternative?"

"Pay the fine and smash the aspirations of all these *children* who would like to follow in your footsteps."

There was that emphasis again.

She paused while adjusting items on the check-out desk. Levi said nothing, quite sure that Mrs. B. had more to say. He was right.

"I'm sorry, Levi. I may have let it slip to the *children* that you might be coming to our group. They're very excited. They all wrote thank you letters this morning," she said, handing him a pile of notes from under the counter.

Levi chuckled. He was beat. He threw up his hands in mock surrender then reached across the desk to shake the small wrinkled hand.

"It's a deal, Mrs. B."

Levi's phone chirped, and he flipped it open.

"We still going to the movie tonight?" Tori said.

"Hell, yes!" Levi replied.

His answer drew a reproachful glare from Mrs. B. After glancing around to make sure none of the beloved *children* were present, he mouthed, "Sorry," to Mrs. B.

"I'm in Calloway. I'm going by the hardware store to buy the shingles for the front porch," Tori said. "Is there anything else you need me to get? I know you were painting this morning. Did you dump paint on anything else?"

Levi snapped the phone shut, well aware that Tori was probably laughing somewhere on the other end. As he turned to go, Mrs. B. came around the counter.

"Could you join me in the audio-video room for a moment?" she said.

He looked at her suspiciously, but she waved him to follow her. She closed the door behind them.

"I was talking to April Jenkins this morning," Mrs. B. said. "I don't usually gossip."

"I've noticed that you say that right before you gossip," Levi said with a smile.

Mrs. B. ignored the remark. "April told me you were having some problems with an individual here in town. Same person you had so many problems with years ago. Chief Malone?"

"Yeah, some old wounds never heal."

"I remembered something after you left the other day," she said. "It's something that might help you in your current situation."

"Really?" Levi said. He was interested.

"You were asking about what was going on over at the house when the Sinclairs lived there," Mrs. B. said.

"I remember," Levi said.

"Perhaps you should ask Chief Malone about that."

Levi looked at her for a minute. He wasn't following. "Doug was in high school at the time. It was Chief Craig who was in charge of the police back then," he said.

"I know that, Levi, but it seems to me, I used to see a black truck over at that house late at night on occasion."

Levi's blank look turned into a big smile. "Really? I wonder what he was doing over there late at night? Buying drugs?"

Shaking her head, Mrs. B said, "I think he was buying something, but I don't think it was drugs."

"Oh, this is too good to be true," Levi said, laughing.

Mrs. B. reached up, grabbed him by the collar, and pulled his face down to her level. She looked him square in the eye. There was no humor there.

"I'll be honest with you. I never liked Doug Malone. The dumbest thing this town ever did was pin a badge on him. But I'll bet if you ask Doug about that sometime, he'd have a stroke. I'll bet he'd stay as far away from you as he could after that."

Levi couldn't believe what she'd just said, but he knew she was right.

"Thank you, Mrs. B."

She released his collar. When Levi reached the door, he paused and turned back to her.

"You know, Millie," he said. She bristled when he used her first name. "You should meet my literary agent, Wanda Sterling, some time. I thought she was tough, but you'd rip her to shreds."

Levi heard her cackling as he left the library.

30

As people streamed out of the double doors after the movie, Levi stood under the marquee of the Comet Theatre, waiting for Tori. He was staring at the hundreds of clear incandescent bulbs that studded the underside of the marquee, a far-away look on his face. The light was blinding after two hours of darkness inside, the copper sheeting reflecting the light from the bulbs. The dazzling marquee stretched clear across the sidewalk to the street. The lights on the underside and the three-story tall purple and white Art Deco era neon sign above lit Main Street for two blocks in either direction—from Harv's Diner to the Post Office.

Levi had never before seen either the Comet Theatre neon or the lights under the canopy since none of those lights had worked back when he was growing up. In those days, the run-down theatre had had only a single light over the ticket booth to indicate it was open.

Levi wandered to the edge of the sidewalk and looked up at the marquee: *Raiders of the Lost Ark. Harrison Ford. The Adventure Begins Again Wednesday.*

Smiling, he recalled that years before everything on the marquee had been abbreviated because the theatre didn't have many unbroken letters. He clearly remembered that when Uncle Ed took him and Tori to see *Star Wars* in 1977, the theatre manager had substituted a dollar sign for the last 's' in *Star Wars*.

"Did you think you'd ever come back here?" Tori said as she walked up to him.

"I don't think I ever completely left. This place was such a big part of my growing up, and I didn't realize until this evening, but it's still a big part of me."

"Like it?"

"It never looked like this when we were kids," Levi said with a smile. "All these bulbs were burned out. I never thought about there being neon above. Unless you drove by during the day, you never knew what was playing since the lights behind the letters on the marquee, the few that worked, used to flicker on and off when they worked at all. The carpets were in shreds, the floors were sticky, the bathrooms often flooded, and the seats had stuffing hanging out of most of them. Do you remember when Ronnie Halston fell through the floor of the balcony and landed in Troy Lewis' lap?"

Tori nodded. "This place was a mess when I started. But it was worth all the effort. Do you know that when this theatre opened in 1924, it was state-of-the-art. It was the most modern building in the whole county. It was only place within fifty miles of Twin Rivers that was air conditioned until the late-40s."

"You brought it back, Tori," Levi said. "It looks brand new—probably just as it did when it originally opened. And the place was full tonight."

"It sells out just about every show," Tori smiled. "They decided to sell tickets for a second show tonight because the first one sold out early. That happens almost every week."

"Think of the memories people relive here every week," Levi said. "Hell, think of some of the movies we saw here that are considered classics today—*The Star Wars Trilogy, Superman, The Blues Brothers, Ferris Bueller's Day Off, The Breakfast Club.*"

"Don't forget the dollar double matinees on Sundays," Tori reminded him. "All the classics in black and white—John Wayne, Jimmy Stewart, Bogie, Cagney . . ."

Levi was lost in the past. "How many hours do you suppose we sat in there watching movies as kids?"

Tori loved it when Levi got like this—all jazzed up after seeing a great movie. She'd glanced over at him a few times during the movie, and in the flicker from the screen, she'd seen such a sense of wonder on his face—pure joy.

"I have no idea," Tori admitted.

"What was your favorite part of coming here?" Levi asked her suddenly.

"I don't know," Tori said. "It was our little escape place—a cool spot to escape to on a sweltering summer afternoon. It always smelled like popcorn. I fell in love with this place—every ratty chair, every creaky step going up to the balcony, every tear in the old movie screen. What made you love this place?"

Levi's face got suddenly serious. "It would definitely be sitting beside you in the dark," he said.

Tori didn't know what to say. She just stared at him.

Levi looked up at the marquee again. "Do you know how many movies I never really saw because you were sitting beside me? I'd sit there, staring at the screen, but my mind was busy thinking about other things. I'd be trying to get up the nerve to reach over and hold your hand. I'd be working it out in my head, over and over again, but I never worked up the nerve. Sometimes I'd just skip ahead and think about how I might just lean over and kiss you. Should I wait until you looked at me and then kiss you? Should I just tap you on the shoulder, and when you turned to see what I wanted, maybe I'd lay it on you? I thought through a million variations while those movies were rolling in front of my face, but I never got a plan worked out—I was too chicken to try anything."

Tori's heart had risen into her throat. She couldn't believe what she was hearing.

"Kids are so stupid," Levi remarked. "It's actually quite simple really. You just do this."

He wrapped his arm around Tori's waist, pulled her into him, and kissed her firmly. She was so stunned she didn't do anything at first. Then when the shock wore off, she wrapped her arms around his neck, knocking his hat off in the process, and kissed him back.

As they stood under the lights of the marquee, they drew whistles and grins from several passersby. An old man and his wife paused as they watched them kiss. The old man reached down, scooped up the hat off the sidewalk, and popped it back on Levi's head. The couple smiled at each other, perhaps sharing their own memories, and walked down the sidewalk hand-in-hand.

Levi and Tori had walked to the Comet Theatre from the Garvey house. They were walking back now, smiling at each other and swinging their joined hands between them. The lights of the Comet Theatre were still bright behind them, but as they got further and further away, their shadows grew darker and longer in front of them.

"So what are you thinking?" Tori finally asked.

Levi laughed. "I'm thinking I'm not that much smarter now than when I was kid. I hardly saw any of that movie. Good thing I'd seen it before."

Tori laughed. "I'll never forget that kiss. It was like something out of one of those black and white movies we used to watch on Sundays. Cary Grant couldn't have done that any better."

When Levi's face lit up, she knew it was one of the best compliments she could've given him.

Levi whispered, "I've never stopped thinking about you, Tori. In all these years, I never got over you. It's weird because we never really had a relationship. I wasn't sure how you felt about me. I only knew I was in love with you. You were always the one that got away."

Tori looked at him oddly. "We never had a relationship? We are still so close we can have an entire conversation with a glance. We were so close then we talked about things nobody else knew—my dad, your folks. That's a relationship. Nothing has changed."

"That's not entirely true," Levi remarked. "When I saw you at the reunion, one thing had changed."

"What's that?"

"You're right. We used to be able to read each other with a glance, but there was something I'd never seen—and you didn't see it either. But at the reunion, I sure saw it. You aren't nearly as good at hiding things as you used to be. When I first saw you Saturday night, I knew in five seconds that you were in love with me. It was right there. I couldn't believe how easy it was to see. That last night at Kingery Pond, I sure couldn't see that for anything, and I was looking for it—desperately looking for it."

Tori squeezed his hand and moved so that their shoulders touched.

"So now what?"

Levi stopped to look at her. "I think we ought to have a long conversation about this, but not right now. Maybe in the morning over breakfast," he smiled.

He pulled her to him and kissed her again—a kiss that was even better than the first one.

As they were walking hand-in-hand towards the driveway, Tori stopped suddenly and said, "What happened there?"

Levi looked where she was pointing. Somebody had smashed his new mailbox and broken off the post at the ground.

"Ah, crap," he said. He leaned over to pick up the flattened mailbox and toss it by the broken post. "Probably kids."

"I don't think so," Tori said, looking towards the house.

The tone of her voice sent a chill up Levi's spine. She started running up the driveway. Old Blue was parked in the driveway in front of the house. She stopped beside the truck and shook her head. Levi jogged up next to her. His face fell when he saw the truck. All four tires were flat.

"Doug," she said angrily.

"It could've been kids," he said tightly, trying hard to keep his temper.

"Not likely," she said, pointing to the rear of the truck. "He left his calling card."

Levi walked around and stood next to her. The same tail light was broken out again.

"That son of a bitch," Levi said through gritted teeth.

He walked the rest of the way around the truck. From the light of the front porch, he didn't see any other damage.

"What are we going to do about him?" she said.

"It's just a truck," Levi said with great effort. She knew he was trying to keep his perspective. "You can fix a truck. And believe me, Tori. I got something to fix old Doug, too. He's not going to be a problem much longer."

He was remembering what Mrs. B. had told him earlier that day. Tori looked at him. His face was unreadable—twisted with mixed emotions.

"I'm not letting this piss me off—that's what he wants," Levi said. "He's trying to push me into doing something stupid. I'll fix that tail light tomorrow. Then I'll call Uncle Ed. He'll haul the truck over to the tire shop on his flatbed, and we'll be as good as new again. No problem. It's just a truck. We built Old Blue from the ground up. There's nothing he can do to this truck that I can't fix."

"And Doug? What about Doug?" she asked, her face taut with anxiety.

"Next time I see Doug Malone, I'm going to drop a bomb on his ass."

Tori looked closely at Levi's face for any hint of what he was talking about. Whatever he'd planned, he was sure about it, and she trusted him. If he wasn't worried, neither was she.

Levi looked at her, and suddenly the anger on his face melted away. "I'm not letting this ruin what has been a wonderful evening," he said. He held his hand out, and she took it.

"And it's not over yet," she said, looking at him with her deep-green eyes and the glimmer of a smile. That errant coil of hair had fallen in front of her face.

"Oh really?" he said.

Laughing, she suddenly bolted towards the house, skipping up the new porch steps. Levi raced after her. He caught her at the door, spun her around, and kissed her under the porch lights.

Across the road, hidden in the field access, Doug Malone had watched the whole scene in disbelief from his cruiser. Rage was surging in his temples. When they disappeared into the house, it took every ounce of his resolve and the rest of his flask to overcome his desire to take the tire iron out of his trunk and beat that old truck to bits. Doug fired the car and popped it into gear.

This is only the beginning of what I have planned for you, he thought. In a week, two at the most, your ass will be packing back to Georgia, my friend.

31

Ed Garvey pulled into the driveway. As he glanced up at the house, a broad smile crossed his face. There she is again, he thought.

Ed had sent some friends out to help Levi with a few things, but he hadn't seen the house since the day Levi had arrived. Now it gleamed in the morning sunlight with a fresh coat of white paint. The weathervane had been fixed. The clean windows reflected the sky and shade trees. Baskets of ferns and flowers hung all around the porch as they always had when Lucille Garvey had been alive. And billowing gently in the morning breeze from the post beside the front steps was the American flag. It had been years since he'd seen that.

Under the flag on the newly installed, freshly painted front porch steps, Levi sat with a cup of coffee. Rosco, who was lying beside him, barked a few times to alert Levi to the fact somebody had pulled in. Since their encounter in Old Blue with Doug Malone, Rosco had suddenly decided he was a guard dog—when he wasn't asleep. When Levi saw Ed, he looked up at the house and lifted both his hands as if to say, How's this look?

Ed pulled his flat bed wrecker around Old Blue, wincing when he saw the dead tires and the broken tail light. Levi walked out to join him. Within a few minutes, Old Blue had been winched and secured onto the back of the wrecker.

"You want a cup of coffee?" Levi asked.

"No, I'm good," Ed said. "I'll get Old Blue over to the tire shop. I should be back by lunch time."

"That would be fine," Levi said with a smile.

"You're in an awfully good mood this morning, considering . . ." Ed nodded towards Old Blue.

Tori walked out onto the porch, cradling a cup of coffee between her hands. She was wearing a long t-shirt and Levi's old robe and slippers. The screen door clacked shut behind her.

Ed rubbed his chin, glancing at Levi and then at Tori. He started checking the straps holding Old Blue on the bed. He said just loud enough for Levi to hear, "There was nothing to be jealous about. Nothing ever happened between us."

Recognizing his own words, Levi shook his head and grinned.

"I think there are more lens for that tail light in the carriage house," Ed said.

"Yeah, there are. I've already used one this week."

"You have a gun?" Ed said nonchalantly.

The sudden change of subject took Levi off-guard. "Huh?"

"A gun. Do you have a gun?"

Levi shrugged. "Granny's old howitzer is still in the closet." Lucille Garvey had an ancient 10-gauge shotgun she used to keep raccoons out of the trash cans. They used to tease her about it because she'd blow holes in the trashcans to scare them off instead of killing the raccoons.

Ed opened the door of the wrecker and reached behind the seat. He handed Levi a well-worn leather holster.

"What's this?"

"Your great-grandfather, Abe, brought that back from World War I."

Ed opened the glove box and handed Levi three boxes of shells.

Levi set the shells on the edge of the truck bed, snapped open the holster, and pulled out a large, very heavy revolver.

"This thing is a freakin' cannon," Levi said as he hefted it in his hand.

"It's a great gun," Ed commented. "British made. It's a .455 Webley Mk VI, issued to Brit officers for decades. They may still be using it. It shoots straight—accurate to about fifty yards. I was going to give it to you years ago, but I was afraid you'd blow your foot off."

"Blow my foot off," Levi said with a chuckle, as he loaded it. He reached into Ed's truck, took an empty pop can out of the drink holder, and tossed it as far as he could down the driveway.

"Be careful," Ed remarked. "It kicks like a mule, and I don't want you to break your delicate little wrists."

Levi raised the gun with two hands, sighted carefully on the pop can, and squeezed the trigger. The revolver fired with a resounding boom. Tori jumped, spilling her coffee. Rosco vanished under the porch. Gravel flew up in the driveway where the bullet struck—at least a foot from the pop can.

Ed exploded into laughter.

"Holy shit!" Levi said. "This thing *is* a freakin' cannon. I thought you said it shoots straight."

"The gun does. The operator, well, I think that's where the problem is."

"It pulls a little left," Levi said, glancing knowingly at Ed.

Levi sighted down the barrel at the can, squeezing the trigger again. The revolver roared. This time the can shot straight up into the air. It had barely returned to the ground when Levi plugged it again and again never missing any of the last five shots. He'd blown the can down the driveway nearly to the road.

After he'd fired the last time, he looked at Ed, who was scratching his head. Levi smiled. "Yeah, it definitely pulls a little left," he said nonchalantly, re-holstering the revolver.

"You're still a dead shot with just about anything you're

handed," Ed said with a nod.

"If I wasn't, I wouldn't be standing here right now," Levi said.

Their eyes met briefly, and there was a long pause as they looked down the driveway at what was left of the can.

"You keep that thing loaded and where you can get to it," Ed said firmly.

"You think I'm in serious danger, don't you?" Levi remarked.

"I know you are," he said resolutely.

Almost imperceptibly, Ed bobbed his head and flicked his eyes toward the road. Levi carefully looked in that direction without being obvious about it. The police cruiser was pulling out of the field access and heading back towards Twin Rivers.

"Saw him when you pulled in?" Levi said.

Ed nodded.

"And we just put on a little show for him," Levi added.

Ed thought for a moment. "I'd think of it more as an educational exhibition."

"What's this?" Levi said, leaning into Ed's truck and pulling out a rifle case.

"Oh," Ed said, "that's my varmit gun."

Tori had joined them beside the wrecker.

"Can I see it?" Levi had already set the rifle case on the side of the flat bed and had flipped up the latches before Ed answered.

"Yeah, sure, Levi," Ed said sarcastically. "Go ahead and have a look at it."

Levi whistled through his teeth as he looked down at the rifle.

"Is that a military rifle?" Tori said, looking over his shoulder.

It had a snap out bi-pod stand mounted under the barrel.

"No, that's the civilian model. It's a Remington 700. But the Marines have used a version as a sniper rifle since the mid-sixties."

"I think they call it the M-40," Levi said. "What is that, a .243?"

"No, it's a .308. And I can tell you that's the best rifle in the world as far as I'm concerned. The M-40 has been the standard sniper rifle for forty years. There's a new version of it now, chambered a little differently. They call that one the M-24."

Levi whistled again as he looked at the enormous diameter of the barrel.

"What kind of varmints are you shooting? Are elephants sneaking into the scrap yard at night? Rhinos? Grizzlies?"

"Coyotes," Ed said.

"That's no civilian scope," Levi remarked, looking at him.

"No, that's an old military scope," Ed admitted. "I paid a fortune for it, but it was worth every cent. With that rifle and scope, I can hit a coyote between the eyes at half a mile on a windy day."

"Oh, brother," Tori said, rolling her eyes.

"That's no shit, Tori," Levi said. "Uncle Ed is a hell of a shot. I've been hunting with him. But why such a large caliber?"

Ed took the rifle, put it back in the case, and pulled the lid closed.

"You stick with what you know," Ed said.

"Weren't you in the Marine Corps in Vietnam?" Levi said. Ed spoke about Vietnam so rarely, Levi knew almost nothing about his service.

Ed nodded. "I was. And that's when I first saw these rifles put to use. The U.S. didn't have a good rifle for sniper action. Vietnam was a very different war from Korea and World War II. To win that war, our soldiers needed a rifle that could be used in the jungle—against guerrilla-style warfare. The Marine Corps basically bought and sent over high powered Remington hunting rifles from the manufacturer. The first ones the Marine Corps put into service had wooden stocks. They're more heavily modified now, but they are essentially that same rifle."

Tori watched Ed as he stowed the rifle case behind the seat of his wrecker. "Were you a sniper, Ed?" she asked.

Even Levi noticed that Ed froze for a moment before turning back around.

"I always liked you, Tori," he said.

Ed walked around the truck, climbed in the driver's door, and looked through the passenger window.

"I'll bring Blue back as soon as she's got her new shoes."

"Thanks, Uncle Ed. And bill me for the towing."

"Please," he said, rolling his eyes.

He fired up the wrecker and backed down the driveway.

Tori looked at Levi. "Tell me that wasn't odd."

Levi nodded. "It was. I wouldn't push him on Vietnam. He's rarely acknowledged that he was even there. But that was the second time the subject has come up since I've been back. Whatever happened to Uncle Ed in Vietnam is something he's never gotten over and something he's never wanted to talk about until now."

"I wonder what's different about now," Tori said as they walked hand and hand towards the porch.

Levi thought he knew.

There's danger in the air, he thought. Uncle Ed feels it, and I've been feeling it, too. And when you feel like you're being hunted, you fall back on your survival instincts.

32

"You want another beer, Ed?" Joyce asked.

She was leaning on the bar in front of him, looking at him down her long pointed nose, a cigarette hanging out of her mouth. Her hair was dyed jet black, and she was wearing a black sweatshirt studded with gold sequins. Though she appeared to be about sixty, Ed knew she was much older than that. She'd owned the Beer Chaser for more than fifty years.

Her voice dragged Ed out of deep thoughts. He seemed momentarily confused as he glanced at the half-empty beer bottle in front of him. He'd been thinking about Levi.

"No thanks, Joyce. I think I'll finish this one and go home."

"You okay, Ed?" she asked.

She knew Ed well. He'd been a regular since he'd come back from the war.

"I'm fine."

"You look like something's eating you. I've never seen you nurse a beer for over an hour," she replied. "You sure you're okay?"

"I'm just tired."

Joyce looked at him doubtfully, then turned and made her way down the busy bar, filling glasses and replacing beers as she went.

Ed picked up his beer, drained it, and stood up. "I'll catch you later, Joyce," he called.

"Be in a better mood," Joyce called back. "You're one of the few customers I have that doesn't bore the shit out of me."

The other customers sitting at the bar all moaned and booed and started giving her grief.

Ed smiled. He'd seen this show many times. He walked out the door and into the gravel parking lot. It wasn't often that Ed Garvey left the Beer Chaser while the sun was still shining. As he walked to his truck, he dug the keys out of his pocket. When he got to the driver side of the big wrecker, he stopped. Chief Malone was leaning against the truck door, smoking a cigarette.

What the hell is this? Ed thought.

"Well hello, Ed," Doug said, smiling. "I didn't expect you out so soon. I thought I was in for a long wait. I brought a whole pack of smokes."

"What do you want, Chief Malone?" Ed said.

He wasn't too surprised to see him, but he was in no mood for games.

"I'm worried about your nephew."

"Is that a fact?" Ed said, his voice dripping with sarcasm.

Doug nodded, flicking his cigarette butt onto the parking lot where several butts of the same brand lay nearby.

He looked at Ed. "I think Levi needs to go home. Twin Rivers doesn't need or want a spotlight shining on it because of some has-been celebrity. We've got a good thing going here—we don't need the rest of the world butting in."

"He *is* home," Ed said. "If you want him to leave, you go tell him. Otherwise, get off my truck. I'm tired, and I'm in no mood for this."

Doug never moved as his face clouded with anger. "You see, Ed, talking to Levi wouldn't do me much good," he said. "He's very stubborn. He won't listen to reason. I certainly don't want any trouble, so I thought perhaps you could talk to him, make him understand."

Ed chuckled. "What I think you mean, Doug, is that you're afraid the next time you try to slash his tires, he'll fill you with more holes than he did that pop can this morning."

Doug's face grew a few shades redder. His fists clenched and unclenched. "I think you should help me, Ed. I don't want to see anything bad happen to Levi—or you."

"Is that a threat?" Ed said, leaning closer to him. There was amusement in his eyes.

Doug smiled with his mouth, but his eyes flashed anger. "Let me run a little scenario for you," he said as he lit another cigarette. "Let's say I begin to see you as a problem in town here. I'm sure you don't spend your evenings at the Beer Chaser just playing pool. Driving under the influence is taken very seriously in Illinois. There are very strict laws against that. I take it very seriously, too, especially in the summer when so many kids are running around the streets. If you were to get pulled over on your way home some night, well, a DUI would be a very bad thing for a man that makes his living towing old heaps back and forth from place to place. I mean, how would you support yourself, Ed?"

"So you *are* threatening me," Ed said with a nod.

Doug shrugged. "We're just talking here, Ed. It's just a little scenario. Think of it as a warning of things to come. But think about it."

Ed sighed as he looked down at the parking lot.

"Maybe you could help me?" Doug asked. He could see Ed softening.

Ed glanced up at him—pain in his eyes. "Maybe I could. Maybe I could talk to him."

Doug grinned.

"But I won't," Ed snapped.

Ed's leg shot out and swept Doug's legs out from under him.

Doug slid down the door of the truck, landing hard on his butt on the parking lot. Furious, Doug put his hand down and began to get up. Just as quickly, Ed kicked his hand out from under him, knocking him on his side. Then Ed fell on him, pinning him to the ground with his knee. Doug tried to punch him, but Ed caught his hand, holding it with such strength that Doug's face went pale. With his other hand, Ed pulled Doug's Glock from his holster and tossed it away. To Doug, it seemed as if Ed had taken him down in one fluid movement. He couldn't believe the speed the old man had—or the strength he possessed.

"You like scenarios," Ed said, leaning over into Doug's face. "Let me run a little *scenario* for you now, Doug. Let's say you piss me off, and I beat you into a coma right now. Of course, I could very easily. I've seen seventy-year-old men move faster than you do."

Ed chuckled at his own joke. He *was* seventy.

It chilled Doug that Ed Garvey didn't seem angry or even flustered. He could've been swapping jokes at Harv's Diner.

"So you're lying here on the ground, bleeding and unconscious, and all my friends are going to come outside like they always do when there's a fight. We'll have to call the police. It'll probably be the County Mounties that show up first—maybe even the State Police. All my friends inside are going to back my story up—the one that I tell them before the cops get here—which is that you threatened me and that you seemed drunk at the time.

"Of course, all of them are going to claim they saw the entire thing. They'll go ahead and arrest me I'm sure, but I know there are those in the County Police *and* the State Police that don't think very highly of you, Chief Malone. They'll probably believe the story because it would be hard for them to believe a seventy-year-old man could take down a big strapping cop like you unless you were somehow impaired.

"I just bet that when they get you to the hospital, or *the morgue*, they'll draw some blood, and the results from that blood test would back up my story, wouldn't it, Doug? Whether you live or die, your days of being Deputy Dawg in this little town would be over. And I'll walk away free as a bird—self-defense."

Ed released his hand. Doug could still feel his iron grip on his wrist. He raised both of his hands, palms out, a few inches in front of his face.

"Let's just say it takes a drunk to know a drunk, and you're a drunk, too, Doug," Ed said. "If I feel like you're a threat to me or my family, that little scenario will seem like nothing. I'll come after you. I've seen things in this life you can't imagine. I've done things in this life you wouldn't even be able to comprehend. I have to live with that every single day. I don't care what happens to me anymore, but I care about what happens to Levi."

Ed pressed his knee harder into Doug's chest and leaned down into his face. Doug could smell the beer on his breath.

"I don't want to hurt you, but I'll put your ass in the ground if I have to. Now you just think about that *scenario,* Chief Malone."

Climbing up from the ground, Ed offered his hand to Doug. He refused it. He got up on his own and walked to his cruiser, brushing himself off as he went. He reached down to pick up the Glock from the parking lot. Holding it in his hand, he glanced at Ed, who smiled and held his hands out on either side. The gesture said, "Now's your chance. You'd better take it."

Doug holstered the Glock. Ed knew defeat when he saw it.

"What are you scared of, Doug?" Ed said as Doug opened the cruiser door. "Levi doesn't mean you any harm. He wants a quiet life in the town where he grew up. Just leave him alone, and he'll leave you alone. There's no reason for any of this. You have the power to take a step back. Let it go before somebody gets hurt. *Just let it go!"*

Doug had paused to hear what Ed had to say, but he never looked at him. He climbed into his cruiser and pulled the door shut. As the car rolled through the parking lot and turned onto the main road, Ed knew he'd won the battle, but he felt the war was yet to come.

I'm not sure I helped the situation, he thought. I just hope I didn't make it worse.

Doug's hand shook as he poured a cup of coffee back at his office. Ed Garvey had rattled him. Ed had taken him down so effortlessly and so quickly that Doug hadn't even had a chance to react. No one had ever done that to him before—no one except his father.

But what really bothered Doug was Ed had acted as if it were a joke—how calm he'd been during the whole exchange, except for the chilling intensity Doug had seen momentarily in Ed's eyes when he said, "I'll put your ass in the ground if I have to."

Doug sat behind his desk and sipped the coffee. He reached down to open the bottom drawer where he kept the bourbon, then changed his mind. He leaned back and rubbed his wrist. He knew there'd be a bruise where Ed had held him.

Maybe Ed is right, he thought. Maybe I should take a step back. Maybe I should just give Levi some distance. Maybe I'm making more out of this than I should. I mean, what could he possibly know?

Doug thought back to the reunion. Seeing Levi and Tori standing in front of Melissa Sinclair's picture had nearly put him into a panic.

But maybe they were just talking about her—reliving old memories, he mused. There was a lot of that going on. Mel was always hanging around that group of losers. It probably didn't have anything to do with me at all.

He thought about Levi's truck in Mrs. B.'s driveway. There could have been a hundred reasons why he was there. He was a bookworm—spent most of his time in the library. Maybe he was just going to say hello. There's no reason for me to believe it had anything at all to do with Mel or the Sinclair house. It could have been nothing more than a social call. There is no reason to think Levi Garvey has linked me to Mel in any way.

Doug began to relax as he realized he'd been overreacting. The more he thought about it, the better Ed's advice became.

I'm being paranoid, he thought. I've worried about Levi and Tori getting back together and comparing notes for so many years that I've convinced myself it's already happened. I've got to leave it alone. If I keep pushing on them, they just might figure something out. It was a long time ago. What are the odds they can put it all together? Zero.

33

Ed put the Remington 700 back in his gun case, closed the glass door, and locked it. He stood for a minute, looking at it.

It was a ritual night. He'd known it that morning when he saw Doug hiding in the weeds across the road from the Garvey house. He'd known it when Levi demonstrated he was still a dead shot with about any gun he had in his hand. He'd known when he passed the farmer mowing a ditch bank, when the wump-wump-wump from the blades on his bat-wing mower became the sound of a chopper over a jungle half a world away. Even Joyce had known it was a ritual night—he wouldn't be seeing her tomorrow. She didn't know anything about the ritual. She knew only that there was a place where Ed had to go periodically, a place where even a friend of forty years couldn't follow. The tension had been building.

But I don't want to go there again, he thought. It kills me a little more each time. I don't know if I can do this. Can I face them again?

It seemed to Ed that the further away in years, the closer on his heels the memories got. They chased him at night in his dreams. They haunted him during his days. He couldn't escape them. They were always there, but sometimes they got closer . . . when they were stalking him. They were stalking him now. The only thing he could do when they were stalking him was to face them.

It was time again. He had to do the ritual.

He unlocked the bottom drawer of the gun cabinet. He had to accept the things he'd done. But there was always a choice. He paused. There were two things in the bottom drawer, and it was always a difficult choice. He looked at the loaded .38. He looked at the carved box.

Will it be life—if that's what you'd call this—or death?

His hand paused over the .38, wondering what his choice would be tonight if Levi hadn't shown up again. He knew the answer without question. Had Levi doomed him or saved him? He could almost hear the late night phone call in Savannah. "Is this Levi Garvey? This is Captain so-and-so from the Illinois State Police. I regret to inform you that . . ."

Ed reached behind the .38 and grabbed the carved wooden box. The contents jangled brightly when he lifted it out. Tucking the box under his arm, he walked into the kitchen, knowing that he couldn't do this many more times. He flipped on the kitchen light and set the box on the table. It jangled again, the sound sending shivers down his spine.

Ed turned away from the box. He stared at the faded kitchen walls, breathing in and out slowly, as he listened to the sound of his pulse pounding in his ears. It wasn't always like this, he thought, as he reflected on happier times.

He remembered buying the house on his GI bill when he'd gotten home from Vietnam in '72. His fiancé, his high school sweetheart, had painted the kitchen bright yellow. He'd laid new linoleum on the floor. It was to be their starter house. They had their whole lives in front of them.

"This is a great house, Ed," she'd said. "But we won't be here long. We'll get something better than a two-bedroom when we start our family—maybe a nice two-story over on Jefferson close to the grade school."

He could still hear her voice as he looked at the walls that had once been the color of lemons and were now the color of parchment. He looked at the floor he'd put down so many years before, now worn through to the plywood below in several places. She'd said that before she knew the fiancé who'd gone to war wasn't the same man who'd come back. It was before even Ed had known that something had followed him home from Vietnam—something he'd never been able to shake.

Their engagement hadn't end ugly. Their plans had just faded away—like the yellow walls in the kitchen. They'd never married. She'd never cooked a meal in her bright yellow kitchen.

I still miss her, he thought, and I still love her, but I couldn't have given her a life. She found a good man who's given her the life she deserves. She's happy with Harv, and they have a great marriage.

When Ed felt a knot forming in his throat, he shook off the old memories. Turning away from the yellow walls, he walked to the counter, pulled the bottle out of the tall sack he'd carried in earlier, and took a glass from the drainer. He sat down at the kitchen table and pulled the box towards him. He twisted the cap off the bottle and poured half a glass of amber liquid—social drinker in public, alcoholic in private. Take it easy now on the hooch, he admonished. You've got to get through them all tonight.

He took a small sip from the glass, the bourbon burning all the way down. He stared at the box. He considered just going to bed, but he couldn't get away. He couldn't hide when he was being stalked. It was time.

He opened the box and slowly began to remove the contents. When the light in the kitchen seemed to flicker, he squeezed his eyes shut. This happened every time. They were coming. The guests were arriving.

Opening his eyes, he finished emptying the box and took a deep breath. His guests were lined up behind him. He never looked, but he knew they were there. He could never bear to look at them all at once, but he could hear them shuffling, waiting for the ritual to begin.

I'll see them. I'll face them just like I did the first time we met, he thought. One at a time.

They were looking over his shoulder as the ritual began—each one waiting his turn.

"Please . . . God . . ." he prayed quietly, "let me get through all of them tonight. If I can just get through all of them, maybe they will let me rest."

34

Levi and Tori had spent the last few hours at a local greenhouse. Old Blue's bed was loaded with trees, bushes, flowering shrubs, and flowers. Now that the Garvey house was back in shape again, Tori thought it was time to rehabilitate the landscaping. Levi had been teasing her as they drove back to Twin Rivers about how she'd robbed the poor man at the greenhouse.

"Well, he should have given us a discount, considering how much we bought," Tori argued.

"I don't disagree," Levi said. "I just think you should've brought it up long before he'd loaded all those plants into the back of our truck."

Tori grinned. "Now why would I do that? I think the fact he didn't want to unload all those plants from the truck worked in our favor."

Levi sighed and shook his head as he turned up Main Street. Rosco was standing up in Tori's lap with his head hanging out the passenger window. As they passed the Comet Theatre, they saw Doug Malone crossing the street from the Police Department to Harv's Diner. Levi looked at Tori, anger suddenly flashing in his eyes.

"I'm hungry," he said, swerving into an empty parking space in front of Harv's.

"Be careful," Tori said. "Don't let your mouth write a check your ass can't cash."

But Levi was like a guided missile. He'd been waiting for just such a chance. Trying to talk him out of it would be pointless. Levi swung the truck door open and walked towards the entrance with Tori trailing behind.

The bell jangled as Levi slammed the door against the back of a booth. Everyone in the full diner looked up when he stormed in. Doug had just gotten a cup of coffee. April was still standing in front of him with the most peculiar look on her face. She reached back to nudge Harv, who had his back to the door. After turning around and seeing Levi, Harv got the same look on his face that April had. Both knew something was about to happen.

"Hi, Doug," Levi said loudly. "I've been looking for you."

Doug swiveled slowly on his stool. The diners were uncomfortably silent.

"What can I do for you?" Doug asked calmly.

"I want to report a crime," Levi said. "Somebody slashed the tires on my truck and ran over my mailbox. They also broke out the tail light on my truck for the second time in a week. Of course, I know who did it the first time."

"Maybe I can come by your place a little later, and we can discuss it."

To Tori, Doug's remark sounded almost like an admission—like he was willing to discuss the damages. But Levi was hot.

"Maybe we could also discuss the damage you did to my tail light when you broke it out with the butt of your gun the other morning," Levi snapped. "You remember? It was when you wrote me that bullshit ticket."

"We can discuss that, too," Doug said, looking uncomfortable, his voice low. "In *private*."

"What? You don't want the people in town here to know what you've been up to?" Levi said. "That didn't seem to be the case when you wrote me the ticket. You couldn't wait to get up here and brag about it."

Doug glanced at April, who stared back. He knew exactly who'd told Levi about that.

"Here, Doug," Levi said, tossing him his keys. "Why don't you go out there and demonstrate to everyone here how I managed to get Old Blue up to 48 miles per hour in the span of two blocks. In fact, if you can do it, you can keep her."

There were a few chuckles around the diner. Tori tried hard to suppress a grin herself.

Smiling tightly, Doug got up from his stool. He put on his hat and walked slowly to the door where Levi and Tori were standing. He handed the keys to Old Blue back to Levi.

Doug leaned in close to them and whispered, "Listen, I'll come by your house later. We'll work something out on the damages—and on the ticket, too."

"I think it's too late for that," Levi hissed. "In fact, I think you'd better make it a full time job to stay out of my line of sight. Next time I see you, Doug, you'll regret it. I *know* your little secret. I just may be tempted to start telling everyone in town what you were up to at the Sinclair house so many years ago."

The color drained from Doug's face. He looked in disbelief at Levi, who was relishing his reaction which was better than he'd hoped. Levi actually thought Doug was going to pass out. He was clearly stunned.

Good God! Levi knows! How could he possibly know? Doug thought, fighting not to show his panic.

Tori squeezed Levi's arm tightly, hoping he wouldn't say any more. He'd already said enough. She was afraid if he said any more, Doug might come out fighting, but Doug only looked at them both before quickly walking out the door.

When Levi glanced at Tori, he could tell by the look in her eyes that she agreed. That had been almost too easy.

April finally broke the silence in the diner. "So what kind of pie would you like tomorrow morning with your coffee, Levi?"

He shook his head. "It wouldn't be right to be rewarded for being insulting. That wasn't very honorable, what I just did."

Levi looked down, appearing to be contrite. No one in the diner spoke. The silence was long. Suddenly, Levi looked up, a shrewd grin on this face. "Of course, I wouldn't say no to a slice of coconut cream," he said.

Levi and Tori had worked on the front flowerbed all afternoon. Rosco was snoring in the shade of the elm tree. Levi knew something had been bothering Tori since they'd left Harv's, but he knew her well enough to leave her alone. She would tell him when she'd worked it out.

They'd planted nearly all the bushes and most of the flowers they'd bought. The sun was beginning to set as they stood back to admire their work. Totally exhausted, Levi was leaning on his shovel, but he couldn't believe how great the front of the house looked. Tori was standing a few feet away, raking and leveling the last bag of mulch.

"Something's wrong," Tori said.

Levi nodded. "I was thinking that maybe a couple of burning bushes on either side of the sidewalk—"

"I was talking about Doug," she said. "Something was wrong with the way he reacted today."

Levi chuckled. "I beat him, and he knew it. That's what defeat looks like, Tori."

Tori shook her head. "That wasn't defeat."

"What was it then?"

"He was beaten before we got there," Tori remarked. "Think

about it, Levi. He was ready to come over here this afternoon and write you a check for the damages. I think he was ready to rip up that ticket, too."

"Oh, bullshit," Levi snorted. "He didn't want me calling him out in public. That's all it was."

"I don't think so. His reaction was all wrong," Tori argued. "He was done fighting before you walked in the door. I don't know why, but he was. The war was over, and he was getting up to leave. You wouldn't have had to say another word."

Levi frowned, clearly not believing what Tori had said.

"Think about how he reacted when you delivered your little bombshell," Tori added.

Levi grinned. He had relived the memory over and over all afternoon.

Tori sighed. She wasn't smiling. "Think about how a character in one of your books would've reacted to being blackmailed like that. I mean, twenty-five years ago he was involved with a prostitute. Embarrassing? Yes. Might it be a problem for him in his current job? Probably not. Did his reaction make sense given the situation? No."

Levi was still smiling, but as he thought about it, the smile faded.

"His reaction was *completely* wrong," Tori said, pressing on. "How should he have reacted, Levi?"

Levi shrugged. "He should have been angry. Frustrated that I'd learned his dirty little secret. I'd expect him to be worried that I'd embarrass him publicly about it." Levi paused, then nodded. "You're right. His reaction wasn't quite right. I have something on him that I can use to twist his arm. He should've been pissed off about it—not afraid."

"There's got to be more to it," Tori agreed. "We're missing something."

"What could it be?" Levi asked her.

Tori sighed and looked down at her feet.

"You think you might know, don't you?" Levi said.

Tori didn't answer, just continued to stare at her feet. He reached over, gently cradled her chin in his hand, and lifted her face up. There were tears in her eyes.

"I just might," she admitted. "I should have told you a long time ago."

35

Tori and Levi were sitting on the porch swing, watching the sunset. She wasn't crying exactly, but tears had been slipping down her cheeks for some time. Levi didn't know why. The tears were unsettling. Despite all the pain she'd shared with him years ago, he'd never once seen her cry.

"I never wanted to tell you about this, but I have to now," Tori said, wiping the tears from her face. "I hope you'll understand why I kept this from you years ago."

Levi knew that Tori telling him whatever it was she had to say wasn't going to be easy for her. He sat quietly, and she said nothing for a long time as if she were trying to figure out how to say it.

"We were sophomores," she said finally. "We'd gone to the homecoming football game. That was the night Jim Anderson tripped coming down the bleacher steps and dumped an entire cup of hot cocoa all over Christine White's cheerleading uniform."

Levi grinned. "I'll never forget that. He pretty much sealed the fact we'd never be members of the popular crowd."

"Your grandma was at the game, too. It was just before you got your driver's license. Afterwards she offered me a ride home, but my dad was supposed to be coming to get me, so I said no. You left with her, and I stayed with Jim, Kathy, and Robin."

"I don't remember," Levi said as he shook his head.

"I do," Tori replied. "One by one, their folks came and got them, and before I knew it, I was standing out in front of the school alone, waiting for my dad. I knew he was probably off drunk somewhere, having totally forgotten about me—again."

Her voice was shaking. Levi reached over and held her hand.

"The football players were beginning to file out of the building. They were laughing and reliving the game out in the parking lot. Then one by one, they began leaving in their vehicles. I pretty much knew I'd be walking home when the lights on the football field went out.

"I'd started walking down the drive when I heard a truck pull up next to me. It was Doug Malone, who, of course, had played in the game. He offered me a ride, but I declined. He idled along the driveway next to me as I walked, trying to convince me to let him drive me. We'd known each other since sixth grade, and he hadn't yet become such a huge ass. It wasn't like he was a stranger. Anyway, it was a long walk to the far side of Twin Rivers, so finally I agreed to let him take me home."

Levi wasn't sure where this story was going, but his heart was pounding. He wasn't sure he wanted to know the rest of it, but Tori continued.

"Instead of taking me straight home, he wanted to stop for gas and to get something to drink. He said it had been a long game, and he was parched. I said sure, and we headed out towards Hillbilly Bob's Convenience Store. But when we got there, he went right past it. He said he wanted to show me something, so I went along. It was kind of fun riding in that big four-wheel-drive truck.

"He turned down a country road, and pretty soon he pulled into an old farm lot and parked the truck. It was dark except for a pole light in the barn lot. I could see Doug fairly well in the light coming through the windshield."

Tori stole a quick glimpse at Levi, then fixed her eyes on the sunset.

"He was telling me how he'd had his eye on me since sixth grade and how he'd been thinking about me. I wasn't worried until he leaned over and tried to kiss me. When I pushed him away, he sort of nodded and smiled. I told him I didn't see him that way—that we were friends. He seemed to understand. He just kept nodding and smiling. When he started to lean forward, I thought he was going to start the truck and take me home."

Tori slipped her hand out of Levi's and clenched both hands tightly in her lap. She said nothing for a long time.

"Out of nowhere, he slugged me hard in the side of the head—really hard. I thought I was going to pass out. Next thing I knew, Doug was on top of me, tearing my clothes and telling me not to scream. I was terrified. I didn't know what to do. He was enormous, and his weight was crushing me. I couldn't move or breathe.

"I was so scared. I knew I couldn't get free with him on top of me, so I told him he was making this a lot harder than it had to be. To be honest, I was thinking maybe that would be the easier way—just let him do it and be done with it. I wasn't sure what to do. He leaned up, but he still had his hands clamped around my wrists. I told him it was going to be hard getting my jeans off with him holding me. 'Well that's more like it,' he said. He leaned back against his door, thinking I was going to undress. I could see just his outline in what light there was."

Levi started to say something, but Tori put a finger to his lips to silence him.

"I was so scared. I was really going to go through with it. I really was. But I didn't want to get pregnant, so I asked him if he had any protection. He said he did, and when he raised his butt up off the seat and dug his hand into his back pocket to get his wallet, I saw an opportunity."

Tori paused. "Do you remember those black cowboy boots I used to have?"

Levi nodded.

"I was wearing those, and when he had one hand under his ass, I leaned against my door and kicked him as hard as I could in the chest. It knocked the wind out of him. I reached for the door handle, but there was no handle there. It had broken off, and I cut my hand on the sharp edge of what was left. I thought I was dead. I wished in that moment I'd just done the deed with him. Doug had one hand stuck in his back pocket, but he grabbed my foot with his free hand and began twisting it. He was gasping, trying to get his breath. I gave him another little surprise. I kicked him as hard as I could with my other foot—caught him right in the side of the head, which banged against the window. He slumped over and let go of my foot. As fast as I could, I cranked my window down and dived out."

Tori took a deep breath.

"I got away. I heard his truck start up moments later, but I ducked into the woods while he drove up and down the road looking for me for a long time.

"I finally made it home, creeping across backyards and through alleys. I was afraid Doug was still prowling for me. I thought a few times I could hear his truck, but who knows, as scared as I was.

"When I got home, Dad's car was idling in the driveway in front of the garage door with the headlights on. He was passed out behind the wheel."

Tori sighed.

"Typical day in the life of an alcoholic's daughter. I was fighting for my life because he didn't come and get me, and he was passed out drunk in the driveway—oblivious to the whole thing. Suddenly, Doug's truck was idling in front of our house. I acted like I was talking to my dad. Doug didn't know he was passed out. Slowly, Doug crept down the street and turned the corner. I heard him roaring down Main Street a few moments later. I reached in and turned dad's car off."

Levi reached over and gently moved the strand of hair that had fallen across her face to the side. She never stopped looking at the sunset. Unsure of what to say, Levi finally decided it was best if he didn't say anything at all.

Tori was sitting on a stool at the kitchen island, her back rigid, her face tight. She was an emotional mess. Levi still wasn't sure what to say or do. He went to the refrigerator and took out a couple beers. He twisted the cap off one and slid it over to her. When all else failed, there was beer. He leaned against the fridge and sipped his beer. Tori wouldn't look at him.

"I always knew there was something wrong with Doug," he said finally. "Now I know. You kicked what few brains he had out of his head with your cowboy boots. I always knew those things were deadly."

When Tori glanced up at him, he smiled at her. She picked up the beer and took a drink as the faintest smile appeared.

"You know why I didn't tell you before," she said, staring at her beer bottle.

Levi nodded. "That part of the story I completely understand, Tori. I'm glad you didn't tell me 'cause I wouldn't have been able to handle it. Doug managed to smash my face in enough just because he didn't like me. I can't imagine what it would've been like if I'd had a reason like that to go after him."

Tori seemed somewhat relieved to hear him say that.

"There's another part I've always felt guilty about," Tori said, her eyes still red and teary.

"You've always wondered if you were the only one," Levi said. "You think he did that to other girls."

Tori seemed surprised that Levi had the same thought. "I've always suspected it. You think that door handle being broken off was just a coincidence? I've always wondered if the next girl who was stupid enough to get in that truck would find the window crank missing, too."

"You think this has anything to do with his strange reaction today?" Levi said.

"I think that's a good possibility," Tori said. "He's hiding something a lot more serious than visiting the local hooker."

Leaning quietly against the fridge, Levi had been thinking. "I'm trying to remember exactly what I said to him when he reacted like that. I never mentioned Sarah by name, did I?"

Tori shook her head. "You didn't. What you said was 'I just may be tempted to start telling everyone in town what you were up to at the Sinclair house so many years ago.'"

Levi nodded. "I'm starting to think Doug's reaction this afternoon wasn't about the hooker mom. . ."

With sudden fear in her eyes, Tori said, "Maybe Melissa Sinclair was the next girl stupid enough to get in that truck. Maybe there were a lot more girls. That's why he's scared, Levi. He thinks you know about what he tried to do to me, and he thinks you know what he may have done to Melissa, too. If more of his victims are still out there, it could ruin him."

Levi nodded. "We need to stay away from him for the time being. We can't prove anything. I have a strange feeling we've seen only the tip of the iceberg."

"And if that's true, that little bombshell you dropped on him," Tori said quietly, "may prove way more dangerous to us than to him."

36

"Lunch!" Levi yelled as he banged out the screen door and set two plates on the round wrought-iron table on the corner of the porch.

Tori had found the table, along with the four heavy iron chairs, at an auction a few days before. She'd had all five pieces sandblasted and enameled in white. Levi was apprehensive about the table at first, reluctant to change anything at the Garvey house. But he'd quickly found a use for the table. He'd worked on his book idea there all morning while Tori planted flowers.

"I'm starved," Tori said, walking around the side of the house. She was wearing overalls and had her curly blonde hair pulled back into a ponytail. She pulled off the heavy leather work gloves and shoved them into her back pocket. Rosco was at her heels, where he always was anymore—she carried treats in her pockets.

"Well, wash up," Levi said as he poured lemonade into two glasses.

Tori looked at her hands, then wiped them a few times on her dirty overalls. She walked up the steps to join him at the table.

"If my grandmother saw you do that," Levi said with a chuckle.

"Little dirt never hurt anyone," she said, taking a seat. "What a nice lunch. You're going to make somebody a good wife one day."

"You're funny," Levi said, taking a seat next to her.

Tori dug into the hotdogs and macaroni and cheese. She was very hungry since she'd skipped breakfast and had been working hard on the landscaping all morning.

"Is this one of Paula Deen's recipes," she asked between bites.

Levi grinned and shook his head, but he said nothing. Tori enjoyed teasing Levi about being on her show almost as much as Ray Billings had back in Savannah.

"It's delicious," she remarked, flashing her green eyes at him in amusement.

"Paula calls this Savannah Pig and Pasta," he said proudly. "The secret is in boiling the water. You know you're doing it right when it starts bubbling."

Tori laughed. The dark thoughts and suspicions they'd shared the evening before about Doug Malone had dissipated in the bright morning sunlight. It was a beautiful day, the Fourth of July, and Doug Malone was the furthest thing from their minds.

"So what's the plan for the rest of the day?" Tori said, feeding Rosco a piece of hotdog off her plate.

"I don't know, but somebody promised me a movie tonight at the Comet, a John Wayne picture."

"*McLintock*—another of your favorites, and the fireworks start at the park thirty minutes after the movie lets out," Tori said.

"The Comet Theatre sure picked a perfect Fourth of July movie, one of a very few comedies John Wayne made. Great cast—Maureen O'Hara, Yvonne DeCarlo, a young Stephanie Powers, and Dick Van Dyke," Levi said.

"Actually, I think it was Jerry Van Dyke," Tori remarked. She didn't bother to mention that they showed the same film every Fourth of July before the fireworks, and she knew it was Jerry Van Dyke.

"No, I'm pretty sure it was Dick," Levi said, deep in thought.

But Tori had noticed something way more interesting than their conversation. She was looking towards the end of the driveway and shaking her head. "Levi, do you hear music?"

Levi paused for a moment to listen. "I don't hear any music. What kind of music?"

"Circus music. You don't hear circus music playing?"

Levi listened again, but he didn't hear any music. Instead, he heard gravel crunching in the driveway as a vehicle approached the house.

"Ah, shit," Levi said when he noticed what was rolling up the driveway. "Christine White, my very favorite person. If I throw up at any point during this conversation, would you please tell her I've had the flu this week?"

Tori smirked.

Christine pulled her black Ford Expedition to a stop in front of the porch and waved cheerfully at them as she talked on the phone. It was an animated conversation. Levi figured she was telling whoever it was that she was at Levi Garvey's house, as if she were there all the time.

She finally climbed out, grabbed an oversized purse, and wobbled over to the house on high heels. She was wearing a wispy little summer dress that was both too short and too low cut. Every time the breeze caught it, Levi was reminded that Christine was breaking one of the hard and fast laws of mid-life—if one's cleavage has crow's feet, it's time to put the pups away.

"Hi!" she said as she clomped up the stairs. "I hope I'm not intruding. I took some pictures at the reunion, and I thought you'd like a set."

She handed Tori an envelope.

"Well, that was very considerate of you. Thank you."

"There are a few really good ones of you and Levi," she said.

Tori and Levi glanced at each other, each suppressing a grin. Christine was obviously looking for something to report to the rumor mill.

"Would you like to join us for lunch?" Levi said, waving her to an empty chair.

"I'm told it's a specialty at Lady & Sons in Savannah," Tori said. "Down in Georgia, they call it Savannah Pig and Pasta."

Christine appeared confused. Their lunch looked okay, but it didn't look particularly special in any way.

"Oh, no thank you. I'm famished, but I'm running late," Christine said. "I've got to get up to Main Street. The parade will be starting soon, and if I'm not there, nobody will know what to do. Then there's the flea market. I'll be lucky if I get a chance to eat or sit down all day."

"And yet you wore those shoes," Tori muttered.

Christine looked at her as if she hadn't caught what she'd said.

"How do you do it all, Christine?" Levi said, looking at her with wonder. "The PTA, cheerleading boosters, church group, school board . . . it's just amazing to me. You must be very organized."

Tori rolled her eyes. He was laying it on a bit thick and heavy. She was afraid she'd be the one who'd throw up.

"We all do what we can in our own way," Christine said, blushing deeply. "It's for the kids, of course."

"Well, I'm not going to let you get out of here without at least packing you a snack," Levi said, getting up from the table. "You just wait here one minute. I have just the thing."

After the screen door banged closed, there was an awkward silence between Christine and Tori.

"He's such a wonderful man," Christine remarked finally.

"That's what he tells me," Tori replied, smiling at her.

Very shortly, Levi came back through the screen door. "Here you are, Christine," he said, handing her what looked like several candy bars.

Tori's eyes got wide when she recognized them.

"These are delicious," Levi said. "They're fiber bars. Very healthy and only about a hundred calories each. Eat two or three of those, and they'll keep you going all day. Try one!"

Christine opened one and took a bite. She smiled as she chewed.

"Good, isn't it?" Levi said.

"Yes, very good. Thank you. I'll eat these on the way over. I guess I'd best be going. They'll start calling me about any time now if I don't get there on time," she said, trying to hide her feeling of self-importance but failing."

"Thanks for bringing the pictures," Tori said.

"No problem," Christine said as she clopped down the stairs and climbed into her Expedition. She fired it up, but before she put it in gear, she opened another fiber bar and took a large bite.

"You know you're going straight to hell, right?" Tori remarked. She was trying very hard to maintain her composure.

Levi smiled and waved at Christine again as she started to back out of the driveway. Christine waved back.

"At least I'll have friends there," he said sideways to Tori. "And I told her the truth—you eat three of those, and they will keep you going all day. And going. And going."

Christine honked twice as she drove by the house.

"Oh my," Tori said, "I hope that was the truck."

They both exploded into laughter.

Tori walked out of the bathroom and stood beside Levi as she checked herself in the big mirror over the dresser.

"Hey," Levi said, looking at her reflection as he rolled up his shirt sleeves, "where did you find that t-shirt?"

She smiled. She knew wearing it would get a reaction. It used to be Levi's favorite shirt—his REO Speedwagon shirt, the one with the winged logo on the front and the three-quarter length black sleeves, the kind of shirt they used to call a baseball shirt. Levi had worn it constantly in high school.

"I found it in the bottom drawer of your dresser," she said, "along with all the rest of your vintage concert t-shirts."

Levi leaned over and opened the drawer, grinning broadly as he thumbed through the shirts.

"These weren't vintage when we bought them at the concerts. I haven't seen these shirts in years—Van Halen, Twisted Sister, Petra, Cheap Trick." He stood up. "You realize that shirt you're wearing hasn't been washed in more than two decades."

"I washed *all* your shirts this afternoon," she said. "Do you mind if I wear it?"

"As far as I'm concerned, you can have them all. They'd never fit me," Levi said, patting his stomach. "And believe me, I never looked that good in that shirt."

Beaming at the compliment, she plucked Levi's Panama off the bedpost and popped it onto his head.

"About ready to go?" she asked, kissing him on the back of his neck.

"Yup," he replied as he finished tucking in his shirt.

When Rosco jumped up on the bed, Levi saw him in the mirror.

"What the hell did you do to my dog?" he said, turning.

Rosco was wearing a red bandana around his neck.

"It's cute, isn't it," Tori said, scratching his ears and kissing his head.

"You're spoiling that dog," Levi said.

When he walked over to scratch Rosco's head, he wrinkled up his nose, then leaned over to sniff Rosco tentatively.

"Tell me you didn't put perfume on Rosco. . ."

Tori shrugged. "Ok, I won't tell you then."

"And why are you getting the dog all dressed up?"

"He's going with us."

"You can't take a dog to a theatre," Levi said, looking at her like she was crazy.

"Well, maybe not to just any theatre," Tori said. "But we're going to *my* theatre."

"I thought you sold that theatre back to the town when you were done renovating it?"

"Are we going to argue semantics?"

"So we're taking the dog," Levi said, smiling.

"Of course," Tori said, tossing Rosco a treat.

They went down the stairs into the front foyer. Levi took the keys to Old Blue off the hook beside the door. He glanced in the mirror on the antique hall tree behind the door, frowning for a moment as if something had just occurred to him. Slowly, he took off his Panama and hung it on the hat hook next to the mirror.

"You're not going to wear your hat? You always wear your hat."

Levi looked at it for a moment, then smiled. "That hat is kind of a trademark of my old life. I used to wonder if people would recognize me without it." He offered Tori his arm. "I've got a different life now. I've turned the page. Maybe it's time for a new hat."

As they walked out onto the porch and down the steps towards Old Blue, Tori said, "You know, Levi, you'd look great in a fedora. My grandpa wore a fedora."

37

Levi and Tori strolled out the double doors of the Comet Theatre after the movie with Rosco trotting behind them.

"I told you it was Jerry Van Dyke," Tori said, grinning.

Levi shook his head. "And you were right about Rosco," he said. "He was very well behaved."

"He slept through the whole thing," Tori said with a laugh.

"After he ate my popcorn," Levi said.

They walked towards the truck, parked at the diner, where they'd had a quick cheeseburger before the show.

"I still think Rosco looks gay with a bandana," Levi said.

Tori suddenly grabbed his arm and stopped dead in her tracks. Rosco came up between them, growling loudly.

Levi looked up the street in the direction Tori was staring. Doug Malone was leaning on the passenger door of Old Blue. Levi sighed. They'd seen Doug lean on his truck like that many times when they were kids, and Levi had usually gotten his ass whipped on those occasions.

"He hasn't seen us," Tori said. "Let's just cut up the alley and walk to the park for the fireworks. Maybe he'll be gone by the time we come back."

"And if he's not," Levi said, "we'll sneak back up the alley and come back for the truck tomorrow or next week."

Tori looked at him—he had a good point.

"He's not going away," Levi said. "He's going to catch up with us eventually, you know. There are a lot of people around now, coming out of the movie, eating dinner at Harv's. It's a public place on a holiday weekend. I can't think of a better place or time to confront him. Would you rather he catch up with us some night when we're alone at the house?"

Tori shook her head. "Let's get it over with," she said with a sigh.

Levi took her hand firmly. They walked up the sidewalk, swinging their clasped hands between them, while Levi whistled "If I Only Had a Brain" from the *Wizard of Oz.*

"Evening, Doug," Levi said. "Lovely night, isn't it?"

"That dog should be on a leash," Doug said, flicking his cigarette at Rosco, who responded by growling and showing his teeth.

"Are you going to write me a ticket, Doug?" Levi asked.

Doug glanced around to make sure their conversation was private.

"Tell you what, Levi," he said. "We'll forget about the ticket if you tell me what you think you know about what went on at the Sinclair house."

Levi smiled and shook his head. "I don't think so, Doug. I think I'll save that info, if you don't mind. I may need it someday."

Doug laughed. "You don't really know anything at all, do you? You *think* you know something, but you're not even confident enough to tell me."

"Then you've got nothing to worry about, do you?" Levi said. "Get off my truck Doug. I'm tired, and I'm in no mood for this."

Doug looked as if he'd been slapped. Levi had used the exact same words Ed had used in the parking lot of the Beer Chaser a few days earlier, right before he'd so easily taken him down. Instantly furious, Doug shoved Levi hard. He stumbled back a few steps and nearly fell.

"What are you going to do, Doug? Beat my ass in the middle of a public street? This ain't high school anymore. And I'm not eighteen anymore. I'll thump you like a melon," Levi said, shaking a finger in his face.

It was all Doug could do not to hit Levi. However, Levi had been overheard. A few people were watching from across the street, some customers were looking out the windows of the diner, and more were coming up the street from the theatre.

"Fine, I'll tell you what I know, Doug," Levi said.

Fear flashed on Doug's face. This wasn't the way he'd worked things out. There were people listening now.

"In fact, I'll tell the whole town about their police chief," Levi announced loudly.

Tori was squeezing Levi's arm hard, but Levi yanked it away from her. He wasn't about to stop.

"I'll tell them about the coward that broke the handle off his truck door so the dates he raped back in high school couldn't get away."

Doug's face went pale as he nervously looked at the people nearby. The crowd buzzed.

"I'll tell them about their chief of police that used to solicit the town prostitute on a regular basis—definitely the kind of man a town would want to pin a badge on."

Doug's jaw was tight as he looked at Levi, waiting for more. But Levi was just standing there grinning at him—gloating. He said no more.

That's all he knows? Doug thought.

Doug waited, but Levi said nothing more. The truth beginning to become clear to Doug, and a faint smile twitched at the corner of his mouth.

That is all he knows! Doug thought again.

Relief washed over him. He looked at Levi and Tori, took a deep breath, and shook his head. But then something suddenly chilled Doug—the look of astonishment on Levi and Tori's faces. It was as if somebody had pulled back the veil and revealed some truth to them for the first time.

Doug's mouth went dry as his eyes darted between Levi and Tori. He knew something had just happened, something had just clicked with them, but he didn't know what it meant.

"You saw it, too, didn't you, Levi?" Tori said calmly.

"I saw it," Levi answered.

Doug's eyes darted between them. He didn't understand.

Tori looked at Doug with a wicked gleam in her eye. "You don't even know what you just did, do you?"

Doug's pulse raced. He had no idea what she was talking about.

"You idiot," she said, shaking her head, "you just told us the truth with your own guilty face. You're the town cop, yet you were relieved when Levi accused you of date rape and soliciting. You looked like you'd just dodged a bullet. You thought Levi knew more. Your face just admitted that there is more—much more.

"I know what your secret is, Doug," Tori said, poking a finger in his chest. "You didn't just rape Melissa Sinclair. You murdered her as well, didn't you?"

The crowd that had assembled in the street let out a collective gasp.

Doug's face went white. He looked at them blankly, his mouth feeling like it was full of cotton as his mind groped to answer that accusation. People in the crowd on the street were whispering, looking at him and pointing. They were beginning to believe her.

Suddenly Doug exploded into laughter. "Rape? Murder?"

Levi and Tori looked at each other.

"Why would I rape or murder her?" Doug said, continuing to laugh. "I'm not proud of it, but I did visit Sarah Sinclair as a teenager. For $5 or $10, I could have either one of them whenever I wanted them. For $20, I could have them both in a little mother-daughter tag team action."

Several in the crowd muttered their disapproval.

"You're a liar," Tori spat. Her eyes were burning embers.

"I certainly didn't have to rape anybody," Doug bragged. "I don't know where you're getting your information, Levi, but anybody that says I did is trying to rewrite history."

He glared at Tori. "You didn't have to make up a story, Tori. I wouldn't have told Levi about our little arrangement back then. Your secret was safe with me."

He grinned at her devilishly and winked.

Tori snapped. She lunged at him, catching him completely off-guard. Her fist connected solidly with his chin. He spun around, hitting his head on the roof of Levi's truck. He fell to one knee beside the truck. Blood flowed from his temple.

Tori went after him again, but Doug was ready for the second attack. He came up off his knee as she flew towards him, brutally backhanding her. With a grunt, she sprawled on the ground at Levi's feet.

Doug heard the guttural growl as Rosco leaped at him, clamping his jaws tightly around his wrist. Doug screamed and kicked Rosco as hard as he could, but Rosco held on, pulling and shaking his head with all his strength, causing Doug to lose his footing. Rosco pulled him to his knees. Levi stepped in and punched Doug squarely in the face. The impact of the blow caused Doug's head to bounce off Old Blue's door panel. Doug's eyes began to roll up in his head. Levi had pulled back to punch him again when somebody grabbed him from behind.

"Let me go," Levi screamed, trying to throw an elbow at whoever it was who held him.

"Just stop," Deputy Alan Haig said, wrestling him back.

Tori was rolling on the ground, trying to get up.

"Stay on the ground, Tori!" Deputy Haig yelled.

Doug was still screaming as Rosco continued to shake his arm violently. Blood flowed from Doug's wrist and dripped off his hand. Blood was also running into his face from the wound on his temple. He finally leaned against the truck. Using it for leverage, he kicked Rosco hard enough to finally get loose. Rosco landed on his back next to Tori. He immediately scrambled to his feet and leaped at Doug for another attack.

A loud crack filled the air. Rosco yelped and fell at Doug's feet.

"No!" Levi yelled.

Doug was shaking badly as he climbed unsteadily to his feet. He was slick with sweat. His Glock fell from his hand onto the ground, and he cradled his mangled wrist tightly with his good hand. He stumbled backwards against Levi's truck, nearly falling. He rested against the truck, his eyes glassy, and tried to catch his breath.

"Alan," he said in a hoarse croak, "these two are under arrest. You know the charges."

He started to say something else when his eyes rolled up in his head, and he slid down the side of Old Blue onto the ground.

Somebody had already called an ambulance. The siren could be heard in the distance. Tori was sitting on the ground sobbing, hugging her knees, staring at Rosco's lifeless body on the street. Levi was standing in disbelief—the carnage in front of him a blur through his tears.

38

There were two holding cells in the Twin Rivers Police Department. Tori was in one, and Levi was in the other. They were sitting on the floor beside each other, a row of bars between them. Tori had been sobbing quietly, her head on her knees. Over an hour earlier, Alan Haig had read them their rights, asked if either needed a doctor, and locked them up. Neither of them had said anything. They could hear the fireworks going off at the park. Levi knew the show had started late because of the fight outside Harv's Diner.

Happy Fourth of July! Levi thought bitterly.

"It's not your fault, Tori," Levi finally whispered to her.

He reached through the bars and put his hand on her back. She shook her head back and forth violently. It was a long time before she raised her head and looked up at the ceiling. Her eye was swollen nearly shut with a bruise darkening beneath it.

"I think I misnamed that dog," Levi said. "Not exactly Rosco the Lethargic in the end, was he?"

"I'm so sorry, Levi. I got your dog killed," she said as more tears slid down her cheeks.

"My dog?" Levi smiled. "Seems to me that from the minute

Rosco met you, he was *your* dog."

"He was protecting me . . ." she said, her voice trailing off, her bottom lip trembling as another round of sobbing threatened.

"They do that," Levi said. "Dogs protect those they love—especially German shepherds. That's the second one that's been killed protecting me."

Tori looked at him in astonishment. Levi's face was unreadable.

"Oh, my God," Tori said as things suddenly tumbled together. "You were a cop. That was the state job you had during the ten years between college and publishing your first book."

Levi nodded.

"And that's where you learned to shoot," Tori said.

Levi nodded again.

"Let me guess," Tori said. "You mentioned Rosco the Big Sweetie, who was a little more aggressive than Rosco the Lethargic. Police dog?"

Levi smiled. "Sergeant Rosco actually."

"What happened?" Tori asked.

"I guess I didn't know what I was getting into," Levi said. "I was young and idealistic. I loved the idea of being a police officer, of making a difference in people's lives and the world a better place. What I didn't understand was the negative impact it was going to have on me."

"How so?" Tori asked, pressing him.

"Nobody can truly understand what it's like being a police officer, especially one on the front lines. It's not like being Andy Taylor or Barney Fife in Mayberry—that's what I thought it was about. And that's what Doug is, a peace officer in a small town. You get in a large city, or like me, involved in the state police drug task force, and you're in a war. And all you ever see is a side of humanity that is so depraved, so violent, that over time it begins to sicken your soul."

"It's so clear now," Tori said. "That's where you got the idea for your first novel, *But for the Grace of God*."

Levi nodded. "I thought my life was tough growing up," Levi said, "but we'd find kids living in crack houses, we'd find babies crawling around the floor of meth labs. I remember thinking, but for the grace of God that could've been me or just about anybody. Instead, I was born into a fairly normal household. My experiences actually made me grateful for my screwed up parents since at least I had a grandmother and an uncle who cared about me.

"I started thinking a lot about that—about how unlucky I thought I was growing up but how lucky I actually was. It took years, but slowly that idea became a novel that explored those very feelings. It's all about luck, Tori. We think we had it tough, but those kids I saw—and kids like Melissa—they never really had a chance. They were doomed from the very beginning of their lives, and so few ever escape."

"What happened to Rosco the Big Sweetie?" Tori asked.

Levi leaned his head against the wall and closed his eyes. "I'd just published the book, and it quickly climbed the bestseller list. I'd put in notice I was leaving the force. I was working my very last shift as a state police officer. Rosco the Big Sweetie was six years old, and he was going to get to retire with me. The dispatcher was being kind to me on my last day, so instead of sending me on the more dangerous assignments, he sent me on a routine domestic dispute in an apartment building. It was a rough neighborhood on the south side of Chicago, and the address was well known to the local police. The perp was a known violent offender, so they wanted the K-9 unit just in case. I met local law enforcement there, and the three of us headed up the stairs and down the hall of this seedy apartment building, thinking we were just going to quickly break up a family quarrel and probably make an arrest. Routine stuff.

"We could hear the yelling as soon as we opened the stairwell door, so we moved down the hall to the address. I pounded on the door and announced, 'Police officers, open up!' Suddenly, bullets started flying through the door of the apartment across the hall—a totally different apartment. One of the rounds hit the local cop, and he went down. I called for backup as Rosco and I took cover on either side of the door the bullets had flown out of. I carefully checked the doorknob and found the door was unlocked. I decided not to wait—I knew the officer I was with was badly wounded.

"Rosco knew the drill. I swung the door in. Rosco rushed into the dark room, growling and barking, and I went in low behind him. Rosco was trained to take down anyone with a gun. In a split second, I saw a gun flash, heard Rosco yelp, sighted on the flash, and fired three rounds. I knew I'd hit him, but I didn't know if he was dead or just wounded."

"But he'd killed Rosco," Tori said, shuddering.

Levi nodded. "There was no question in my mind about that. The back-up I called must've been close by because I heard them coming up the stairs while I was searching for a light. When I finally found the light, I discovered Rosco was dead and so was the perp. He was twelve years old—a gang member. No doubt he'd heard 'police' shouted outside his door and thought we were coming for him. There was a large stash of narcotics found in the apartment."

"My God, that's awful," Tori said.

"It gets worse," Levi said. "The local officer I was with died on the way to the hospital, and the domestic dispute also turned violent. While Rosco and I were dealing with the shooter in the apartment, the ex-con across the hall strangled his wife to death."

Tori shook her head in disbelief.

"I guess that explains why I was so surprised when I read your first book," Tori said. "It didn't seem like you. It was so dark and complicated. I had a tough time imagining you writing something like that. I expected something warm and funny, like the author."

"It took two books to purge those feelings. That's why I should've never written the third one—the intensity was gone," Levi said. "I'd worked my feelings out in fiction."

"I can't imagine living through that," Tori said.

"I can't imagine anyone retiring after doing police work for twenty-five years," Levi said. "I've been trying to forget that whole experience for more than ten years now—not just that last day, but all of it. I guess I just wasn't strong enough. I just couldn't detach myself from what I saw every day, and it was sucking the life out of me. I didn't want to see the world like that anymore, so I've tried to put it behind me. I created a completely different life in Savannah. Of course, Uncle Ed knew I was a cop—Grandma knew, too—but I've hidden it from everyone else. I didn't want to be asked about it. But lately, with this whole ugly confrontation with Doug, those survival instincts have kicked right back in again—almost as if they never left."

"I think the danger in this situation has got your Uncle Ed's instincts on high alert, too," Tori said. "That's why he's been bringing up Vietnam lately, isn't it?"

Levi nodded. "We can't ever truly get away from the things we've done and the things we've see. I found a way to work it out and at least live with it, but I don't think Uncle Ed ever has. I have a feeling that what I went through in those ten years was a walk in the park compared to what he's done and seen."

"And Melissa?" Tori asked. "Do you really think she's dead?"

Levi nodded. "I do. You saw the look on Doug's face—you can't deny that look. I think he raped her. Then something went wrong, and he killed her. She vanished graduation night. Nobody has seen her for years. She never put her escape plan into action, and according to Mrs. B., she was determined to do that. Only one thing makes sense to me—she's dead."

Tori sat quietly for a minute. "We're in a lot of shit, aren't we?"

"Oh, yeah," Levi said. "We're looking at serious charges. I don't see how we can avoid going away for awhile."

"I was thinking about something earlier," Tori said. "I've got a theory, and if I'm right, it will tell us for sure if Melissa is alive or dead."

"What's that?"

"It's up to Doug whether we're charged. We assaulted him, right?" Tori said.

"If he admits he started it by pushing me, which he won't, then we could be released. But he won't, Tori. He wanted this, and now he's got it. He's going to punish us."

"I'm not so sure. Here's what I think," Tori said. "If Doug presses charges, Melissa Sinclair is alive and well. If he doesn't press charges, then she's dead."

Levi chuckled. It sounded incredibly simple, even stupid to him. Knowing Tori as well as he did, he couldn't believe she could be so naïve. But then he started thinking about her theory. The more he thought about it, the more he understood her logic.

"Holy crap, Tori," he said. "You're right! If he killed her, the last thing he'd want is for us to be in court. Our suspicion that he committed a homicide would be our defense in court. There'd undoubtedly be an investigation. The trial would be high profile because I'm a famous writer—I've got some credibility. He'd want that only if he knew for a fact he had nothing to worry about, and there was nothing that could come out of an investigation."

Tori nodded and smiled crookedly—the whole side of her face was starting to swell.

"And let's not forget, you arrogant ass, that I'm the president of the First National Bank of Calloway—not exactly a stripper at the local hoochie hut. I've got a little credibility myself."

Levi laughed. That was the Tori he knew.

"So if he lets us go—" Tori said.

"That means she's dead," Levi said, finishing her thought.

There was a long silence between them as they considered what that actually meant.

Levi reached through the bars and carefully turned her face towards him. "I don't think I've actually said it, Tori, but I love you."

Tori grinned and winced at the pain from her face. "I love you, too, Levi. If I go to prison, I'm going to have your name tattooed on my knuckles."

Levi chuckled and rested his head against the wall.

"You know, Tori, I'm kind of torn," he said. "On one hand, I don't want to go to prison, but on the other hand, I don't want to be set free because I'll know what it means."

Tori was quiet for a moment before she responded, "For Mel's sake, I hope we're charged."

39

Wiping the sweat off his forehead with a hankie, Ed leaned on his shovel and watched the finale of the annual fireworks show a mile or so away at the park. The show had started more than an hour late, delayed because of the "excitement" on Main Street after the movie, he'd heard someone say.

Ed looked down at the small mound of earth in front of him. It didn't look like "excitement" to him.

Ed wondered if Alan Haig knew he'd likely ended his career by calling him. Rosco was evidence and should have been preserved as evidence since he had Doug Malone's blood all over him, yet Alan had called him to come and get Rosco. When Ed arrived on Main Street, Alan handed him the keys to Old Blue he'd taken from Levi when he'd booked him and helped him load Rosco into the back of the truck. Old Blue was evidence too with Doug's blood all down the side of it, but Alan must have known what he was doing. Perhaps he'd done it out of friendship for Levi. Whatever his reasons were, Ed was grateful to him.

Ed sighed as he looked down at Rosco's grave, just a few feet from the grave of his namesake. The first time Ed had seen Rosco at the Garvey house, he'd been sleeping on that very spot. Ed remembered making a joke of it because Rosco was so soundly asleep he looked dead. Before he'd started to dig, Ed had noticed in the moonlight the way the grass was matted down on that spot. Rosco had obviously continued to nap there.

"I'll get you a nice stone," Ed promised aloud. He had a knot in his throat. "Levi just didn't know you very well when he nicknamed you Rosco the Lethargic. I'll come up with something a little more befitting a dog of your character. You're the best dog I've ever known. Thanks for protecting my family, Rosco."

Ed was tired, too tired even to put away the shovel. He leaned it against the tree and walked down the driveway. His wrecker was parked on Main Street.

Ed drove his wrecker home, his eyes so heavy he nearly dozed off several times. Finally, he reached his driveway and parked in front of the garage. For a moment, he considered sleeping in the wrecker, but instead, he slowly got out of the truck. He barely had the energy to walk to the house.

Ed walked into his house and flipped on the kitchen light. As he walked across the kitchen towards the living room, the light seemed to flicker. They were stalking him again, coming much more often than they used to. He wanted to be alone tonight. He was exhausted.

But they were coming whether he wanted them to or not. He could feel the wump-wump-wump of the chopper blades in his chest. He could smell the cordite burning his nose. He could hear the screams as the napalm fell from the sky.

He walked to the gun cabinet and opened the bottom drawer. He had his choice to make. Life or death? His hand paused, shaking, much longer than usual over the .38 before it went to the wooden box.

I've still got some work to do in Twin Rivers, he thought. It won't be much longer now. I'm tired, and I'm almost ready to go.

He set the box on the kitchen table, pulled a bottle out of the cabinet under the sink and a glass from the sink drainer. He twisted the cap off, filled a glass, and took a long drink.

I'll never get through it, he thought.

He opened the wooden box. The light flickered as the dark shadows of his guests joined him. He knew they were all standing behind him as he reached in to begin setting up the ritual.

When he finished, he had the brass shell casings of sixty-four .308 rounds standing upright on the table in front on him. He heard them shuffling, anxious to get started.

He picked up the first casing. A Vietnamese soldier walked around from behind him and took the chair across the table. He couldn't have been more than sixteen years old. Ed looked at him. He'd seen him many times before. In the flickering light, he saw the boy as he had the first time—with the crosshairs of a sniper scope hovering over his forehead.

"I'm sorry," Ed said. "I don't know your name. You weren't carrying ID. I know you had brothers and sisters because I found pictures of them in your pockets."

The soldier nodded.

"We met on Hill 881 near Khe Sahn, South Vietnam, on May 3rd, 1967. You killed our lieutenant. He was a young man, probably twenty-three. Lieutenant Willam "Wild Bill" Silvernail. You also killed a friend I went to high school with. Buck Taylor."

The soldier nodded again.

"You would've kept picking us off one at a time until we were all dead unless I stopped you," he said.

The soldier nodded.

"I crawled through the reeds on my belly for hours, an inch at a time, looking for you. I had no idea where you were. I knew the only way I was likely to find you was if you fired again. I also knew what that meant. Another one of my friends would die at your hands before I could kill you."

The soldier nodded.

"You did fire again, killing a nineteen-year-old kid from Missouri. I knew about where you were, but it took me a while to spot you. You were very cleverly concealed in the second branch of a tree. You were almost invisible. I plugged you in the center of your forehead at 220 yards."

The soldier sighed.

"I regret it," Ed said, placing the shell casing in the box.

The soldier looked down, nodded, then vanished.

Ed picked up the next shell casing off the table and looked at it.

Another soldier took the chair across from him. He was older, maybe twenty-five, wearing fatigues . . .

40

Levi wasn't sure if he'd fallen asleep or not when he heard a door open. Alan Haig walked in, looking weary. Without saying a word, he unlocked and opened both cell doors.

"What's going on, Alan?" Tori asked.

"I've got your stuff out on my desk. You're both free to go."

Tori looked at Levi, whose face showed his disbelief.

"We're not being charged with anything?" he asked.

"I spoke to Doug this morning," Alan said. "He doesn't want a media circus in town. And he admitted he actually shoved you first."

"How is Doug?" Levi asked.

"He's in the hospital, but he'll be out by lunch time," Alan said. "He's got a dozen stitches from the gash on his head and over a hundred on his left wrist and arm."

"I hope it hurts," Tori said.

Alan glared at Tori for a moment before returning his gaze to Levi. "As a condition of your release, Doug said he'd appreciate it if you'd cover any medical charges not covered by his insurance," Alan said.

Levi nodded.

Tori and Levi rose stiffly, followed Alan into the outer office, and collected their possessions.

"You want a ride home?" Alan said. "I called Ed last night to come for the dog. I asked him to take your truck, too. I didn't want it sitting out there all night, drawing attention. It had blood all over the side."

"I appreciate that," Levi said, shaking his hand. "You've always been a good friend. What do you think, Tori? You want a ride?"

"I'd rather walk," Tori said, rubbing her butt. "I don't know about you, but I've been sitting on that floor all night, and my ass is sound asleep."

"Levi," Alan said, "there is one more message I'm supposed to give you from Doug."

"What's that?" Levi asked, eyebrows raised.

"Doug wants you to stay clear of him, and he'll do the same," Alan said. "I think that's a good idea. You and Tori said some pretty ugly things about him last night in front of a lot of people. It'll be all over town by the time church gets out this morning. The things you said and the things he was forced to admit were very embarrassing for him, especially considering his position. He's doing you a big favor, not pressing charges, and I think avoiding him is the least you can do."

Tori stepped forward. Levi knew she was about to say something that wouldn't do either of them any good. He put his hand firmly on her shoulder and squeezed. She got the message.

"I think that's a very good idea," Levi said. "Thanks for everything, Alan."

Levi and Tori walked out of the Police Department and turned up Main Street towards the house.

Glancing back towards the Police Department, Tori said softly, "She's dead, isn't she?"

"Yup," Levi said with a nod, "there's no doubt in my mind now. You got it right last night."

"What do we do now?" Tori asked.

"It's Sunday," Levi remarked. "Not much we can do today, but I may still have a few friends in the Illinois State Police I can call tomorrow. Doug's not going to get away with it."

Levi and Tori walked up the driveway, hand in hand. It had rained overnight, and there were puddles in the driveway. As they walked on either side of a large one, hands linked, Levi suddenly pulled on Tori's hand, yanking her into the puddle. She shot him an ugly glance as water seeped into her tennis shoes. Just as suddenly, she yanked back, and he stumbled into the ankle deep water as well.

"Nice, isn't it?" she chuckled.

"Not really," Levi said, looking down at his feet. "The water is a little cold." He smiled as he wrapped his arms around her waist and kissed her.

After they took a few more steps up the driveway, Levi noticed the shovel leaning against the elm tree. Tori saw it at the same time. They walked over to the muddy mound under the elm tree and stood silently for a moment.

"I'm going to miss that lazy damned dog," Levi said.

"He wasn't lazy," Tori said. "He followed me everywhere. Maybe it's just that you were boring."

Levi smiled, but he had tears in his eyes. "Maybe it's because I didn't walk around with my pockets full of treats."

Tears welled up in Tori's eyes when she realized she still had treats in her pocket.

Turning towards the house, Levi said, "I'm hungry. Make you some breakfast?"

Tori nodded as they headed for the porch. Suddenly, she started running. She bounded up the steps and stopped on the porch in front of the door.

"What the hell?" she said in an angry tone.

Levi walked up the steps behind her. She was looking at the mangled screen door. Somebody had ripped it off the hinges and stomped it to pieces. The front door was standing open, the door jam splintered where it'd been kicked in.

"I didn't even lock the damned door when we left," Levi said, puzzled.

Tori disappeared inside the house. Seconds later, he heard her exclaim, "Oh my God, Levi! Come quick!"

When Levi walked into the foyer, he couldn't believe what he saw. The large foyer was a mess. The furniture had been tipped over, drawers emptied on the floor, pictures ripped off the wall. Every knickknack Lucille Garvey had collected during her long life was broken on the floor. The closet door was standing open, its contents thrown all around. Levi had been on a lot of robbery calls as a state cop, but he'd never seen anything like this.

Walking around the mess, Tori stepped into the library. "Oh, no," she said in a whisper.

Levi followed. The books on every floor-to-ceiling shelf on every wall in the library had been dumped onto the floor. The room was two-feet deep in books.

Tori climbed over the books and went through the den to the kitchen. He heard her cries of dismay from where he stood. He was still staring in disbelief at the mess around him when she returned.

"There's not a dish that hasn't been shattered in the kitchen," Tori said.

Levi picked up a wooden chair, set it upright in the doorway between the foyer and the library, and sat down. The contents of his grandma's house had been destroyed. Tori went upstairs, but a few minutes later, she came back down.

Levi glanced at her. "Upstairs, too?"

She nodded. "Every drawer is dumped. The mattress is shredded, and the stuffing is everywhere up there. He found your concert t-shirts in the bottom drawer. They're gone—shredded."

Levi sighed. "How is this possible? Doug's in the hospital."

Tori snorted. "He did this while we were in the movie. He'd already done this when we met up with him last night."

Levi sighed. "This is the biggest mess I've ever seen."

"Insurance?" Tori said.

"I have insurance."

Suddenly, Levi chuckled. Then he laughed as he surveyed the mess.

"You're laughing?" Tori said, eyes wide. "At what?"

"I've been wondering all week what I was going to do with all Grandma's treasures. I mean they're not exactly my style, and I still have all my stuff in Savannah. I don't think I would've ever been able to throw any of her stuff away. Doug did me a favor really. He broke a bunch of dishes I don't have to haul to the attic now. He ripped up a lumpy mattress and rid this house of Grandma's collection of ceramic pigs and paintings of flowers—fields of flowers, children picking flowers, flowers in vases, brides with flowers in their hair. He destroyed a stereo circa 1971 and broke a couple of old chairs that were so rickety nobody could sit on them."

Tori looked at him as if he'd gone insane. "How can you not be mad?"

"It's just stuff," Levi said. "It's not the stuff that matters, Tori. It's what Grandma meant to me that matters. It's not the relics we leave behind after we're gone; it's the things we do while we're alive. Doug couldn't shred or break her legacy."

Levi stood up, picked up the chair he'd been sitting on by its back, and shattered it against the library doorway. He waded into the library through the books.

"So this is what we do. We're going to clean up this damned mess. We're going to build a big fire and burn what was destroyed. We'll sweep up the broken ceramic piggies, the flower pictures, and the broken dishes. Then we'll buy things to replace them that reflect our style. This is our home now, Tori. That's what Grandma wanted.

That's why she made the improvements to this house in her last days. She knew I'd come back, and she wanted me to fill this house with my own memories—our memories. And the rule for the day is even if something isn't damaged but we just don't like it, it goes into the fire."

"You're something else," Tori said, grinning.

"I'm a realist. And the first thing I saw when I walked into the foyer was an omen of good fortune."

Levi walked into the foyer, his shoes crunching on pieces of broken pigs. He pointed to the antique hall tree, which was leaning over against a small table. His Panama hat was still hanging on the hook where he'd put it the night before. It hadn't fallen off. Laughing, Tori reached over to grab the edge of the hall tree. Levi leaned down to help her. They hoisted it back upright in one swift movement. It was undamaged. The mirror hadn't broken. The hat wobbled on the hook, but it never fell off.

Levi grinned. "That's where that hat stays from now on. Right there—a little reminder of the past."

"So where do we start?" Tori said, looking around.

"I'll start in the library," Levi said. "I may never get all these books organized like they were, but I'll get them back on the shelves. With his foot, Levi nudged a book from the foyer, where it had spilled out, back into the library.

Tori leaned against the doorway, looking at all the books on the floor. "I'll run over to the hardware store," she said. "I'll repair the door jam and fix the screen door Doug wrecked."

"They close at noon on Sunday," Levi said as he tossed the keys to Old Blue to her.

Tori looked at the keys in amazement and then at Levi. "Really? You're going to let me drive Old Blue?"

"It's a truck, Tori. It's just a truck," Levi said. "But—"

"I know. I'll be careful 'cause she's your little baby," Tori said.

Levi grinned.

"I wasn't going to say anything, but maybe I should," Tori said, looking down at the floor.

"What?" Levi said.

Tori reached down to pick a book up off the floor. Then she tossed it to him.

"Are you shitting me?' Levi said as he caught it.

It was a copy of *Christine* by Stephen King. The edges of the pages were stamped Twin Rivers Public Library. Levi opened the cover where the check-out card had been and laughed. Mrs. B. had stamped it. As she'd said, it was due back on April 24, 1985.

Levi carefully waded through the books and set *Christine* on one of the library shelves.

"So that's one down and a couple thousand yet to go."

"Aren't you going to return that to the library?" Tori asked.

"No way. That book cost me nearly a thousand dollars yesterday!"

41

April couldn't remember the last time the diner had been so full this late in the morning. She was trying to do it all—take the orders, deliver the orders, and keep the coffee cups full. Nichole Larsen, the waitress they'd let go when the recession hit, had come in with her family. When she saw how hard it was for April to keep up, she went back to the kitchen and took her apron off a hook, where it was still hanging, and began working the counter.

Harv was whistling happily in the kitchen as the grill, filled from one side to the other, sizzled with pancakes, eggs, and bacon. It was as if every time he rang the bell to tell April or Nichole to take an order out, they brought him a couple more to fill.

Just like the old days, Harv thought.

Everyone in town had come out to learn what'd happened the night before. The rumors were flying. The main conversation had been about Melissa Sinclair and the claim that Chief Malone had murdered her. Everyone seemed to know something about the story—how Melissa and her mother had disappeared so many years ago. People were talking about the things that had gone on over at their house back then, about how Doug Malone had admitted he used to go there for prostitution.

But the main topic of conversation was what was going to happen to Levi and Tori. Almost everyone knew they were sitting in holding across the street, waiting for transfer to the county lock-up. There were rumors Doug might not make it, that he was in intensive care fighting for his life. People speculated. If Doug died, Levi and Tori would be charged with homicide. If Doug lived, he might be charged with homicide—for the murder of Melissa Sinclair. Many spoke as if speculation had become fact.

April had listened to the gossip all morning. If Doug lived, he'd go down for murder. If he didn't make it, Levi and Tori would go down for murder. She was sick at her stomach. Since she'd seen the entire fight the evening before, she might be called as a witness against Levi and Tori if the case went to trial.

"Hey!" Larry Fremont exclaimed, standing up in his booth and pointing out the window. "Levi's not in jail. Here he comes up the street!"

The entire population in the diner shifted so fast to the windows, April thought the building might tip over on its side. Those that couldn't find a spot where they could see out the windows rushed out the door onto the sidewalk in front.

April peered out the window next to the cash register. Sure enough, Old Blue had just stopped at the stop sign and was proceeding by the diner in jerks and starts. Knowing Levi never drove Old Blue like that, she grinned when she saw the long, curly, blonde hair flying around in the breeze from the open window of the cab.

"That's not Levi," she said. "That's Tori."

Larry Fremont announced loudly enough for all to hear, "They aren't under arrest. They're free. Do you suppose that means they were telling the truth. Why else would they be let go? He paused as he glanced around the hushed diner. Then he said, quietly, his eyes wide with wonder, "Maybe Chief Malone did murder Melissa

Sinclair."

Behind Old Blue was a black Ford Expedition, which swung into the handicapped space. Christine White wobbled inside on high heels as the diner began to buzz with new information. The only place open was a spot at the counter. When she sat down, Nichole slid a cup of coffee in front of her. The level of conversation rose to a dull roar.

"What's going on?" Christine asked Nichole.

"Chief Malone has been charged with murder!"

"Of who? That dog last night?"

April walked up behind Nichole. She had little patience with Christine White. "No, you fool," she said to Christine. "Doug killed Melissa Sinclair."

Christine stared, her mouth hanging open. "When?"

"Like twenty-five years ago."

Christine sat for a moment, then said to April, "That's not possible."

Several at the counter looked at her.

"What do you mean?" April said.

"Melissa Sinclair isn't dead."

The counter went quiet, and the conversation in the diner faded as whispers spread the news Christine White had just added.

"At least she wasn't dead a month ago," Christine said. "She's been in contact with me several times over the years. The last time was just over a month ago. She let me know she couldn't come to the reunion. Melissa Sinclair is alive."

The silence in the diner was complete. The only sounds were Harv's whistling in the kitchen and the sizzle of bacon and eggs on the grill.

But the silence didn't last. Within moments, the buzz began again. In started in small groups in booths and then spread throughout the diner. This gossip was of a different type.

"Chief Malone warned us about this. Levi Garvey is the problem."

"He's been causing problems for Chief Malone ever since he arrived. Now he's spreading lies. Why?"

"Probably to make the news—promote a book."

"Tori Buchanan attacked Doug—split his head."

"Levi Garvey's vicious dog attacked Doug and nearly killed him. It was only a miracle that Doug was able to kill that dog."

"Levi probably hired the best attorneys his money could buy—made bail, I'll bet. He'll never do a single day in jail for what he's done."

April felt sick, but she couldn't stop the gossip. She loved Levi, but she wondered herself if maybe he hadn't let his old rivalry with Doug Malone get out of control.

Melissa Sinclair is still alive, she thought. Oh, Levi. I hate to say it, but maybe Doug is right. Maybe you'd be better off somewhere else. We don't need this in Twin Rivers.

42

Levi was sitting on the porch, listening to the rain fall through the tree leaves. It was late afternoon, and a thundershower had rolled through. The gutters were gurgling with runoff from the roof. There was an occasional flash of lightning followed by the distant rumble of thunder. These were the pleasant, relaxing sounds that took him back to summertime when he was a kid.

He was tired. It'd been a long day, cleaning up the ransacked house, and a long night before that, sitting on the floor of a holding cell. Levi had called it quits a few minutes earlier. Tori was still running the vacuum upstairs. They'd thrown a lot of stuff out and burned a lot more. The house was pretty much back in order, but it looked empty. There would be a big shopping trip in the near future.

Tori walked out onto the porch and took a seat on the swing.

"I quit, too," she sighed. "I'm wiped out."

Levi glanced at her and began laughing.

"What?" she said.

"You got a little mattress fluff there in your hair."

She shook her head. "I'll be honest with you. I think I got a little mattress fluff everywhere. In fact, I'm going upstairs to take a shower, and when I get back down, I expect you to have dinner ready."

Levi laughed again. "Unlikely," he said. "Even if I had the energy to do such a thing, we'd have to eat out of the pans on the stove—we don't have any dishes."

"Oh, yeah," Tori said as she stretched her sore back. "I knew that. I spent an hour sweeping them up."

"Dinner at Harv's?" Levi suggested.

"Perfect," Tori said. She stood up, put both hands on the small of her back, and stretched again. "If I'm not back in twenty minutes, you'd better check on me."

She walked into the house but returned a moment later.

"I almost forgot," Tori said. "I stopped by my house on the way back from getting the stuff I needed to fix the screen door."

She plopped a hat on his head.

"Grandpa's fedora?" Levi asked.

She studied the hat on his head. "Not only does it fit, but it suits you."

Levi walked into the house to look in the mirror of the hall tree.

"I think you're right," he said, cocking the hat over one eye.

It was a wide-brimmed gray fedora with a black ribbon band.

"If it was good enough for Bogie and Cagney, it's good enough for me. Thanks, Tori."

Levi parked Old Blue in front of the diner. When they walked in, they knew something was wrong. The diner was nearly full, but it was unusually quiet. Everyone was looking at them. Levi shrugged as he glanced at Tori.

"It's the new hat—they don't recognize us," he whispered.

Tori snickered and elbowed him.

Actually, the quiet reception didn't really surprise him. They'd been involved in one of the ugliest scenes the town had probably seen in decades. It would likely take awhile for things to get back to normal.

April was standing behind the counter, a testy look on her face.

"Evening, April," Levi said.

She didn't answer as she continued rolling silverware into napkins.

"Aren't you going to say hello to me?" a large man, wearing a plaid shirt and jeans, said. He was seated at the counter with his back to them. When he turned, Tori grabbed Levi's arm.

"Evening, Doug," Levi said.

Doug had a huge bruise on the side of his face and a black eye filled with blood. He had a jagged cut running across his forehead to his temple. His left arm, resting in a sling, was heavily bandaged to the elbow.

Doug turned the rest of the way around on his stool and leaned his back against the edge of the counter, staring at them both.

"Let's go somewhere else," Tori whispered to Levi.

Ignoring Tori, Levi said to Doug, "I'm glad you're here. I'd like to report a crime."

"Levi, don't—" Tori urged, pulling on his arm.

"A rape or a murder maybe?" Doug said with a twisted grin.

"No," Levi said, "breaking and entering. Somebody kicked in my front door with his big, size-twelve boot and ransacked my whole house last night while we were at the movie."

"Let me guess. Once again, you think it was me who did that?"

There were murmurs around the diner. Tori realized that something had changed in town since yesterday. She could tell from the way people were looking at them that they weren't on their side anymore.

"Well, if the big, size-twelve shoe fits," Levi said with a smile.

But nobody laughed.

"You know, Levi," Doug said, "ever since you've been back in town, you've been accusing me of things. I give you a ticket, and you accuse me of pulling my weapon and breaking out your tail light. You tried to embarrass me last night by bringing up the fact I used to visit a working girl more than two decades ago. That was true, but I was young and it was a long time ago. Then you accuse me of raping girls I dated in high school. . . and finally murder. Now I've ransacked your house."

"Once again, Doug, if the shoe fits," Levi snapped at him.

"I do you a huge favor," Doug said. "I don't press charges on you for what you did last night. I've got over a hundred stitches. I'll need several surgeries on this hand before I can use it again. It will be a long time before I can return to work in my full capacity, but I let you go. I don't want a media circus in town, and I hoped maybe you'd realize I'm not your enemy. I hoped you'd realize we could both live in this town without all this shit going on."

"You didn't press charges, Doug, because you started the fight," Levi said, shaking a finger at him. His face was growing redder by the minute. "The last thing you'd want is for us to be in court because you know what our defense would be."

Doug smiled and shook his head. "Why don't you go ahead and tell everyone what your defense was for beating me up and having your dog maul me."

"You raped and murdered Melissa Sinclair," Levi announced.

Laughter erupted throughout the diner. Levi couldn't believe his ears. He looked around, dumbfounded. Doug was laughing, too.

"You stupid, arrogant bastard," Doug said, shaking his head. "Before you accuse somebody of murder, maybe you should make sure the victim is dead."

There was more laughter. Levi didn't understand, but he could feel his face growing hot.

"What do you mean?" Levi said.

Doug looked at him and sneered. "You idiot, Melissa Sinclair is alive!"

Tori's face went pale.

"That's not possible," Levi stuttered.

"Everyone in town knows it," Doug chuckled. "You were so intent on making me look like a fool, you wind up looking like a fool yourself."

More laughter.

Levi glanced at April Jenkins. She was shaking her head, her eyes down.

"Now, what's this about me ransacking your house last night?" Doug said. "What possible motive would I have to do something like that before you beat me up? And I sure couldn't have done it afterwards."

Levi's mouth had gone dry. Tori was tugging on his arm as he glanced around the diner. Everyone was looking at him with disgust. Tori tugged on his arm again, and he stumbled back a few steps.

This just isn't possible, he thought. She's alive? I imagined all of this? I accused Doug of a murder that never happened? And now I'm the village idiot and Doug is the hero?

He glanced at Tori. Her eyes were pleading with him. Let's get out of here! they said.

He followed her out the door.

Doug turned on the stool, slowly surveying the room from side to side. "What's next?" he said with a loud laugh. "The thing is, people, Levi wanted a big show trial. That's why I dropped the charges. He's pissed off about it. He wanted the publicity. He still wants it. That's why he's now accusing me of vandalizing his house. You can't sell books unless your name is in the papers. You all just watch. Levi isn't done yet. He'll figure a way to get some publicity out of this yet. You just wait and see."

Later that evening, Doug was still laughing as he sat in his office. He took off the sling, and flung it into the corner—he wasn't nearly as injured as he'd let on. He poured himself a strong drink and leaned back in his chair, chuckling. He'd managed to turn the whole thing around, snatching victory from the jaws of defeat. He couldn't believe his good fortune. Christine White had dropped the bomb that made everything work out. Even before he'd gotten out of the hospital, everyone in town knew Melissa Sinclair was alive.

And now it was time to finish Levi off. Doug knew Levi was right on the edge. He was so close to leaving Twin Rivers, he could be packing his bags right now. And the beautiful thing about Doug's plan was that everyone would blame Levi for what was about to happen next.

Doug had made a list. He was just waiting for his chance to use it. From his desk drawer, he pulled out the yellow legal pad on which he'd listed every major network, news agency, and tabloid in the United States. He reached for the phone on the corner of the desk pulled it in front of him, and dialed the first number on the pad.

"Is this the *Examiner*? I'd like to speak to Stephanie McBride. I have a story about Levi Garvey. . . yes, that's right, the best-selling author."

As he waited on hold, he chuckled to himself again.

43

Something woke Levi. He wasn't sure what it was. He sat up on the settee, one hand on his throbbing forehead, and looked across the coffee table, covered in beer cans, at Tori who was snoring in the wingback chair. His phone buzzed in his pocket again. He fumbled for it, finally found it, and flipped it open.

"Hello?" he croaked.

"You have a pretty house." He recognized the raspy voice immediately. He heard her sip her coffee. "My grandma lived in a house like that in Pennsylvania when I was a girl. Does it have the stained glass panels at the top of all the windows? I'll bet it does. That's very Victorian."

"Wanda?" Levi said, rubbing his temple. "What are you talking about? Are you here?"

"No, I'm in New York. But I'm looking at your house on TV right now. You're getting a lot of coverage. You want to tell me what the hell is going on out there in Hickville, U.S.A?"

Levi picked up a pillow and threw it at Tori. She woke up in a mood and threw it back, hard. She glared at him. He could tell she was just as hung-over as he was.

"Turn on the TV!" he snapped at her.

She looked at him blankly but got up to turn it on.

"What the hell?" she said.

They were looking at the Garvey house in the background as a reporter talked about Levi. Tori ran into the foyer but quickly returned.

"You'd better go look," she said.

Wanda was talking in his ear. "They're saying you assaulted a police officer, put him in the hospital. They say you accused him of rape and murder. They say you've lost your mind. They just interviewed a few townspeople. They don't seem very happy with you, Levi. You've turned that sleepy little town into a three-ring circus."

Levi walked into the foyer and looked out the window. Alan Haig had his cruiser pulled across the end of the driveway with the lights flashing. Half a dozen media vans were parked on the road, and one was in the process of raising a satellite tower.

"You listening to me, Garvey?" Wanda snapped.

"Yeah, yeah, I'm here."

"They're saying you orchestrated this whole thing to publicize some book you're writing. Is that true?"

"I am researching a book, but I didn't do this," Levi stuttered. "I really thought the chief of police murdered somebody."

"Well, they're saying he didn't. Everyone they've interviewed knows this murder victim isn't a murder victim. Hard to be a murder victim when you're still alive," Wanda said with a growl.

"I know, I know."

"You need to get the hell out of there, Levi," Wanda said. "That police chief you beat up? Well, they just interviewed him on CNN. He looks pretty pissed off. Everyone they've talked to looks pretty pissed off, as a matter of fact. You'd better get your ass out of there before your cop buddy decides to charge you with something."

"Yeah, I think maybe you're right," Levi said, but the phone was dead. Wanda was done talking.

Tori had been going from room to room on the first floor and the second, looking out the windows.

"There are more news vans coming up the road," she said. "There's a helicopter flying around out there, too."

"We need to get the hell out of here, Tori," Levi said. "If we stay here, Doug will have us arrested again. He planned this whole thing. He wants us to go. In fact, I think the whole town wants us to go. So let's not stay where we're not wanted. Let's go."

"I'm not leaving," she said, her arms crossed stubbornly across her chest.

"What do you mean you're not leaving? Are you kidding?" Levi said, dumbfounded. "Look out the window! Look at what's going on outside! What choice do we have?"

"This is my home, Levi. I grew up here. I love it here. I have a life here. If he wants to arrest me, then so be it. I'll fight it. I don't regret anything."

"But I can't stay here," Levi said. "It was a mistake to come back. I caused this whole problem."

The words stung Tori. "It was a mistake? Was I a mistake, too?" she said, her eyes glistening. A single tear slid down her cheek, which she quickly brushed away with the back of her hand.

He smiled. "No, you're the one good thing I've gained from this, one I'll never let go of again," he said, pulling her into his arms.

She took a step back and put her hand on his chest. "And now you and I just leave all this and go back to Savannah? We run away together?"

Levi's face grew dark. "We don't have a choice."

"There is always a choice," Tori said. "You go out there and tell those reporters what happened. You apologize for the whole thing. If Doug decides to press charges, we'll hire good attorneys, we'll tell the truth about what happened, and we'll take whatever a jury dishes out for us. I personally don't think Doug will do that. I don't think he'll want me to tell my story about him trying to rape me. I told you I think there are others he may have done the same thing to. If I'm right about that, he'll be too worried about them coming forward, too. We can stay and fight this together, Levi."

"That's what you think I should do?" Levi said, shaking his head. "Dig in and fight?"

"Yes," Tori said emphatically.

"Then what?" Levi asked. "The town forgives us? We live happily ever after? Is that what you believe?"

"I don't know," Tori said.

"We turned this town into our own personal battlefield. We were fighting a decades-old battle out of habit. We were so full of our own righteousness we saw plots and conspiracies at every turn. We tried to make him a bigger villain than he actually is. We weren't fighting the good fight. We were fighting Doug out of pettiness for things that happened long ago. He's a bully—someone to be pitied. All he has in his life is being the big fish in this little pond. I've hated him for so long, I just couldn't let him have that one small thing."

"You were reacting to the things he did," Tori said.

"Doug didn't even start this, Tori," Levi snapped. "Don't you understand? *I* started this at the reunion. I don't know why, but I pushed Doug that night into that rage. I did it on purpose, and I knew it would be easy to accomplish. I knew exactly what to do to get him to explode. I'd done it a million times before. He didn't disappoint me either. He made a huge ass out of himself, and I loved it."

"But—" Tori started.

"I could've left him alone. Uncle Ed urged me to leave him alone. But I couldn't. I started this because part of me is still that teenage boy with the black eye and bruised ribs. Those injuries healed a long time ago, but my ego was still bruised, and I wanted to exact a price for it. I wanted to make him pay. And in the end, look at what I've done. I've destroyed my dream of coming back here, living a quiet simple life, and writing my books in the family house."

"It'll all blow over," Tori said.

"It won't," Levi said. "You're dreaming."

"If you leave, I can't go with you," Tori said.

"I can't stay here, Tori," he said. "I think you know that."

Tori sighed as she wiped fresh tears off her face.

"You'll love Savannah," Levi said, smiling at her. "You really will. I found a book on the history of Savannah yesterday when I was cleaning up."

Tori looked at him doubtfully, her arms wrapped tightly around her. Tears were coursing down her face.

Levi walked to the bookshelf. "You can read it on the plane. I read it when I was a kid," he said, running his finger along the spines of the books. "I think that's the main reason I decided to settle in Savannah. And, of course, there's John Berendt's book."

As he pulled the book off the shelf, he heard the front door open and close. When he turned around, Tori was gone. He knew what it meant.

It was over.

44

Harv was scraping what was left of a burned hamburger off the grill when April banged through the swinging doors into the kitchen.

"Harv," she said, sounding annoyed, "Jim Finney is beginning to wonder where his lunch is."

As soon as she saw the burned hamburger in the trashcan sitting on top of an order of blackened fries, her face dropped.

"Tell Jim Finney it's going to be a minute," Harv grumbled as a fresh burger hit the grill with a hiss.

"Are you feeling okay?" April said. "You haven't been yourself lately. Maybe you should go see Doc."

"I'm fine," Harv growled.

"Well, something's been wrong with you the last couple of days," she said. "You've been like a bear with a sore ass around here."

Harv nodded toward the TV he kept in the kitchen on top of the refrigerator. "I get a little tired of watching CNN and MSNBC rip on Levi Garvey. Bill O'Reilly on FOX just called Levi a pin-head."

"Then turn it off," April said.

Harv sighed.

"There's something bothering you," April said, pulling a bag of fries out of the freezer and dumping them into the fry basket.

"I think I'm going to punch out the next person I hear blame Levi for this media blitz."

April smiled. "Well, it has been good for business. That usually makes you happy."

"I don't think Levi did this," Harv said, laying a square of cheese on the burger.

"Well, something has you wound up," April said. "In forty years, Jim Finney has never ordered a cheeseburger."

"Shit," Harv mumbled, scraping the cheese off the burger with his spatula.

"You don't think Levi did this, do you?" April said. "Why not?"

Harv nodded towards the TV. "That's why."

April looked up at the screen. She'd seen this story a dozen times. The news networks had been playing the same story in rotation every hour since it'd started, but there had been no fresh breaks in the story since it'd first aired. They were just running the same clips over and over again. In the clip that was on the TV now, Doug Malone was standing in front of the Twin Rivers Police Department, talking about the events that had taken place in Twin Rivers over the last two weeks and describing how Levi Garvey had attacked him on Main Street during the Fourth of July weekend.

"Look at the way he had his head bandaged," Harv said. "He never had his head wrapped like that when he was in here right after he got out of the hospital. Look at how he's got his injured hand clear up in the middle of his chest so the cameras can see it. When he was in here, he had it in a sling down around his waist. Is this a media circus to promote Levi's book, or is this Doug Malone's media circus to destroy Levi Garvey?"

April looked at the TV. "And if this is Levi's show, where has Levi been?" she said.

"Exactly," Harv said. "If he did this for publicity, why hasn't he been out there soaking up the attention? But there hasn't been one word from Levi Garvey—not even a formal statement from his attorney or his publisher or his agent. Nothing. I mean, surely, if Levi had planned all this as a publicity stunt, wouldn't we be seeing a whole lot of Levi Garvey?"

"You think Doug did this," April said.

"You're damned right I do," Harv said. "And there's another thing that bothers me. I watch these damned network news shows all day every day. What should've happened by now?"

April shrugged.

"You think those reporters are stupid? You think they're not looking for every possible angle on this story?" Harv said. "I've been waiting for it. I've been back here watching and waiting for them to find and interview Melissa Sinclair, the woman Levi accused Doug of murdering. And they haven't."

"What are you saying exactly?" April asked, chills beginning to form on the back of her neck.

"I may be just a short order cook, but something stinks here. These news guys break a story that some senator has been dicking his intern, and within three hours, they've dug up three more women the senator had been doing the same thing with. By the end of the news day, they'll find a love child the senator fathered five years earlier."

"But what does it mean?" April asked, staring at Harv.

"I think we've all been very stupid," Harv said, flipping the burger. "How do we know Melissa Sinclair is alive exactly?"

"You were here, Harv. You know the answer to that question. We know she's alive because . . ." She trailed off as the realization of what Harv had been thinking hit her.

"Because the biggest gossip in Twin Rivers said she was," Harv said. "That's it! That's the evidence! And two days later, there is not one interview with the murder victim even though the entire national media is looking for her."

"Oh my God, Harv! You don't really think . . ." April gasped, not finishing the thought.

"I think a lot of things back here sweating over this grill. And I think you should take Jim Finney his burger before he has a stroke," he said, dumping the hot fries on the plate next to the hamburger.

45

Tori couldn't sleep. She couldn't eat. She'd cancelled her vacation, hoping work would take her mind off Levi. She'd accomplished little besides sitting behind her desk, staring at her computer monitor, and worrying about Levi.

Something had happened during the last couple of weeks. She'd known the minute she'd sat down behind her desk at the bank that returning to her old life again was impossible. She had a difficult choice to make—either run away and make a new life with Levi or continue living a life that no longer appealed to her.

She'd spent the morning in her office with the door closed, but by lunchtime, she realized she needed to see Levi. She'd had second thoughts. She'd decided that maybe they should run away for awhile, maybe take a long cruise or spend a few months in Mexico. Maybe once they were away from this mess, they could figure out what they should do next.

Tori got into her car and drove the eight miles to Twin Rivers. When she got to Levi's house, she felt a glimmer of hope. The news crews were gone. It was certainly a much different scene from the one she'd seen when she'd weaved out of Levi's driveway amid the shouts of reporters and the flashes of cameras.

Old Blue was sitting in the driveway. She pulled up next to the truck and got out. When she walked up the steps to the door, she was surprised to find it locked. She let herself in with her key.

She'd taken just a single step across the threshold when she realized she was too late. She stood, staring at the antique hall tree. Levi had left a message just for her, a message that would've meant nothing to anybody else.

Levi's Panama was gone. Hanging on the hook in its place was the fedora.

I guess Levi has made his choice, she thought, as she pulled the door shut behind her.

46

After the doors were closed, the airplane began to taxi to the end of the runway. Levi Garvey pulled his Panama down over his eyes and leaned back against the seat.

Uncle Ed had driven him to Peoria to catch the flight. With any luck, he would be sitting on his front porch in six hours, looking out at Pulaski Square. He might even call Ray Billings when he got home to invite him over for a few.

Considering he'd booked at the last minute, he'd found a very fast route home—Peoria to Chicago to Atlanta then home to Savannah—much better than the grueling, twelve-hour, five-city marathon he and Rosco had endured on the flight out. He couldn't believe he'd been gone only two weeks.

He felt the plane roll to a stop, then swivel around as it prepared to take off. As the engines wound up and the plane began to move forward, he took off his hat and set it in the empty seat beside him. He looked out the window as Peoria flew past in an ever-increasing blur. Then there was the moment when the plane went weightless, and the city dropped away below.

As they climbed, Levi looked over towards the horizon where he knew Twin Rivers lay—and Tori. He snapped the shade closed over the window.

"Is there anything I can get you, Mr. Garvey?" the flight attendant said, smiling down at him. He smiled back at her—she had lovely brown eyes.

"How long is this flight?" Levi asked.

"About fifty minutes to Chicago," she replied. "Your connecting flight will leave Chicago for Atlanta about twenty minutes after we land. You'll have to move fast, but we'll have transportation arranged to take you to your next gate."

"Thank you," Levi nodded.

He loved the way this airline treated its first-class passengers.

"Can I get you a beverage?" she asked.

"How about a rum and coke?"

"Coming right up."

Staring at the empty glass in his left hand, Levi replayed images of the past two weeks. The fact he was leaving without Rosco hurt a lot, but losing Tori so soon after finding her again would haunt him for the rest of his life.

He also couldn't stop thinking about Melissa. The idea that she was alive was beginning to soak in. She'd probably seen on TV that two of her "best friends" from the Zoo Crew thought so little of her they hadn't even noticed her absence in the past twenty-five years. She would be caught up in the middle of the Levi Garvey scandal. Some reporter would find her and drag her into it. Levi winced every time he thought about Doug's public admission that she was a slut. She'd be humiliated in front of her family, her friends, and her co-workers. He knew the scandal would open up a lot of old memories for Melissa, memories she'd obviously wanted to leave far behind her.

The plane landed in Chicago. As he was whisked through O'Hare

International Airport in a golf cart, he called Christine White.

"This is Levi Garvey," he said.

"Hello, Levi," she said coldly, clearly no longer the president of his fan club.

"Uh, listen," he said. "I was hoping you could give me a phone number or address for Melissa Sinclair. I feel like I owe her an explanation. I know you've been in contact with her over the years."

There was silence for a moment. "Had you asked *me* about her sooner, I could've saved everyone a lot of embarrassment," she retorted. "Hold on a minute while I get my reunion files."

The golf cart finally reached the gate at the opposite side of the terminal. The attendants were waving Levi to the door. They'd been holding the plane for him. Levi was walking briskly towards them when Christine came back on the line.

"Levi," she said, "I don't seem to have an address."

"If you can just give me a phone number or an email, that would be fine," Levi said, digging a pen out of his pocket as he was hustled into his first-class seat and the doors were sealed.

"Well, that's the weird thing," Christine said. "I don't seem to have anything on her."

The airline attendant tapped Levi gently on the shoulder. "I need for you to hang up your phone, Mr. Garvey. We're preparing to leave the gate."

Levi held a finger up at her.

"Christine," Levi said quickly, "you told everyone you'd been in contact with her. I saw you say that on CNN this morning."

"I was in contact with her," Christine snapped defensively. "She always sent back her RSVP cards. She never attended, but she was very considerate to let me know."

"Mr. Garvey," the attendant said pleadingly, "the captain has been holding the flight for you. You need to hang up your cell phone so we can depart."

"That's it, Christine? You call that being 'in contact' with someone?" Levi said, as his face reddened. "And how the hell does that even make sense, Christine? If you don't have her address, then how did she get the invitation to begin with? How do you send back an RSVP for an invitation you never received?"

"I don't know, Levi," she answered, her voice shaking.

"Just answer one more question, Christine," Levi said. "Did she write the information on the RSVP herself, or did she type it?" Levi knew the answer before he asked the question.

"She typed it," Christine said. "That's kind of odd now that I—"

"Mr. Garvey," the captain said. He had appeared suddenly in front of him. "If you don't hang up that cell phone right now, you'll be escorted from the plane and handed over to airport security."

"Where was it mailed from Christine?" Levi said quickly.

No answer.

"Christine! Do you still have the return envelope?" Levi shouted.

"Hang on," Christine said impatiently. "I'm looking."

"That's it, Mr. Garvey," the captain snapped. "We have a schedule to keep, and believe it or not, there are other passengers on this plane besides you."

He turned and walked back up the aisle toward the cockpit.

"That's weird, Levi," Christine said. "It was mailed from Twin Rivers—"

Levi snapped the phone shut.

"I'm sorry, captain. That was an emergency call. Please accept my sincerest apologies," he said, standing up in his seat.

The captain turned around and glared at him over the top of his glasses—he couldn't have been any more perturbed. He said to the flight attendant, "Collect Mr. Garvey's phone and *don't* give it back to him for any reason until we land in Atlanta."

Levi gladly handed the phone to the flight attendant.

"Mind if we go now, Mr. Garvey?" the captain asked, his voice dripping with sarcasm. "Is that convenient for you?"

Levi didn't answer. He knew a rhetorical question when he

heard one.

"You're lucky I'm in a good mood today, Mr. Garvey," the captain muttered as he walked to the cockpit and slammed the door.

I can't believe I could've been so stupid, Levi thought as he stared at the banks of white clouds outside.

He knew he'd been duped. He wasn't sure what pissed him off more—the fact he'd been duped or the fact that Doug Malone had pulled it off.

Levi figured Doug didn't have anything to do with Christine's part. Her coming forward at the diner with the claim Melissa was alive was nothing but a happy coincidence for Doug.

But Doug had played a part in the deception. Levi knew what he'd done. Doug had sent in his own RSVP card with Melissa Sinclair's name typed on it. Levi bet Doug had done that with every invitation he'd received for the last twenty-five years. And Levi knew exactly why. If anyone asked about Melissa, Doug knew Christine, the queen of the local grapevine, would let them know she'd been in contact with Melissa—because Christine White knew everything that went on in River County. It was her life's work. Levi couldn't believe that when Tori asked about Melissa at the reunion, she never thought to ask Christine. If she had, none of this would've happened. Christine would've answered the question, and Tori would've walked away believing Melissa was fine.

It'd been very lucky for Doug that his little game with the RSVP cards had finally paid off in a way he never could've anticipated. It had convinced an entire town—actually an entire nation—that Melissa Sinclair was alive. It had, just as quickly, convinced the town—and the nation—that Levi was an idiot. .

Levi was also certain that Doug had called in the press, knowing that the negative attention would likely push him over the edge. Doug might've even figured out it was negative press that had driven him back to Twin Rivers to begin with.

He finally figured out my weakness, Levi thought. I can't stand up to ridicule. I used that same thing against him all through high school. I made him look like a fool repeatedly. He finally figured out what I was doing, and he used it against me. He finally beat me at my own game.

"Is there anything you need, Mr. Garvey," the flight attendant asked cautiously, breaking into his reverie.

She'd been watching him closely since takeoff from Chicago—probably at the direction of the captain. She appeared to be a little afraid of him. Levi could understand that since it'd been widely reported in the press that he was a lunatic, that he'd lost his mind, that he'd gone on a rampage of unfounded accusations and beat up a cop in a small town. The flight attendant and the captain had likely known that before he boarded the plane. Holding up the flight hadn't helped their preconceived opinion of him.

"Maybe some coffee?" he said.

She nodded and turned back up the aisle, glancing briefly over her shoulder as if to make sure he wasn't following her.

Levi's thoughts returned to Doug Malone. Two big questions remained: If Doug had killed her, when did he do it and where was her body?

Partially reclined in his seat, Levi stared out the window again, his thoughts turning over and over in his head, the coffee he'd ordered untouched. He was three decades in the past, trying to recall anything that might provide some answers. As he mused, something touched his ankle. The same panic that had seized him at Tybee Island—and Kingery Pond—returned. He jerked upright in his first-class seat and gasped audibly. When he looked down at his foot, he saw that he'd stepped into the strap of his carry-on bag which was under the seat in front of him.

Levi smiled sheepishly at the flight attendant who'd been watching him closely. She'd obviously seen his strange reaction moments ago. She was clutching the cabin intercom mike tightly to her chest.

As he pulled his foot out of his carry-on, the answer to one of his questions suddenly struck him. He knew exactly where Melissa was. The idea sent a shiver through him. It was too horrible to conceive, but it made sense. Levi knew that the answer to a single question could remove any remaining doubt from his mind, and he knew exactly how to get the answer to that last question.

The minute they landed and he was well clear of Miss Nervous Nellie Flight Attendant and Captain Cranky Pilot, he headed to an empty waiting area. He had two phone calls to make during the forty-minute layover in Atlanta.

47

April Jenkins was sorry to see the press vans leave. As soon as the reporters saw Levi load his bag into Ed's old Cadillac and leave the Garvey house, amid the flashes and shouted questions, they knew there was no story left in Twin Rivers. They vanished almost as quickly as they'd appeared. The national press horse and pony show was heading to Savannah.

The diner was back to being dead again. Except for Ed at the counter and an older couple in one of the booths, it was empty. Ed had confirmed what she'd heard from several reporters earlier—Levi was headed back to Georgia.

April was filling salt and pepper shakers, and Harv was in the kitchen scouring the grill, which had seen a lot of action since the July Fourth weekend. They'd just had their best week since the recession had hit over a year ago.

Ed was unusually quiet as he sipped his coffee. He appeared to have a lot on his mind.

When the phone rang, April wiped her hands on her apron and answered it.

"Harv's Diner," she said. A look of surprise crossed her face when she recognized the voice. "Hang on, Levi."

Ed's head snapped up. April shrugged.

"Harv," she called into the kitchen, "telephone for you!"

"I'm busy. Find out who it is. I'll call 'em back," he bellowed.

"It's Levi Garvey."

There was a loud clatter in the kitchen followed by a stream of foul language. Harv banged through the swinging door. April and Ed both shrugged when he looked at them. He took the phone from April.

"Levi?" he said. "Where the hell are you?"

"I'm waiting for a plane in Atlanta, Harv," Levi said. "Listen, I don't have much time, and I've got to ask you a favor. I need for you to keep this just between the two of us."

"Too late, Levi. It'll have to be between just you, me, April, and your Uncle Ed. April and Ed are eavesdropping."

Levi got a lump in his throat. He wanted to be there more than anywhere else on earth.

"There's a picture of the old gang hanging over my favorite booth," Levi said.

"Yeah, the Zoo Crew. You pointed Melissa Sinclair out to April and me in that picture," Harv said. "What about it?"

April's brow knitted when he mentioned Melissa's name.

"In that picture, I've got my foot up on the bumper of Doug's truck. If I remember right, the plate number is visible. I need that plate number, Harv."

Harv paused for minute, then walked back through the swinging kitchen door, stretching the phone cord to its limit. When he was out of earshot, he asked quietly, "Levi, what's going on?"

"There's still something that's bothering me, Harv. I have to know, and I think that plate number will tell me what I need to know."

"She's really dead, isn't she, Levi?" Harv asked.

Levi paused. "Nobody is going to believe me."

"There are a few that will. Hold on, Levi."

Harv walked out of the kitchen, handed the phone to April, picked up a ticket book and pen, and strode toward the booth where the older couple was sitting. April and Ed were watching him with a dozen questions on their faces. The couple looked at Harv questioningly as he leaned over and squinted at the picture from the end of the booth. He couldn't make out the plate number from that distance.

"What's on earth is wrong with you, Harv Jenkins?" the old woman said sharply.

"Margie, can you see that license plate number on the black truck in that photo?"

She put on her readers, which were hanging on a chain around her neck, and squinted at the picture. "Sure," she said.

Harv wrote it down and returned to the phone. "I got it, Levi. You ready?"

Levi scribbled the number down on the back of his airline ticket. "Thanks, Harv," he said, shutting the phone.

Levi glanced at his watch, which was finally accurate again. It'd been two weeks since he'd been sure about what time it was. His flight left for Savannah in thirty minutes.

He dialed another number and waited. When a familiar voice answered on the other end, Levi couldn't help but grin.

"Hello, Officer Billings? I'm a wanted fugitive from the law, and I'd like to turn myself in."

Ray laughed. "Well, Mr. Garvey, I kind of thought I'd be hearing from you. But I don't believe being stupid is against the law. If it were, the prisons would be full. *And* I would be drinking the large regular coffee I ordered right now instead of this mocho crap-uchino something-or-another that moron just gave me in the drive-through. So what do you want?"

"I need to ask a favor," Levi said, glancing at his watch. "It's a big favor, Ray. A really *big* favor."

"I don't think you've ever asked me for a favor before," he said. "This must be important."

From Ray Billings, that was an invitation. Levi took a deep breath. He knew he could count on Ray.

"If I were to give you an Illinois license plate from twenty-five years ago and tell you it belonged to a 1982 Chevy Silverado, could you pull the Vehicle Identification Number for that truck?"

"A VIN number?" Ray asked. "I should be able to."

"And with the VIN number, you could pull a history of the vehicle? Right?"

"Well, yeah, that's what they're for," Ray said. "Even back in the 80s, they used the VIN number any time the vehicle was sold. There would be a record of every owner of that truck. There would be a record if the vehicle was ever totaled. There would be a record when it went to the scrap yard. I could probably even track what happened to the engine block and any other major parts that were sold. Old clunkers turn up abandoned all the time, and it's rarely a problem to track their history and last owner."

"Now here's the big question, Ray," Levi said. "Would you?"

Ray chuckled. "Give me the plate number."

Levi read it to him. "How long is this going to take?"

"I'm not real familiar with Illinois, but our guys should be able to get those records with a few key-strokes. I'll call it in now and pull a few strings. It might take me an hour. Probably less."

"I'll be back in Savannah in about two hours," Levi said, glancing again at his watch.

"Tell you what," Ray said. "I'll have the information when I pick you up at the airport."

Levi smiled. "Thank you, Ray."

"I'll see you when you land, Brother Garvey."

After Levi pulled his bag off the carousel, he looked around for

Ray Billings. When he didn't see Ray, he decided he'd wait outside the terminal. He didn't want to hang around very long because he'd already been picked up by one aggressive reporter as he left the concourse. The guy had obviously been waiting for the plane to land.

"Mr. Garvey! Can I get a statement from you about what happened in Twin Rivers, Illinois? Is it true you beat up a police officer on the Fourth of July?" he'd yelled as he followed Levi.

Airport security had finally detained the reporter, but Levi knew it was only a matter of time before that jackass turned up again or another just like him.

"Looking for somebody?" a voice said behind him.

Levi turned around. Ray was standing a few feet away in his uniform, grinning at him through his curled up mustache, with his bald head gleaming in the bright lights of the baggage claim. Ray towered over him as they shook hands. Then Ray got a puzzled look on his face. He turned Levi's hand over, then grabbed his other hand and examined it as well.

"What?" Levi said.

"Damn, Levi, you've got blisters and calluses on your little girlie hands," he said with a chuckled. "Either you've been working hard in Illinois, or you've been spending too many hours alone thinking about Brittany—with both hands."

Levi laughed. "I've sure missed those amazing powers of observation. You're a sight for sore eyes, Ray. I feel like I've been gone a year instead of a couple of weeks. What happened to your head?" Levi asked, pointing to a fading bruise on the temple of his bald head.

Ray rubbed it and smiled.

"You remember that last night in Savannah? On your porch?"

Levi nodded.

"Good thing I decided to walk home that night. As I was whistling my way through the square, I turned the corner up by Bull Street and walked right into one of those damned iron lampposts. I rang it like a bell."

Levi laughed until he had tears in his eyes.

"I know what *you* were thinking about," Levi said with a wide grin. "*You* were thinking about Brittany and that little naked trot up the stairs that night."

Ray laughed. "Put a goose-egg on my head the size of a golf ball. It started black and blue, then turned green and purple. My friends on the force have had a great time taking pictures of my head every day and printing them out. We have a whole collection of photos now. It's kind of like a flip-book. They stack them up and flip through the pictures, and you can watch the bruise on my old wrinkly head bloom like a flower and fade. It's about gone now."

Levi smiled at him, but Ray knew Levi had a pressing question he was eager to ask.

"I have some information for you," Ray said, tapping the notebook in his pocket. "I'll tell you what I found out if you'll buy me a cup of coffee." He pointed to a coffee shop in the airport. "And I'll tell you right now, if I get anything other than a regular coffee from the *barista* in there, I'm going to arrest him."

"Ray," Levi said, grinning, "you've learned new words since I left. You used to call them 'coffee dudes.'"

"No," Ray said, "I used to call them 'coffee fairies.' Did I mention I had to go to sensitivity training last week?"

"I can't imagine why," Levi said, laughing.

"Captain Hippie made me go," he muttered.

"Captain Hippie?"

"I mean, Captain *Harper*. Now you know why he sent me."

"Oh, Ray," Levi said.

"It was a great experience. I'm a new man now. From now on, when I break up a knife fight outside a titty-bar at 2 a.m., I'm not going to cuff them. I'm just going to have them hug each other, and we're all going to sing Kumba-Freakin'-Ya.

After they were seated at a table in the back of the coffee shop, Ray pulled the notebook out of his pocket. "Here's what I know," Ray said.

Levi leaned forward, his eyes focused intently on Ray.

"That cop who's been all over the news was the second owner of the truck. Douglas William Malone bought it slightly used from a dealership in Peoria. It had about 5,000 miles on it. He financed it through the dealership. His mother co-signed the loan, and she made all the payments. I got that information from the dealership.

"There is only one record of the truck after the sale. The auto body shop did $400 worth of work on it. They didn't have any details other than they replaced the bumper. But it wasn't an insurance claim. Their records showed Momma Malone wrote a check for it, not an insurance company."

"I'll bet anything that bumper they replaced had blue paint all over it—from Old Blue," Levi said.

Ray flipped his notebook closed.

"That's it?" Levi said.

"That's it. There are no other records on that truck."

"What's that mean, do you think?"

"You know what it means," Ray said with a shrug. "Douglas William Malone has a rusty old 1982 Chevy Silverado up on blocks in his pasture somewhere. The truck was never sold. It was never scrapped either." Ray leaned over the table and looked at him knowingly. "Of course, you suspected that when you called me, didn't you?"

Levi leaned back in his chair and pushed the brim of his Panama back on his head with one finger, a look of grim determination on his face.

"Did that help?" Ray asked.

Levi nodded as he stood up.

"Where are you going?" Ray said.

"To hell if I don't change my ways," Levi said with a tight smile.

He picked up his bag and started to walk away from the table.

"You let me know if you need anything, okay?" Ray called after him.

Levi paused and turned. "Watch out for those lamp posts, Ray. They'll kick your ass."

48

It was dark when Tori bumped her suitcase down the steps and rolled it to her Impala in the driveway. She pushed the button on her keychain, and the trunk popped up. She picked up the suitcase and heaved it in. Then using the light emanating from the trunk, she opened her purse for the tenth time to be sure she had the tickets. Her stomach knotted as she checked the departure time—she'd never been much of a traveler. Besides, she still wasn't convinced she was actually going on this trip although she'd booked the flight which was leaving in less than three hours from Peoria.

When she'd left the bank that day, she'd informed the bank manager she was taking the rest of the week off. She wondered if that was a lie since she might never be back. Her life as a small town bank president might be over.

But as Tori started to close the trunk, doubt seized her again.

My life is here, she thought. It always has been, but Levi isn't going to come back. I'm wasting my time. But does it really matter? Do I want a life here without him, or do I want a life, wherever it may be, with him?

She slammed the trunk. She'd made her decision. She couldn't imagine her life now without Levi.

I guess I'm running away, too, she thought. We're back to that same thing we talked about after the reunion. Levi can't commit, and I can't seem to let go.

He'd told her at the jail that he loved her. She knew he'd never said those words to a woman before, but there was no question in her mind he'd said them to at least four dogs. Tori smiled at that thought.

She walked around the car, opened the driver's door, and started to climb in.

"Where do you think you're going?" a voice said from the shadows behind her.

She froze. She knew the voice.

"I'm going to Savannah," she said.

"Are you running away, Tori?"

"No, I'm coming back. I'm just going there to shoot my ex-boyfriend," she said coldly. "I'll be on the next plane back."

"You can't take a gun on a plane."

"Oh, I'm not going to," she said. "Officer Ray Billings of the Savannah Police Department said I could use his gun."

"You talked to Ray?"

"He's worried about you, too, dumbass," Tori said, turning around. "Where the hell have you been? Ray said you left three days ago."

Levi stepped out of the shadows. She could see his outline from the streetlight. He was wearing the Panama.

"You looked better in the fedora."

"Yeah, well, I'm not quite done with the past yet," Levi said.

"I can't believe you came back for me."

"I didn't come back for you. I came back for *Doug*. He did it, Tori, and we're going to prove it. We'll fight this together, just like you said."

"That's good enough for me," she said.

She wrapped her arms around his neck and kissed him.

"You know this is going to get ugly," Levi whispered in her ear.

"Please tell me you have a plan," Tori said, still hugging him.

"Nobody is going to listen to us," Levi said. "We have no credibility. So we're going to get Doug to confess."

She pulled back and looked at Levi's face. "You can't be serious. That's your plan? What the hell is wrong with you? He'll never do that."

Levi laughed. "Oh, Tori, ye of little faith. He'll do it, believe me. He won't be able to help himself. I'm not going to give him a choice in the matter."

"How?" she demanded.

Levi kissed her again. "I'll tell you what. We'll have a long conversation about that—after breakfast."

He took her hand and pulled her toward the house.

49

"I tried to tell everyone what Levi was up to," Doug said. He sipped his coffee and grinned. "That's okay. In my book, it's never too late to say I told you so."

During the week since Levi had left, Doug had changed his habit. Instead of getting a cup of coffee to go, he usually sat in the diner and drank coffee for an hour, all the while gloating over how he'd been right all along about Levi Garvey.

April was sick of it. Everyone in town was getting sick of it. Harv stayed in the kitchen when Doug was ripping on Levi because Harv didn't trust his own ability to keep his mouth shut.

Doug reached over the counter, lifted the glass lid of the pastry display, and helped himself to a glazed donut. He took a big bite and, with his mouth full, continued on his daily rant.

"I did that son-of-a-bitch a big favor by not pressing charges. My doctor says I'll need at least three surgeries on this hand before I can use it again," Doug said. "I may sue Levi yet."

"Thank God, your injuries haven't impeded your ability to lift that heavy glass lid and get yourself a donut," April said as she wrote the donut down on his ticket.

Doug glanced up at her coldly, then smiled the smile that never reached his eyes. He shook his finger at her. "You're a funny lady, April."

Harv walked out of the kitchen with his coffee cup and filled it from the pot on the counter.

"I can't believe you haven't taken Garvey off your wall of fame, Harv," Doug said, pointing to the display. "After what he did to this town, I think it's time to put Levi Garvey behind us. Forget about him."

"And how are we going to do that, Doug?" Harv grumbled. "You're in here rehashing the whole thing every damned day. I don't know if you've noticed, but the news crews have gone. Levi's gone. Rosco's dead. Ed has listed the Garvey house, and it won't be on the market long even in this economy. Levi's not coming back. The story is over. It seems to me, you're the one keeping the story alive here in Twin Rivers, not that picture on the wall." Harv leaned on the counter in front of Doug. "Maybe if we want to put Levi Garvey behind us for good, we ought to throw you out of here."

Several of the customers in the diner laughed.

Doug stood up from the stool and glared at Harv. Then the artificial smiled appeared again. He shook his head, and said, "You and April are both funny, funny people. I'll see you both tomorrow."

The thought sickened Harv.

Doug picked his flat-brimmed hat up from the counter, adjusted it on his head with both hands, and started for the door.

"Doug," Harv said, "I think you're forgetting something."

"What?" Doug said, turning back toward the counter.

"You forgot to pay your ticket," Harv said, waving the green ticket at him. April looked at Harv in amazement.

Doug's face hardened as he walked to the register. "How much do I owe you?" he said, pulling out his wallet.

Harv's laugh was humorless. "You've had coffee and a donut in here every single day for years, and you don't know how much it is?"

Doug's eyes flashed angrily. Everyone in the diner was now listening.

"Oh, that's right," Harv said. "You've never actually paid for anything in here."

"How much?" Doug snapped.

"I'll charge you just for the coffee. That seem fair to you?" Harv said. He pulled the adding machine next to the register closer to him and began punching buttons.

"What the hell are you doing?" Doug said, his face turning redder by the moment.

Harv ignored him as he continued to punch buttons. Finally, he ripped off a piece of adding machine paper and looked at it.

"That'll be $21,060."

Doug exploded. "Have you lost your damned mind?"

Harv looked at him as if he didn't understand why he was angry. "I pro-rated it, Doug. I figure three cups a day, six days a week, for fifteen years. That's what it comes to."

"I'm not paying that," Doug said, shoving his wallet back into his pocket.

Harv smiled. "That's a bargain, Doug. I could always charge you what you actually owe."

Harv reached under the counter and pulled a large cardboard storage box out. He popped the lid off and dumped the contents onto the counter. There were thousands of green tickets, which fluttered all over the counter and onto floor. The customers in the diner muttered amongst themselves.

"Every single one of these tickets is yours," Harv said. "You haven't paid any of them. But if it takes me all day, I'm going to add up every one of these damned tickets, and I'm going to send you a bill. This is *my* restaurant, and you're going to pay me what you owe me, and until you do, I don't want to see your face in here again."

"You'd better think about what you're saying," Doug said, leaning over the counter and staring into his face.

"Are you threatening me?" Harv snapped back.

The sound of chairs scooting across the wood floor filled the diner as four big farmers stood up at the center table all at once and walked up behind Doug. April couldn't believe what she was seeing—those farmers were backing Harv up.

"You get the hell out of my restaurant, Doug, and don't come back," Harv said.

Doug glanced at the four angry faces that had suddenly surrounded him and walked to the door.

"Oh, Doug," April said cheerfully. "You want one last cup to go? I can always add it to your tab."

The diner exploded into laughter as Doug banged out the door in a rage.

The sound started somewhere in the back of the diner. One person began clapping, and it soon spread. Soon every customer in the diner was standing to applaud Harv. At first, Harv looked confused, but finally he took an exaggerated bow.

When Harv turned back towards the kitchen, he leaned over to April and whispered, "We're so screwed."

"Yes, we are," she said. Then she did something nobody in Twin Rivers had ever seen her do before. She threw her arms around his neck and kissed him right there in front of everyone. "I love you, Harv Jenkins."

He shrugged. "Whatever it takes to get you off my ass, April," he said as he smiled. "I told you I'd take care of it."

50

After storming out of the diner, Doug stomped across the street. Suddenly, he froze. His police cruiser was parked in front of the police department—all four tires flat and one tail light busted out. Parked right next to it was a familiar blue truck.

"Levi Garvey!" he shouted. "I'll kill that son-of-a-bitch!"

He looked up and down the street but didn't see anyone. Then he looked back towards the diner. Leaning against a lamp post, Levi Garvey was smiling from under the brim of his Panama.

"Seems like you're having a really bad day, Doug," Levi called over to him. "Did you just get kicked out of Harv's?"

From the corner of his eye, Levi could see the customers in the diner rushing towards the windows.

"You shouldn't have come back here, Levi," Doug said, fuming.

"I live here," Levi said.

"Not for long," Doug hissed, storming towards him.

Levi never moved, never flinched as Doug closed the gap between them. When Doug was a few feet away, Levi pulled the revolver from the back of his belt and aimed it at Doug's forehead. It was that same lightning speed and fluid movement Doug had experienced from Ed—with that same Garvey calm. Doug froze.

"You haven't met my friend, Mr. Webley, have you? He's a really old guy, but he has a nasty temper and a hair trigger."

Stepping forward, Levi pressed the Webley into Doug's forehead as he reached over and plucked the Glock out of his holster and tossed it in front of the diner.

"Why did you come back here?" Doug snapped as he took a few steps backwards.

Levi shrugged. "I felt bad about the way we left things. I've been thinking about how I could make it up to you. I wanted to do something nice for you, Doug," Levi said, his voice full of sarcasm.

"Really?" Doug said.

"Really," Levi said as he began to pace around Doug in a wide circle, waving the revolver around erratically. It was the same way he'd paced around Doug at the reunion. "I've been busting my brain trying to think of something nice I could do for you. Suddenly, I thought of the perfect gift. Actually, you told me what you wanted that first day we ran into each other."

Doug looked confused.

"Don't you remember, Doug?" Levi said.

As Levi had circled him and Doug had inched away from him, they'd slowly worked their way out into the center of Main Street.

Doug shook his head. He had no idea what Levi was talking about.

"You got all misty-eyed about it," Levi said with a smile. "The Reaper, Doug! Your old truck!"

Doug's face went pale.

"Don't you remember? You said, 'I'd do anything to get that old truck *back*.' It was an interesting choice of words, Doug. Get that old truck *back*. You didn't say, you'd love to get another truck just like it. You said you'd like to get *your* old truck *back*—like you knew where it was and if you could get it *back*, you would. I study language. Only a writer would notice something like that, but it was kind of telling in a way."

"Listen, Levi, this isn't helping you any. We can talk this over. We can work things out between us."

"Yeah?" Levi said, pausing. He lowered his gun. "Maybe we could go to couple's counseling. Maybe with a good counselor we could get at what it is that makes us fight like this."

Doug felt a moment of hope. He could tell from the crazed look on Levi's face that something had snapped. He wasn't himself. Levi had gone a little crazy. Maybe Doug could find a way out of this.

"Sure, if that's what you want. We can find a way to live here together," Doug said, nudging a little closer to him. "Things got a little out of control. That's all. We'll put all this behind us."

He'd been inching his way closer to Levi. Just a little further and he'd be in position to make a grab for the gun. He'd have no trouble overpowering Levi.

Suddenly, the gun was planted on his forehead again. "No, Doug, I just don't think so. But it was a really nice try," Levi said with a chuckle. "I know what I'm going to do. I'm going to give you a little present—the very thing you said you wanted."

Doug slowly backed up.

Levi leaned into him. "I know where *The Reaper* is," Levi whispered. "I figured it out. I'm going to go and get your old truck back for you."

Fear flashed in Doug's eyes. When he stepped forward, Levi cocked the revolver.

"I wouldn't," Levi said.

Doug stopped short.

Slowly, Levi edged towards Old Blue, the revolver now pointed at Doug's chest. As he reached the trunk of Doug's cruiser, he looked up at him and smiled. He flipped the gun over, caught it by the barrel, and used the butt to smash out the other tail light. Just as quickly, he flipped the gun back over and grinned.

"I think we're just a few scratches away from being even," Levi said.

Levi climbed into Old Blue and fired it up. He had the revolver pointed at Doug through the window as he slowly backed out of the parking space.

"I've got to get out of here, Doug," Levi said. "I'm sure somebody in the diner has called the *real police*, and they'll be here soon."

As Levi pulled down Main Street, his laughter rang out.

Doug started for his cruiser before remembering the flat tires. He rushed over to pick up his gun in front of the diner. His hands were shaking so badly, he had trouble holstering it.

Then he pulled out his cell phone. "Alan, I need your cruiser, right now!"

51

"You look like hell, Ed," Joyce said, placing his favorite hangover cure in front of him—a poor man's bloody mary, made with beer and tomato juice. "You want some bacon and eggs?"

"Yeah," Ed said, rubbing his temples.

It'd been a ritual night. Those nights were coming more and more frequently, often times two nights in a row. He didn't know how much longer he could keep up the pace.

"You've got to stop doing this to yourself, Ed," Joyce said. "You look like death warmed over. You're killing yourself. I've seen this too many times before, and I don't want to see it happen to you. You're drinking yourself to death."

Ed looked up at her. His eyes were bloodshot, and his face was ash-gray. He reached for his drink with a trembling hand and drained half of it. "You think I could get the eggs without the sermon, Joyce? I appreciate it, but I don't need it."

"Believe it or not, Ed, you're not like these guys," she said, waving her hand down the bar at the other three customers in the tavern. "Those guys were in here until last call last night, and they're back this morning already. Eleven o'clock in the morning and they're drinking."

Ed looked at them—he knew all three. He probably looked as bad as they did as they drank draft beers and stared at their mugs with dead eyes.

"They'll be in here all day," Joyce said. "Booze is all they've got. They drink because their wives have left them. They drink because their kids won't talk to them. They drink because they're lonely. All three will be dead within ten years. Keep up like you have been, and that's going to be you, too. And you've got so much more than they do. You've got friends, a business, and you've got Levi."

Ed glanced at the men again, then stared at his glass.

God, I hope I don't live ten more years, he thought.

Joyce walked down the bar and leaned through the doorway into the kitchen. "Eggs for Ed," she hollered.

She was walking back toward Ed to finish the sermon when the phone rang. She stopped to answer it.

Thank God for small miracles, Ed thought.

"Beer Chaser," Joyce said. Suddenly, her face was a mask of urgency when she looked at Ed. "What? When? Oh, no!"

Ed perked up. He knew something bad had happened, and by the way she was looking at him, it had something to do with him.

Joyce put her hand over the mouthpiece and said hastily, "It's April Jenkins. Levi is back. He was holding a gun on Doug Malone in the center of Main Street. They called the police, and the county and state are on their way."

Ed jumped off his stool and headed for the door.

"Wait! There's more, Ed! What was that last part again, April?" She put her hand over the mouthpiece again. "Levi left in his truck heading north out of town. He slashed the tires on Doug's cruiser, so Doug couldn't follow him, but Alan Haig brought his car up for him. Doug's not far behind Levi."

"How long ago?" Ed said.

She asked April. "Levi left maybe ten minutes ago. Doug isn't more than five minutes behind him. The state police are rolling in now."

"He can't outrun Doug in Old Blue," Ed said. "Why in the hell would Levi be heading north? There's nothing out there but—" he trailed off.

"The old Kingery Mining property," Joyce said, shrugging.

It all clicked together in an instant. Ed suddenly realized exactly where Levi was going and what this was all about. He also understood what a deadly game Levi was playing.

Ed ran towards the door.

My God, Levi is leading Doug back to the scene of the crime, Ed thought.

52

Tori was standing just inside the edge of the woods when she saw Old Blue roaring up the road. She'd never seen Old Blue move that fast before. She rushed to the edge of the two lane highway, and Levi came to an abrupt stop.

"Well?" she asked.

"He's coming all right," Levi said. Tori could tell his adrenaline was pumping. "You make damn sure he doesn't see you. Call the cops the second you see him coming up the road. Better yet, call Harv. There should be quite a gathering of law enforcement on Main Street by now. It will take them maybe two minutes to get here. Wait for them. Make sure they don't miss the lane that leads back to Kingery Pond."

"I know, I know," Tori said. "Now go before he shows up."

Levi popped the truck into gear, pulled off the main road, and drove up the lane to Kingery Pond.

"And be careful," Tori called after him.

She quickly ran back into the woods and waited for Doug Malone to follow.

Levi pulled his truck in sideways across the place he usually parked at the overlook. He climbed out and looked down at Kingery Pond seventy feet below. The green shallow water was as smooth as the surface of a mirror, and the old mine shaft, dark as ink, looked like a malevolent eye staring up at him—as foreboding as it'd looked the first day he'd seen it. It sent a shiver up his spine.

His heart pounding, Levi positioned himself behind Old Blue's hood and waited. Even if everything went as expected and the cops were right behind Doug, it was a dangerous gamble. There was a good chance Doug would come out of his car shooting. It was an imperfect plan, but it was the only way Levi knew he could prove that Doug Malone had something to hide here.

Levi glanced over the hill one more time at Kingery Pond. What a horrible place to be left, he thought.

Levi looked up the lane anxiously, listening for Doug's car, but he heard nothing. Doug should've been there by now. It seemed as if he'd been waiting a long time. He was about to call Tori on her cell when a shadow fell over him. Levi realized something a second too late—too late to do anything about it. Doug Malone knew the woods around Kingery Pond as well as he did. He knew the other way into the old mine property.

A flash like a super nova bloomed across Levi's vision. The pain from the back of his head exploded, and the world around him began to fade away as the ground came up to meet him.

Levi's eyes slowly blinked open. He squinted against the sunlight as his head throbbed. He was trying to remember what had happened. Suddenly, Doug's form appeared over him, a tight grin on his face.

"Oh good," Doug said as he chuckled. "I was afraid I'd have to throw you in unconscious. This is much better."

Terror seized Levi as he understood what Doug meant. He sat up quickly. The world spun wildly around him as his head throbbed and his stomach lurched. He nearly passed out again, but he fought against the darkness edging in on him. Slowly, his vision cleared. He looked around.

Doug had carried him down to the other side of Kingery Pond. The overlook was above them. He could see just the top of Old Blue's cab in the distance. They were at the same place where they'd waded into Kingery Pond more than thirty years before.

"Get up, Garvey," Doug ordered.

"I'm not sure I can stand," Levi said.

"Try," Doug said, planting the gun between his eyes. "You like that? Having a gun shoved into your forehead? I didn't like it much either. I'm pretty pissed off about it, actually. If you don't get up, so help me, I'll kill you right now."

Levi looked up into Doug's eyes and stumbled to his feet.

Doug nodded. "Very good, Levi. Now start walking," he said, motioning with the gun barrel out toward the water.

"I'm not going out there," Levi said.

Doug shoved him into the edge of the water. "Oh, you're going to do exactly what I tell you," Doug screamed at him. "You are not going to tell me what you will and won't do. You'll either march out on your own, or I'll drag you out there with a half dozen holes in you. Either way, you're going swimming. We're going to see how long you can tread water. You want to do that as you are now or with a few bullet holes in you?"

"Doug," Levi said calmly, "it's over. You can't get away with this."

Doug shoved him again hard, opening a gash in Levi's chin with the barrel of his gun and knocking him over backwards into the two-foot deep water.

"You think I don't know that?" Doug shouted. "You think I'm so stupid, I don't realize there's nothing I can do at this point to escape prison? Whether you live or die, I'm going away at this point. You figured it out. I don't know how, but I'm sure Tori knows, too. She's not here, so it doesn't matter now. I'm screwed. But if I'm going to spend the rest of my life in prison, I'm going to at least have the satisfaction of knowing you're dead, Levi. Now, get up!"

Levi scrambled to his feet.

"Move," Doug ordered.

"Listen, Doug," Levi said.

Doug grinned and shook his head. He aimed his Glock and fired. Levi fell over backwards into the water. Doug stood watching as Levi floundered in the shallow water struggling not to drown. Doug finally reached down, grabbed Levi by his hair and pulled him to his feet. Levi looked down at the hand he had clamped tightly against the wound in his shoulder. His whole body was trembling as blood flowed freely through his fingers.

"I have fourteen more shots," Doug said, waving the gun in his face. "I may not be as good a shot as you are, Levi, but even if I'm the worst shot on earth, you'll be dead long before I have to reload. I haven't decided where I'm going to put the next bullet. If you piss me off, Levi, I'll be a real bastard and put one in your other shoulder. That'll make treading water an interesting challenge for you."

Levi turned slowly and began wading towards the dark center of Kingery Pond.

53

It's been too long, Tori thought, glancing at her phone. She couldn't call Levi. That was one part of the plan they hadn't considered. The old Kingery Mine property was in a dead-zone—no cell service. It'd been nearly thirty minutes, yet there had been no sign of Doug. She was beginning to believe their plan had failed. Maybe they were wrong about Melissa . . . again. Doug should have been out there by now. If Levi was right, Doug wouldn't be able to help himself. He wouldn't have a choice.

Suddenly she saw the glint of sunlight off a windshield as a vehicle rounded the bend and came roaring up the road. Tori's felt her stomach flutter with nerves. Here we go, she thought. That's got to be Doug.

She crouched out of sight as the vehicle approached the lane leading back to Kingery Pond. She couldn't see it from her hiding spot behind the trees. Her heart pounded as she heard the vehicle slow. He was turning down the lane. It had to be Doug! When she heard the vehicle make the turn, she risked taking a peek from her hiding place. It was a white tow truck.

"Ed!" she shouted as she jumped out of the woods and ran

toward the road after the tow truck.

Ed heard her and locked the brakes. The truck came skidding to a stop in a cloud of dust.

"Where is Levi?" Ed said as Tori ran breathlessly up to his window.

"He's up the lane waiting for Doug," Tori said, "but Doug hasn't come by yet."

"Melissa Sinclair?" Ed asked. "She's in the shaft, isn't she? In Doug's truck?"

Tori nodded first but then shook her head. "I don't know now. That's what we thought, but it's been too long. If Doug had done what we thought he'd done, he would've known exactly where Levi was going. His showing up here was proof of his guilt. He should've been here by now."

"You two idiots! That was your plan?" Ed snapped. Tori had never seen Ed angry before. "Did you think about what would happen if you were wrong? There's no way for Levi to walk away from this now. He should've left it alone. There are police all over Twin Rivers looking for Levi—there's a warrant out for his arrest."

Tori sighed, "We were so sure."

From the direction of Kingery Pond, the distinctive sound of a gunshot echoed through the woods. Ed and Tori looked at each other in shock.

"Get in," Ed yelled. She barely had the door closed when Ed floored it, throwing gravel and dust everywhere. "The back lane—I didn't think it was still passable after all these years. There's another way into the mining property, and Doug used it. He flanked us. Damnit!"

54

Levi stood in water up to his knees at the edge of the shaft. He'd dreamed about this place many times over the years, and everything about it was as horrible as he remembered—the blackness of the abyss, the smell of sulfur, the slimy mud. He was reliving the nightmare.

"Any last words, Garvey," Doug said with a cackle that echoed off the steep walls which surrounded them on three sides.

"Why did you do it, Doug?" Levi said. "I just don't understand."

Doug laughed. "She didn't give me any choice."

"She was going to tell everyone what you did," Levi said.

"What I did? Listen, she'd been playing her little prick tease game with me for a week. I saw her walking, and I offered her a ride. I didn't force her into the truck. She knew what was going on. I drove her out to the old Davis farmstead—I used to take dates there. I took your woman there, too," Doug said, leering at Levi.

When Levi started to lunge for him, Doug raised the gun in his face. "Easy there, stud," Doug said. "Things were going along fine with Mel, and then she wants to play hard to get all of a sudden. She scratched me down the side of my face. I don't play that game. It pissed me off."

"So you raped her," Levi said, staring at him.

"Call it what you want. She didn't struggle much. I'd call it consensual."

"Yeah," Levi said. "I'm sure the fact you weighed a hundred and fifty pounds more than she did didn't have anything to do with it."

Doug ignored Levi's sarcasm. "She's quiet as I drive her to the convenience store. But when she's outside the truck, she screams at me, telling me I'm going to pay for what I'd done—I'd raped her, and she knew there were other girls I'd done the same thing too. She's going to report me to Chief Craig."

"Good for her," Levi said.

"When I start to get out of the truck," Doug said, "that little bitch runs. I chased her through town in my truck, but I lost her. She was running through backyards and up alleys. But do you think I'm going to let that daughter of a junkie-whore ruin me? It ain't happenin'. I got tired of looking for her, so I parked the truck at the end of Ash Street, walked to her house, and waited in the dark for her to come home. I knew where she was going eventually. It wasn't that hard to figure out where to wait for her. And sure enough, the stupid little bitch shows up all right. I grabbed her—I just wanted to talk to her. But when she started screaming, I hit her really hard, and she went down like a sack of potatoes."

"You killed her," Levi said, shaking his head.

Doug shrugged.

"Then the porch light comes on, and her junkie whore mom steps out, sees her trashy little slut daughter on the sidewalk, and starts screaming too," Doug said tightly. "There was a shovel leaning against the side of the house, and I grabbed it. I don't even remember hitting her. I just reacted. Well, now I had two problems. I turned off the porch light and sat there for some time trying to figure out what I was going to do. I realized nobody had heard the screams. They were probably used to all the shit that used to go on over there and figured it was the same shit. I got the truck, loaded them in the back, and went into the house and packed up their clothes, like they'd left in the night. I'd been over there enough times to know Sarah was planning on sneaking out of there. I threw their stuff in the truck and drove out to Kingery Pond. I knew nobody would miss them. I was sure right about that."

"Why did you dump the whole truck?" Levi said. "That makes no sense."

"Listen, smart-ass, I hadn't planned on killing anybody," Doug said. "First of all, I didn't have anything to weigh them down, and I didn't want them popping back up again. Besides, I'd crushed Sarah's head with the shovel—there was blood everywhere. There was blood all over me, blood all in the cab, blood in the bed of the truck. Then there was all the stuff we'd taken from the house. And I had to clean the front porch and sidewalk. I didn't have much time left. The sky was already getting lighter, and I knew the sun would be coming up soon."

"I know the rest," Levi said. "You drove your truck out to the edge of the mine shaft. You unspooled your winch cable, and walked around the shaft to the other side of the pond and hooked it to a tree or something. You put them in the cab, popped the transmission into neutral, and then turned on the winch."

Doug grinned darkly at him. "You always were a smart guy. Truck went over the edge, battery in the truck shorted out and stopped the wench, and all I had to do was cut the winch cable and let the truck sink to the bottom."

Levi looked at the shaft and felt sick. They had been down there all those years, and nobody had missed them. Not even Mel's friends.

"Of course, I did make one mistake," Doug chuckled. "Right as the truck started over the edge, I see Melissa's face in the back window. She wasn't dead after all! She was screaming and trying to break the glass. I guess I'd just knocked her out. Too bad I didn't know that before I crushed her mother's skull with that shovel."

Levi looked at him in horror.

"Oh, don't give me that look, Levi. You'll be joining her soon," Doug said nudging him towards the hole. "Let's see how long you can swim."

55

Ed rolled to a stop beside Old Blue, and Tori jumped out of the truck. She ran around the side and stopped short. On the ground next to the passenger door was a pool of blood, Levi's Panama, and the .455 Webley.

"Ed!" she gasped.

When Ed ran to see what she'd found, something caught his eye down below them. "Oh, no," he said as the color drained from his face.

Tori spun around to look. Doug Malone was standing in the shallow water, and Levi was thrashing in the water in front of him. Leaning down, Doug pulled him up by his hair. Even from a hundred yards away, Tori could see Levi was injured.

"He's been shot," Tori gasped. She began running down the lane towards the low side of Kingery Pond as fast as she could.

Ed stood frozen. He knew Doug would kill Tori the minute he saw her, and then he'd kill Levi. There's only one thing I can do, he thought. But Ed was paralyzed. You've got to. You have no choice, he urged himself.

When he saw Doug raise his gun to Levi's face, it broke his

panic. He ran to his truck, grabbed the rifle case, flung it open, and pulled out the rifle. Back on the edge of the cliff, he dropped to one knee and looked through his scope.

But there were problems. The first was he couldn't hold the rifle steady—the scope wobbled erratically over Levi and Doug. It was the booze. His nerves were rattled. He couldn't make the shot anymore.

But even if he could have, there was another problem. Doug and Levi were walking side by side to the mineshaft in the shallow water, Levi obviously injured and Doug half heaving him along under the arm and half dragging him. Even if Ed could hold the rifle steady at that range, he couldn't hit Doug without hitting Levi, too.

But it was the final problem that bothered Ed the most. Even if I can hold the damned rifle steady, he thought, and I have a clear shot, I still won't be able to do it. I can't do it again. I just can't.

Ed lowered the rifle, put his hand over his face, and sobbed.

"Come on, Levi," Doug said, edging him closer to the edge of the abyss.

Levi nearly fell, but Doug was holding him up firmly under his arm. If he'd fallen, he would've slid over the edge. His heart was hammering in his chest.

"Enough stalling," Doug said. "You going in alive, or are you going in dead?"

Levi sighed. He saw the end of his life differently. He knew there was no escaping this fate. He twisted his legs and began struggling in the shallow water.

"What the hell are you doing?" Doug barked.

"I'm taking off my shoes," Levi said. "At least afford me that small favor."

Doug waited as first one tennis shoe bobbed to the surface and then the other.

"Are you ready now?"

Levi nodded.

Ed sobbed in his hands. Then he looked down one more time. Levi and Doug were still exchanging words. My nephew is pleading for his life, and I can't save him, he thought.

Ed knew that at any moment Tori was going to come rushing out of the woods and into the clearing beside Kingery Pond. He'd have to watch her die, too.

A breeze blew through the trees, and the sunlight flickered through the leaves. Ed felt the familiar presence as he had so many times before. His guests. He could feel them, smell them. He could hear their boots shuffling on the gravel behind him. He could actually see their shadows on the ground in front of him. All of them were there. They'd come to watch his final punishment for what he'd done four decades earlier. They'd come to witness his atonement.

"I won't do this," he said, not turning to face them. "I can't take another life. I can't live anymore with the lives I've already taken."

Ed jumped when he felt the hand on his shoulder. He saw the shadow of one of the soldiers on the ground in front of him as the soldier knelt behind him. He smelled the jungle, he smelled the man's breath, and he heard the words he whispered in his ear. "Bạn phải. Nếu bạn không ông sẽ chết."

The words surprised him. He knew what they meant—he'd learned some Vietnamese during the war. He felt the other guests gather in closer around him. He felt the hand pat his shoulder reassuringly, and the urgent whisper came again. "Bạn phải! Nếu bạn không ông sẽ chết."

"You must! If you don't he will die."

With hands that no longer shook, Ed raised the barrel of the rifle, flipped open the bipod stand, and flopped down on his belly. He perched the rifle on the edge of the cliff. He found his target in the scope and adjusted it for range—the same scope he'd used so many times before nearly four decades ago. His pulse slowed as he listened to his own breathing. There were no ripples on the pond below—no wind. It sickened him how quickly it all came back, how the sounds and sights around him faded away. There was nothing left but his rifle, his finger on the trigger, and his view through the crosshairs of his scope.

It was an easy shot, but Levi was still in the way.

Patiently, Ed waited for the opportunity to take Doug out without hitting Levi. He watched as Doug jerked Levi around. His pulse raced when Levi nearly fell into the shaft, and the scope jiggled slightly.

Oh, God, he's going to kill him before I get a clear shot. Please, just give me this one last shot, he prayed.

Levi stood near the edge, Doug standing right beside him. He almost wished the edge of the shaft would collapse and take them both with it so he wouldn't have to jump in himself.

"It's funny," Levi remarked.

"Something's funny about this?" Doug said.

"Sure," Levi said. "Last time we were here, you saved my life. Now, you're taking it. You've gone from pulling me out to pushing me in."

"I wish I'd let you drown the first time" Doug said. "I'm tired of playing with you, Levi. It's time to go. I'm going to count to three. If you're still standing here, I'm going to shoot you in the head. You got that?"

Levi knew he meant it.

Maybe it's better that way, he thought. I'll never be able to jump in there on my own.

"One..."

Levi turned and faced Doug, looking squarely into his eyes.

If he's going to shoot me, he's going to look me in the eye when he does it, Levi thought.

"Two . . ."

Levi was staring into Doug's eyes when he saw the sun reflect on something up on the top of the overlook behind Doug. He glanced up to the cliff over them, and saw Old Blue's roof. Tears filled his eyes.

I'll never drive that old truck again, he thought. Goodbye, Blue.

The sun glinted again, but the reflection wasn't off Old Blue. It was lower.

Could it be? he thought. Uncle Ed?

He prayed he was right. But knowing it left him with an impossible choice.

I know why he hasn't fired, Levi thought. Doug's head won't stop a .308. It'll hit me too.

"I've changed my mind, Doug. I'll buy you a drink in hell," Levi yelled as he leaped into the abyss.

A slow evil smile lit up Doug's face. He lowered his gun, ready to enjoy watching Levi drown.

As water closed over his head, Levi heard the dry crack of a rifle.

His final thought was, at least I'll go to my death knowing I sent Doug to his first.

56

Tori burst out of the woods, covered in sweat, and ran to edge of the water. Doug was holding his gun to Levi's head when she began charging into the water. Suddenly she saw Levi leap into the water over the mineshaft. A split-second later, Doug's head exploded like a melon. He spun around and fell into the water. She knew he was dead before she heard the shot a second later.

She could see Levi thrashing frantically as she ran as fast as she could through the knee-deep water. She was only half-way to him when the thrashing stopped, one hand visible briefly before he slowly sank below the surface.

Tears streaming down her cheeks, she tried to run faster, but the muddy bottom made that impossible.

Levi had thrashed in the water, but he couldn't move his right arm because of the slug Doug had put in his shoulder. He felt his strength flowing out with the blood. As the water soaked into his jeans and his shirt, he knew he was growing too heavy to stay up.

The reflection had meant death for Doug, but it'd also meant death for him, too. If he'd jumped away from the shaft instead of towards it, Doug would've reacted, and Ed might've missed. Doug would've unloaded the Glock into him before Ed could snap the bolt for another shot.

I never had a chance either way, he thought.

Levi desperately lunged upwards towards the surface, managing to snatch one more breath before he began to sink again. His waterlogged clothes were pulling him down. He was sinking fast. He struggled against it. It was just like it'd been once before when he was a kid and in so many dreams since.

"Wake up! Wake up!" he silently yelled at himself. He prayed to wake up, covered in sweat, sitting bolt upright in bed at home. He prayed this was just another nightmare.

But this was real. He saw the shimmering surface of the water slipping away and the darkness around him deepening. He remembered something from back when he was a boy, something he'd thought to himself last time he was sinking into this awful abyss. *So this is what it's like to drown.*

The silence became complete as he sank lower into the water. He closed his eyes. He didn't know how much longer he could hold his breath. He didn't know how much longer he wanted to.

Suddenly, something touched his foot. Panic set in as the old memory surged forward to the front of his mind. Suddenly, something grabbed him around the neck and began pulling on him.

My God, there is something in here! he thought in a panic.

He opened his eyes and thrashed against it, but he wasn't being pulled down. He was being pulled up. His face broke the surface of the water, and he gasped for breath.

"Kick with your legs, Levi," Tori said breathlessly in his ear. "I can't pull you much further."

Levi kicked and Tori kicked. Soon his foot hit the muddy bottom of Kingery Pond. They sat on the bottom for a minute, trying to catch their breath. Tori still had her arm around his neck.

"He get him?" Levi gasped.

"Ed is a hell of a shot, Levi. I should've never doubted him. It's over."

Levi sighed, leaned heavily against her, and closed his eyes. It was over.

Ed laid his head down on the scope of his rifle. Tori and Levi were lying in the shallow water near the shaft. Doug was floating a few feet away, face-down in a growing circle of bloody water. Ed could still feel the soldiers behind him and see their shadows on the ground.

"Thank you," he whispered.

He felt the hand pat his shoulder as the shadow that had knelt behind him rose.

"I've tortured myself for years over the lives I took," Ed said quietly. "I wasn't a murderer when I was drafted—I was just a kid who was a really good shot. The Marines put that skill to work. I didn't kill you because I wanted to. I killed you because I had to. I've carried you with me all these years out of guilt—I didn't want to forget what I'd done. But all I was doing was trying to save those men I cared about. That's the same thing I had to do today."

When Ed popped the bolt on his rifle, the spent shell flipped out onto the ground. He started to pick it up but stopped himself.

"You think I should put that shell in my little box?"

No one answered as the shadows moved back.

"I've made you real over the years, so I could face you on my terms—the ritual. You were ambushing me in my sleep. You'd show up when I least expected. I'd be reminded of Vietnam by a helicopter flying overhead or somebody burning trash. I'd be thrown into a complete panic. So I created that ritual as a memorial. I thought I could control my fears and guilt that way, but I couldn't. You're just a figment of my tortured mind. I've let you run my life. I've let you ruin my life. A few times, I've almost let you take my life.

"It's time for me to move on. I killed all of you a long time ago half a world away. I've apologized to all of you many, many times. But the truth is, I'm not sorry. I'd do the same thing again."

Ed climbed to his feet. He paused for a moment. He could still feel them behind him. He closed his eyes, took a deep breath, and turned around to finally face them all at once. Tears slipped from beneath his closed lids and ran down his cheeks. He heard nothing except his wildly beating heart. Slowly, he opened his eyes. There was nothing there but the woods and the lane leading out to the main road.

The ritual was over. There were things he'd have to learn to deal with, but he'd taken an important step. He was free.

A rising cloud of dust was coming up the lane. It was the police—a lot of police. Ed leaned his rifle against the side of Old Blue and raised his hands over his head.

Alan Haig was in the lead car. He stopped and got out as the other cop cars pulled to a stop up and down the lane. There were five or six cars behind him with flashing lights.

"What's going on here, Ed?" Alan said.

"Call for an ambulance, Alan," Ed said, nodding over his shoulder toward the pond. "Then I'll tell you all about it."

57

"Morning," Levi said as he walked into the kitchen.

Tori was sitting on a stool at the kitchen island. A single strand of hair hung in front of her face. She didn't speak. Tori wasn't a morning person.

Levi got a mug from the cabinet and poured himself a cup of coffee. He stood at the kitchen island sipping it. When he reached over to tuck the loose strand of hair behind her ear, she smiled at him.

"Anything of interest in the paper?" Levi asked.

She knew what he meant and shook her head.

It'd been three weeks since the shooting, but they still hadn't pulled Doug's truck out of the mine shaft. Men with chainsaws and wood-chippers had worked over a week to widen the old mine road enough to get a large crane back to Kingery Pond. But getting the crane there had proven to be the easy part. Construction workers, highly skilled at operating a crane, had been working day and night since then. State police investigators had confirmed there was a vehicle down there—they'd pinged it with a sonar device. But it wasn't easy to hook something that couldn't be seen in the dark water

660 feet below—a job none of the construction crew had tried to do before.

The water was too deep and too dangerous for divers to assist. There was also a real risk that the edges of the shaft might collapse. The recovery of the truck was turning out to be a very difficult challenge.

Finally, officials had decided to bring in experts who did this kind of work for a living—a deep-sea underwater salvage crew from Louisiana. The residents of Twin Rivers had been anxiously awaiting news since the crew had arrived the day before. They'd gone to work immediately.

At first, the news networks had carried the recovery effort story live 24/7. But as hours became days and days became one week and then two without new information, the networks had scaled back their coverage. The media frenzy in Twin Rivers had abated. Now there were only a few reporters and cameramen waiting around to break the story if and when the truck was finally recovered.

Smiling, Tori reached over the counter and touched Levi's face. "You know, you're finally getting your color back. You don't look like Nosferatu this morning."

"Gee, thanks. That's so sweet," Levi said. "Actually, I feel pretty good today. I may wander the grounds if there are no news crews around. I'm about to go nuts trapped in this house."

He walked behind her, wrapped his arms around her waist, and nuzzled the back of her neck. She leaned into him and reached back to wrap her hands around his neck.

"I'm not even going to ask you why you're not wearing your sling," Tori said. "You rip those stitches open and—"

"Nag, nag, nag," Levi said, his hand slipping under her robe.

Tori slapped his hand. He walked back around the counter, looking at her with feigned hurt in his blue eyes.

"You're not strong enough yet," Tori bragged as she smiled at him.

"I'd die happy."

It'd been a long recovery. Levi had lost a lot of blood, and the pain from the injury had been like nothing he'd ever experienced before. Then there had been the infection—probably due to the heavily polluted water of Kingery Pond. He'd spent two weeks in the hospital—asleep most of the time, groggy and muddled when awake.

When he was finally released and sent home, Tori worried it was too soon since he was so weak and confused. However, two days later, he did something she hadn't thought was possible. He'd gotten out of bed. Tori had caught him coming down the stairs. His face was gray, the circles under his eyes so dark they looked like bruises.

"You shouldn't be up," she said.

"If I see one more episode of Judge Judy," Levi croaked, "so help me, God, I'll jump out the damned window."

Tori had felt relief wash over her as he brushed past her at the base of the stairs. It was the first lucid thing he'd said in over two weeks. She watched him weave down the hall, steadying himself against the walls as he made his way to the kitchen.

"What the hell!" he shouted moments later. "There's no coffee made? Tori! Where's the freakin' coffee?"

She'd smiled. Thank God. Levi was back.

From that point on, Levi had made dramatic improvement every day, becoming increasingly more difficult to deal with. When she'd seen Levi looking out the window yesterday morning, she'd known what he was thinking. As the press coverage dwindled, it wouldn't be long before Levi would make a break for it—jump in Old Blue and take off for coffee at Harv's most likely.

"Did you take your pills this morning?" Tori asked.

"No," he said. "You want to go upstairs and fool around?"

"No. Are you going to take your pills?"

"Hell, no. Come on, let's go upstairs."

"No," she said, trying to look annoyed. "Why haven't you taken your pills?

"I read the bottle. It says on the label 'do not take with alcohol.'"

"So?" Tori said.

"I thought after we see the movie tonight at the Comet, we'd go have a few cold ones at the Beer Chaser. It's Wednesday, you know."

"Are you asking me out on a date?"

Levi nodded.

"Then what?" she asked.

"Then maybe we'll test that theory of yours. We'll find out whether I'm strong enough or not."

"You're not," Tori said with a grin.

"After three weeks—" Levi paused, then chuckled. "If I were you, Tori, I'd take my vitamins."

58

Levi was standing under the elm tree in the side yard. It was the first time he'd wandered around outside since he'd gotten out of the hospital. The press was gone, having finally given up on staking out the house. There wasn't even a local news van in front.

Levi looked down at the red stone. He wasn't sure when Uncle Ed had left it, but he'd just noticed it from the porch that morning. It'd been engraved simply Rosco the Brave. Levi approved. That moniker was much more appropriate than Rosco the Lethargic.

The distant squealing of tires and the scream of an engine being pushed to its absolute limits broke the stillness. The Twin Rivers cruiser was racing up the road towards the house, lights flashing. It swerved into the driveway and skidded to a stop in front of the porch in a cloud of white dust.

"Alan, what's wrong?" Levi yelled, as he tried to run to the patrol car.

"The crane has hooked something at Kingery Pond," Alan said. "They're bringing it up now."

Alan followed Levi as he hurried into the house. Kingery Pond was only a few miles away, but the coverage on national television would be better than what they could see if they drove out there.

"Tori!" Levi yelled as they entered the library. He flipped on the television. Tori rushed in a few seconds later. She clutched Levi's arm as all three stared at the screen.

The talking head was standing in the foreground with the crane and work crew in the background. ". . .we were told a few moments ago that the crane has hooked something at the bottom of Kingery Mine Shaft No. 3. As we've been reporting over the last few weeks, it has been alleged that Melissa Sinclair and her mother Sarah were murdered by former Twin Rivers Chief of Police Doug Malone back in June of 1985. It is believed that Doug Malone dumped the bodies here, in his truck, in order to conceal the crime. Doug Malone was himself killed by Ed Garvey, a former Marine sniper and Vietnam vet, a few weeks ago while he was attempting to murder Ed Garvey's nephew, best-selling author Levi Garvey. Levi Garvey, a former resident of Twin Rivers, was visiting his hometown to attend his 25th class reunion when he stumbled upon the grisly truth of this two-and-a-half-decades old crime.

"We're being told that the object the crane has hooked should be breaking the surface any minute now. If Levi Garvey is correct, what we should see within a few moments is Doug Malone's 1982 Chevy Silverado."

The camera zoomed in on the crane as Levi, Tori, and Alan watched. For several minutes, they stared with rapt attention at the close-up shot of the cable inching upwards from the surface of the water. Suddenly, the nose of a black vehicle broke the surface.

Levi shook his head and turned away. "I can't watch this," he said.

He walked out onto the porch and down the steps. Thoughts raced through his mind. *This doesn't seem real. I can't believe Doug was capable of this. How could I have been so wrong about him. I toyed with him because I thought he was nothing more than a bully. I had no idea he was a monster—even then.*

Tori banged through the screen door. At the bottom of the steps, Levi spun around. Her face was ashen.

"What's wrong?" Levi asked.

"What they pulled up—it's not Doug's truck. It's a car. . ."

"What?" Levi said, not understanding.

They rushed back into the library. The crane was maneuvering a car around in a wide circle. Then it was lowered to the ground near the edge of the pond as water poured from around the doors.

Tori and Levi stared at the screen, dumbfounded. "My God, that's not an old car," Levi muttered. "Maybe a 2007?"

Tori and Levi looked at each other, horror and shock on their faces.

Alan only stared at the screen silently, his face immobile.

59

If the days and weeks leading up to the discovery of the first vehicle had seemed long, the days afterward were interminable. Every day or two for the past two weeks, the salvage crew had hooked and pulled up another vehicle, each one a little older than the one before it. And in every one of them so far was a body stuffed in the trunk.

The last car they'd pulled out was the twelfth—a 1990 sedan. Each time a vehicle was found, Alan Haig rushed to the Garvey house in the squad car to notify them personally.

Now the three of them were watching the coverage on television as they had over and over again during the past two weeks.

". . . and you just have to wonder, this being the thirteenth car pulled from the mine shaft and most likely containing the thirteenth victim of serial killer Doug Malone, how many more victims are yet to be recovered. The question is, were there more victims between 1985, when the supposed first victims of Doug Malone were dumped into the mine shaft, and 1990, when the most recent car was made? Each time, as we wait for the crane to pull the next vehicle from the shaft, Americans hope to see Doug Malone's truck containing the bodies and Sarah and Melissa Sinclair."

Levi glanced at Tori. The reporter had just said what they were both thinking.

"Are you going to write the book?" Alan asked.

Levi had been struggling with that question. Even though it didn't feel right to profit from such a horrible crime, he knew that until he told every detail, the story would never go away.

"I am going to write the book," Levi said. "I have to at this point—if for no other reason than to purge the horror from my mind—but I haven't started writing yet."

"You're going to have to make a statement, too," Tori said. "You know that, right?"

"I'll be releasing a formal statement when they pull up Doug's truck," Levi said.

"Is that what you and Wanda Sterling were talking about this morning?"

"Yes."

"There is still one thing I don't understand," Tori said. "How did Doug get those cars into the mine shaft? The water is shallow along the edges, but it's too deep to drive a car out there. You wouldn't be able to push them out to the edge of the shaft with another vehicle either—not only because of the water but because of that sticky mud. You'd get stuck for sure."

"Oh, I found the answer to that," Alan said quickly, his face suddenly alive. "On the opposite side of Kingery Pond across from the entrance road, we found a tree with a cable pulley chained around it. We figure he tied one end of a very long cable to the front of the victim's car and then walked the other end of the cable around the pond and pulled it across the mine shaft. He ran it through the cable pulley and walked it back to his own vehicle."

Tori suddenly understood. "Then he attached it to the front of his vehicle and just backed up the road. He'd pull the victim's car right into the mine shaft."

"Then when it began to sink, he'd walk out to the edge of the shaft and cut the cable," Levi said. "Just like he'd done the first time with his truck."

Alan nodded. "Every car we've pulled up so far has had twenty to thirty feet of cable attached to the front bumper." Alan was looking quite pleased to explain the details.

"How do you suppose he tricked those girls?" Tori said.

"We're taught at a young age to trust police officers," Alan said, his hands moving to indicate his own perfectly pressed uniform. "We know all of the victims were traveling alone along Interstate 57. All of them were attractive women in their twenties, and all were driving newer model cars. Now, he wouldn't have pulled them over on the interstate in his cruiser since he didn't have any jurisdiction there. He would've been too afraid some state trooper would come along and question him. Instead, he likely abducted his victims from gas stations or rest areas." Alan smiled, seeming to enjoy his explanation. Then he continued.   "He was smart though. The reason the missing victims were never put together was because that route runs hundreds of miles—between Chicago and St. Louis. The police never connected the missing victims because they never pinpointed a specific location along that long stretch of highway where the girls disappeared."

"We'll probably never know for sure how he tricked his victims," Levi said, glancing over at Tori.

Her face suddenly looked perplexed, a slight frown between her eyebrows.

She caught Levi's gaze and recognized "What?" in his raised brow. Rising suddenly, she left the room. Alan didn't even notice as he stared at the television.

"I hope to God the next one is Doug's truck," he said.

"Me, too," Levi said, as Tori returned and took a seat on the back of the couch behind Alan.

Levi looked at her again. She'd had such a strange look on her face before she left the room, but now her face was a blank canvas.

"That seems unlikely," Tori said. "There's been a car every year or two so far. There could still be two or three more vehicles down there."

"It would be anybody's guess," Levi said.

"Somebody has to know," Tori said. "Don't they, Alan?"

"What do you mean?" Levi said.

"Doug had an accomplice," Tori said. "Surely, the investigation has come to that same conclusion, hasn't it, Alan?"

"No, it hasn't. Why do you say that, Tori?" Alan said, a tight smile on his face.

"Doug couldn't drive two cars," Tori said bluntly.

The smile faded from Alan's face.

Levi thought for a minute before he suddenly remembered something. When Doug had told him the details of how he'd killed Sarah and Melissa, his words had betrayed him again. Doug had said, "Then there was all their clothes and stuff *we'd* taken from the house . . ."

"He used the word *we* . . ." Levi said, staring hard at Alan, whose face was again expressionless. "When he was telling me about the crime, Doug slipped up. He'd meant to protect that conspirator even from a man he was about to murder. But there's no question in my mind that he said *we*."

Alan stood up and turned towards them. "You're seriously suggesting there was another person involved in this?"

"There had to be," Levi said. "Tori is correct. They figure most of those girls were abducted as they traveled the interstate. That's fifteen miles away. How did Doug get the victim's car to Kingery Pond—and his too? He couldn't pull the car into the mine shaft without a second vehicle, and he couldn't drive the victim's car and his own at the same time. There was a second person."

"Alan knows that, Levi," Tori said. "Tell us, Alan. How many more cars are in the mine shaft?"

"What are you talking about?" Alan stuttered. "Have you lost your mind?" The smile on his face didn't match his ashen skin.

Levi walked over and stood behind Tori with his hand on her shoulder.

"It had to be you," Levi said. "You helped him with Sarah and Melissa, and after that, there was no turning back, was there? He couldn't have done it all himself that night—loaded the bodies, cleaned up the blood at the house, packed up their clothes, dumped the truck in the mine shaft. You helped him, didn't you? You were the *we*."

The smile faded from Alan's face. He looked down at his feet and shook his head. "Just can't leave things alone, can you, Levi?"

Levi eased his hand slowly down the small of Tori's back where he found what he expected to find. He wrapped his fingers around the grip of the Webley that was stuck into the back of her jeans.

"I'd have figured it out eventually," Levi said, slowly easing the gun free. "I hadn't thought much about it—I've been trying not to. But I'd have figured it out once I started researching the book. Doug had no close friends or family, just you, Alan. I wouldn't have been able to miss it."

"Did he force you to help him cover up his crimes?" Tori said. "Did he blackmail you because you helped him cover up Melissa and Sarah's murder?"

Alan laughed. "Oh, Tori, you can be so naïve. Let's just say we shared in everything. Damn good thing you got away that night back in high school. Doug was so angry with me for letting you get away, even though I thought taking you out to the farm was a bad idea to begin with."

"Why's that?" Tori said.

"Why else?" Alan said. "Levi—you'd tell him if you told anybody, and Levi wasn't afraid of shit." Alan paused as a twisted smile crossed his face. "I was waiting for my turn back off the road."

Tori gasped.

"Oh, grow up, Tori. You think you were the first girl we took out there? You think you were the last? Those girls they're pulling out of the shaft—those were just the mistakes. There are many more—alive and well today and probably still regretting the night they decided to stop at a well-lit public rest area to get a soda or use the restroom."

Tori flinched at how casually he'd said it. This was an Alan she'd never seen before—he was proud of what he was saying.

Alan smiled, "That night we took you to the farm, I heard the commotion in the truck. That wasn't unusual. But suddenly you slid out of that truck window. You ran right by me in the dark. You don't know how close I came to tripping you. If I had, Tori, your evening would've ended a lot differently than it did. You were the only one who escaped with her honor intact." Alan chuckled as Tori shuddered.

"I'm sorry about this, Levi," Alan said, reaching for his sidearm.

"So am I," Levi said, raising the Webley from under Tori's arm.

Alan froze, then slowly lowered his hand. Once he figured out where the gun had come from, he chuckled again.

"Very good, Tori," Alan said. "You figured it out while we were watching the TV and got the gun, didn't you?"

"You're going to pay for what you did, Alan. You and Doug murdered all those girls," she said, her face hard as stone.

He sighed and shook his head as he looked at Levi. "And I know you well enough to know you won't hesitate to shoot me—right? And with Tori standing in front of you like a human shield, you'll shoot to kill, won't you?"

Levi nodded.

"You'd really kill me, Levi? One of the Zoo Crew?"

Levi's pulse surged. He knew what Alan was thinking.

"I'd have to."

Alan nodded. A moment later, he made a sudden grab for his gun.

The Webley roared.

Alan was dead before he hit the floor.

60

Wearing his fedora, Levi was writing at the wrought iron table on the corner of porch, his reading glasses perched on the very end of his nose. It was a beautiful early spring day. Even so, he was wearing a heavy jacket since it was still chilly out. The leaves on the trees were budding, and the daffodils were pushing up through the last remnants of snow.

Levi looked up from his laptop when he heard a truck honk. Ed's flatbed was pulling up the driveway with an old wreck on the back. Levi smiled as Ed pulled to a stop. He'd seen very little of Ed all winter.

"Where have you been hiding?" Levi called as Ed slid out of the cab.

"Here and there," Ed said, climbing the porch steps.

Ed had lost some weight, and the dark circles under his eyes were gone. He sat down on the swing as Tori walked out onto the porch. She'd heard Ed honk. Noticing the wreck on the back of the truck, she walked to the top of the steps to get a better look at it.

"That old heap has been around a while," Tori said, sipping her coffee.

"Old heap?" Ed said as if shocked. "What are you talking about? People keep telling me I look better than I have in years!"

Tori and Levi laughed. "You are looking better, Ed," Tori said. "I was talking about the old heap on the back of your truck."

"Old heap? Don't you know what that is?"

Tori looked at him suspiciously, aware that she was about to hear a bunch of bullshit. "No, Ed, why don't you enlighten me."

"That's Old Blue's daddy," he said with a grin. "I bought it last fall. It's been in an old barn for the last fifty years or so. It's a 1949 Ford F-1 with a V-8 flathead. I spent all winter tinkering with the engine. It has kept me busy between head shrinking sessions."

"What are you going to do with it?" Levi asked.

"I thought I'd restore it," he said, glancing at Levi with a shrewd grin on his face. "Actually, if you didn't mind, I thought I might work on it here. Restoring it might be good therapy for me, like painting a house, for instance."

Levi glanced at him and smiled.

"There's not much room in the garage at the scrap yard, and most of the tools I need to work on it at this point are in the carriage house. It'll take a lot of work, but when we, I mean, when *I* get done, I'm going to give it to you, Tori, as a belated wedding present."

Levi was suddenly very interested in the old truck. He stood up and walked to the porch rail, staring at it thoughtfully.

Tori looked at Ed with a huge smile on her face. "Really?" she said. "You're going to give it me when it's finished?"

"Oh, I don't know, Ed," Levi said. "Tori is a Chevy girl. She'd never lower herself to drive a Ford truck."

"The hell I wouldn't," Tori said. She ran down the porch steps, jumped up on the back of the flatbed, and peered into the cab. "This truck is a disaster, but you said Old Blue was a mess when you first saw it too—right?"

"Worse than that," Ed said. "Hell, there were weeds growing in Old Blue's cab when I brought it home. Old Blue had been sitting on four flat tires on the ground behind a barn for twenty years. There were many times while Levi and I worked on Old Blue that I wondered if we'd ever get that truck on the road again. There's hardly a piece of Old Blue that didn't come off another truck. We called that truck Frankenstein while we were working on it."

"Ed's right," Levi said, smiling at the memories. "There's not much of the original truck left in Old Blue. It's a collection of the best pieces of about three trucks."

"If you don't count bumpers and tail-lights that have been replaced since," Ed said with a smile.

Levi shot him a sharp glance. "It'll take us, I mean *you*, a couple of years to rebuild this one."

Ed nodded. "The frame's in great shape. We'll strip it down to the frame, sandblast it, and paint it."

Levi nodded as he sat down next to Ed on the swing. "Then reassemble it one piece at a time from the ground up."

"The bed and the floorboard have some issues," Ed said, "but other than that, it's surface rust. Not a rusted out place on the body anywhere. Nothing like the problems we had with Old Blue."

"I know what's going on here," Tori said. "Living with Levi, I've learned to listen for words like *we*. Ed needs help working on it, and Levi needs a little something to tinker with between chapters. Am I right?"

Ed and Levi both shrugged innocently.

"Okay," Tori said as she turned to both of them from the back of the flatbed. "But if it's going to be my truck, I want it to be purple."

Ed and Levy looked at each other in horror.

"Whatever you want, Tori," Ed said, elbowing Levi in the ribs to shut him up.

"Sure, purple it is," Levi said.

Tori grinned and turned back to look at the old truck again.

Ed leaned over and whispered to Levi, "I'm thinking red, right?"

Levi nodded enthusiastically.

"I love it," Tori said. "Thank you, Ed." She pulled on the passenger door, which creaked loudly, then stuck half way open. She jerked back. "What is that awful smell?" she said, the words muffled by her hand that was clamped over her nose and mouth.

"Oh," Ed said, "there was a dead raccoon in there when I bought it. It'll air out. Don't worry about it."

Tori looked at them doubtfully, her hand still clamped over her face as Levi laughed.

"It'll be fine," Levi said. "Believe me."

"Oh, I got something for you, too, Levi," Ed said. "Hey, Tori. There's a box on the floor of my truck. You want to bring it here?"

Tori jumped down from the flatbed and opened the tow truck door. After looking into the box, she smiled at Ed. She pulled out the box and walked up the porch steps with it.

"That's a big box," Levi said, standing up. "What is it?"

Tori set the box on the swing. When Levi peered in, his face went blank. For an instant, Ed thought maybe it was the wrong gift, but then a big smile filled Levi's face, and his eyes got teary.

"I've given you a lot of presents over the years," Ed said, "but there were two you loved more than any of the others, Old Blue and . . ." his voice trailed off.

Levi reached into the box, pulled out the wriggling little fur ball, and held it in his arms. The German shepherd puppy began yipping and licking his face.

"I wasn't sure you'd want another dog," Ed said. "Maybe it's too soon."

Levi walked to the porch rail and leaned on it, stroking the puppy, which was playing with his hand—pushing it back with his paws and growling with his little puppy voice.

"Well, he's a vicious little monster," Levi said, rubbing his belly. The puppy grabbed the sleeve of his jacket, tugging on it as he shook his head back and forth.

"I still catch myself starting to call Rosco when I get ready to go somewhere in Old Blue," Levi said, his face a mixture of sadness and joy as he looked down at the puppy.

Tori had taken a seat on the porch swing next to Ed. She reached over and held his hand.

"Do I even have to ask what you're going to name him?" Ed said.

Levi glanced over at the two rocks under the elm tree. "How about Mycroft? That's a good name for a dog," he said, placing the puppy down on the porch. "That was Sherlock Holmes' brother."

They watched the puppy as he ran from one of them to the other. Each reached down to play with him as he bounded by. They laughed when he grabbed a pant leg here and there, growling and shaking it. He was adorable. Finally tiring, Mycroft curled up on the welcome mat and closed his eyes.

"Are you okay, Ed?" Tori asked, breaking the silence.

He knew what she was talking about. "I will be," he replied. "I've been working through some stuff with some new friends of mine. They've been through some of the same things I have."

"Like a therapy group?" she asked.

Ed nodded. "Wish I'd done it a long time ago. And of course, I had to do something about my drinking, too."

"You quit?" Levi said.

"I have quit drinking," Ed said firmly. He paused, then added quickly, "As much."

Tori and Levi laughed.

"You heard the news about Kingery Pond?" Ed asked.

Levi nodded. "They're going to fill it in."

"They'll begin in a few weeks when the ground finishes thawing," Ed said. "They'll use the dirt from the overlook to fill it—that's where the dirt came from to begin with. They'll level the entire area."

They sat silently for several minutes, watching the puppy twitch with puppy dreams as he dozed.

"It still doesn't seem real," Tori said. "Fifteen vehicles down there—sixteen victims over a twenty-five year period. I just can't believe what Doug and Alan did."

"We stopped them," Ed said.

"I could have stopped them sooner," Tori said quietly. "Back before they ever got started."

"You don't know that," Levi said.

"He's right," Ed said. "Let's say you reported Doug back when he tried to attack you. What do you think would've happened?"

Tori shrugged.

"Nothing would've happened," Ed said. "Doug would've been in some trouble, and they would've questioned him. He would've denied the charge. They would've thought it was a case of horny teen football player versus reluctant girl, and that would've been it. It would've been filed away as a misunderstanding. That kind of thing has been going on since Henry Ford invented the automobile."

"I can't think of a teenage boy who hasn't pushed that envelope a few times," Levi said.

"Levi is right," Ed said. "You couldn't have known, and you couldn't have stopped him even if you had. It was too common. Good little boys and girls do many very naughty things out in the woods after football games and school dances. It would've made no difference even if you'd reported him."

Tori's mind knew Ed was right, but it was taking her heart longer to accept the idea that she wasn't responsible—she'd been working on that idea for months. Tori looked over at the puppy, who was back to running around the porch, and laughed.

"What?" Levi said.

"Your stupid damned dog just pooped on our new welcome mat," she said.

"Mycroft!" Levi said, trying to look stern.

"Uh, what do you say we get that truck unloaded in the carriage house," Ed said.

Levi quickly agreed as they stood up in unison. They bounded down the steps as Mycroft followed them to the edge of the porch. There he stopped at the top of the steps, realizing he was too little to get down the steps. He yipped at them—one ear standing straight up and the other leaning over into his face.

"And who's going to clean up this little puppy mess?" Tori called after them.

Having suddenly gone deaf, Levi and Ed quickly jumped into the wrecker.

"That's what I thought," Tori said, scowling down at the puppy. "You and I are going to have to have a little talk, dog." She held the screen door open. "Let's go in the house, Mycroft!"

The puppy had seemingly gone deaf as well. Not moving from the top of the steps, he continued yipping at Levi and Ed as they backed the wrecker further up the driveway towards the carriage house. Levi and Ed were both smiling and waving at Tori through the windshield as if they couldn't hear her as they retreated—as if they knew nothing about a little pile of puppy poo on the welcome mat.

"Come on, Mycroft," Tori said louder.

Ignoring her, the puppy continued to yip at Levi and Ed.

What kind of name is Mycroft for a dog? she thought.

"Hey, Rosco," she said softly.

The puppy's head snapped around, and he looked up at her with one ear up and one ear down. He was so cute she couldn't help but smile at him.

"Let's go in the house."

Rosco bounded across the porch and followed her inside.

ABOUT THE AUTHOR

Todd E. Creason, the father of two daughters, lives with his wife, Valerie, near his hometown in Illinois. He considers writing a hobby. *One Last Shot* is his first novel. He works full-time as a business manager at the University of Illinois. As an active Freemason and Past Master of his lodge, he is the author of the award winning *Famous American Freemasons* series. When he's not reading or writing, his hobbies include fishing and music. An accomplished piano player, he has spent more than twenty years playing everything from rock and roll to country and blues.

Visit the author's website at

toddcreason.org